THE ESSENTIAL CARL MAHOGANY

ZACH BODDICKER

LAST CHANCE PRESS

ISBN: 978-0-692-63863-7

The Essential Carl Mahogany is a work of fiction.
Names, characters, places, and incidents either
are the product of the author's imagination
or are used fictitiously. Any resemblance to actual
persons, living or dead, events, or locales
is entirely coincidental.

Printed in the United States of America

First Edition, January 2017

For my parents

1

Like it or not, you've heard at least one of the hundreds of songs I've written during the course of the last few decades. Some of them just can't be avoided anymore. Aside from ubiquitous radio play, they've adorned many a television and film sound-track, and a handful of commercials that've made heavy rotation during the NFL and NHL postseasons in recent years.

But you'd have to be a country music completist to have heard me actually singing any of them. Some say I have a voice made for print; and, for a dyslexic, this should've been a setback, but I've earned the respect of my peers, and have taken home dozens of awards from various industry organizations. I've vacationed, schmoozed, and boozed with countless names more household than my own. However, such credentials and connections don't help whatsoever when you're scratching your head over the next thing to do.

My publicist insists that I speak about my songwriting as though it were a passion. He claims it helps "maintain the fourth wall" and "keeps the dream alive."

Whether I call it a passion or a habit makes no difference to me. I can say for sure that it was the latter that placed me on the couch several weeks back, guitar in my lap, wringing the last anemic drop out of a song idea. It was well past midnight, and an hour since I'd written down a lyric that I hadn't scribbled over in paper-curling strokes.

I slapped the spiral notebook on the coffee table, blew out my candles, sat back, and gazed out the front window toward my landlord's mansion. A thunderstorm was underway, and the lightning's proximity concerned me. I grew up in storm-happy Eastern Iowa, and knew to take precautions, so I unplugged my recording gear from the wall, and went to the fridge for a beer.

The lightning bolt hit close enough to rattle everything in the house and trip the breakers. Half-blinded by the flash, I rushed to the window in time to see the silhouette of an enormous elm branch crash down on Percy, my 1982 Ford Econoline cargo van.

After more than 30 years of service, one of the few things to have endured both my fickle showbiz career and personal life looked to have all four wheels in the grave.

And, before I even had a few seconds to react to that, I noticed a faint E minor 11th sus 4 chord resonating from my bedroom. This is the chord that blossoms after a standard-tuned acoustic guitar falls from a poorly-secured wall bracket and makes contact with hardwood flooring. This was not just any guitar, but a museum-quality 1941 Martin D-45, passed down to me by my paternal grandfather as a reward for finishing high school, and an instrument worth more on the vintage market than I'd ever earned in two or three of my best fiscal years.

I couldn't bear to inspect that wreckage, so I took a long swig and stared out at Percy, angry with myself for parking it beneath the most prominent dead tree on the property. I'd known the storm was coming, and that lightning seemed to have a sexual attraction to that particular tree. I also knew that a wall bracket worthy of upholding the holy grail of flat-top acoustic guitars should be secured into wall studs and not just a half inch of 50-year-old drywall.

I guzzled what was left out of my beer can, and then squeezed it until it looked something like my van. Then, as though a high-pressure hose had come unfastened in my head, I charged outside and across the muddy driveway, determined to show the fallen elm branch its proper place. I jerked and pulled at it from every direction. It was two feet thick at its base, at least a dozen in length, and had no bark with which to gain and maintain a grip. I was no match.

So I started the van and floored it out into my landlord's pasture, attempting to buck the branch off. We thrashed and fishtailed through thick patches of Canada thistle, spiraling around the field wayward as a wind-up toy, bouncing over prairie dog mounds, brush, and yucca. The rain sounded like the applause of many thousands at a rodeo. Eight seconds turned into twenty-eight, and that doubled and doubled again; an exhilarating, cathartic ride, until three of the five warning lights on the dash lit up. I watched them flicker as I let off the gas, and Percy slid and spun to a stop. The smell of coolant wafted up through the firewall. I rolled the window down and looked out. The elm branch hadn't budged at all. In fact, it was probably more embedded in the roof than it had been before.

I leaned my head back and closed my eyes, taking in the symphony of pneumatic hissings, radio static, and distant thunderclaps. It'd been a few days shy of a year since I'd fled the tired promise and aesthetic letdowns of Music City. Why I chose to settle on the high plains of Eastern Colorado is a question I'm often asked, but still hesitant to answer in any other way than "why don't we talk about you?" Many other reasons aside, the only woman I'd ever come to love deeply had run off with my manager and close friend of 20 years.

I'd never seriously considered retirement from the music business. Even after Sheila split, my instincts led me right back to the guitar, notebook, and tape recorder. Setbacks, disappointments, and heartbreak had always strengthened my resolve.

And, I don't have a speck of superstitious belief in me, but there's something about a lightning bolt, strategically placed, that'll make anyone re-examine their facts.

After a long year in Forsyth, I had nothing to show—nothing, minus a van, and possibly the Martin. I'd settled there intent on taking full advantage of a do-over, but this hadn't come to pass with any degree of success. Depression, self-doubt, and persistent, intrusive thoughts of Sheila had squashed my efforts toward community outreach. Sure, I'd met some friendly, jocular locals, but it was almost as though I no longer knew how to proceed beyond a basic introduction. Conversations dried up, interest waned. The awkwardness became embarrassing and unbearable, so I decided to stop imposing myself on the good people of Forsyth and rededicate myself to what I knew best, and what'd led me into just about every trouble I'd ever known.

Seventy half-finished songs later and I was sitting in my crushed van, wearing only my briefs, wondering if and when things might start to turn around. I did have a tour to look forward to, though I was disgusted with the album I was being sent out to support. The suits had decided to call it *The Essential Carl Mahogany*. It was the most incongruent, flaccid collection of songs ever to have my name branded upon it.

I crawled to the mattress in rear of the van, careful not to hit my head on the collapsed roof. Not careful enough, however. I landed face-down, feeling for the lump that was sure to rise from my skull. Then, like a high-centered tortoise, I reached around in the dark, hoping there might be a guitar to strum.

2

The rev of what sounded like a small motorcycle engine woke me, my throat and sinuses parched and burning from having spent the night under a damp sheet. I stared bleary-eyed at the ceiling as the reality of the previous night's events began to take hold. I sat up, rubbed my eyes, crab-walked to the driver's seat, and opened the door. A ribbon of blue-gray two-stroke engine exhaust hit my gag reflex as I stepped onto the wet pasture.

Bill, my 82-year-old landlord, stood with his back turned to me, performing subtractive surgery on the tree limb with a chainsaw. He wore the uniform of old guard Forsyth aristocracy: white loafers, khaki slacks, a faded yellow Polo shirt, and a white visor. The elastic band of his protective goggles mussed the thin, white-blond hair on the back of his head. He let off the throttle once he noticed me bent over, shivering, on the verge of retching.

"What the Sam Hell is going on here?" I couldn't tell if he was angry or forestalling laughter. He revved the motor again. "What were you chasing after in your goddamn underpants?"

I looked around at the smear of tire tracks leading every which way in the slick topsoil, wondering how I was going to explain certain decisions I'd made the night before. My eyes ached, adjusting to the unfiltered Colorado sunlight. "Nothing that I caught, apparently."

Bill didn't look like he was going to turn off the saw, so I did it, and then took a few steps back and had a look at Percy. As expected, the damage looked far worse in the glory of daylight. Its new contours resembled a swayback whale, convincing me there was little hope for it.

He looked at me, then the van, then back at me.

"Bite your lip, ol' man," I said.

He shook his head and restarted the chainsaw. "Go get some drawers on before the neighbor zeroes in on you. I'll get this branch outta the way so we can go get this thing looked at."

Had I been able to run to the house barefoot without the threat of slipping in mud or stepping on goat-heads or thistle, there would've been no issue. But, I had to tiptoe each of the hundred yards, sure that the neighbor to whom Bill had just referred (a self-published, anti-government xenophobe) had me in the sights of his binoculars, or the scope of a rifle, laughing his dentures loose.

I inched toward the house, pulling stickers from my feet every few paces, anticipating the lecture I was sure to receive. Its form would be challenging, but its content would be vintage Bill. He'd go on and on about the virtues of taking a wife, settling down, and starting a family. There'd be stories from his past, lessons learned, and advice aplenty.

And I would indulge him, out of genuine respect and gratitude. Although I'd never spoken to him in any detail about the mess with Sheila, he'd always given me the sense that he understood my struggle. Above all, he had the patience to let it work itself out without forcing his hand. Allowing him some occasional room to proselytize was the least I could do. His wife was ten years deceased and his estranged son lived in Houston and never came to visit, or phoned, so he didn't have many people he could count on for an ear.

I showered, and then stepped out of the bathroom, naked, drying my hair.

"It's a great relief to learn that someone half my age has worse handwriting than I do," he said, sitting on the couch, flipping through my notebook of failed lyrics, psychedelic doodles, and forgotten reminders.

"Gimme that," I said, grabbing the notebook from him. As I hurried toward the bedroom, I managed to stub the ring and pinky toes of my right foot on the corner of an end table. The pain brought me to the floor and into a fetal position. I moaned and cussed, rolling about the hallway like an egg.

"Today is not your day," Bill said.

I moaned again.

"But it's early yet."

The pain stabilized after a minute or so. I crawled to the bedroom and put on the previous day's jeans, aggravating the pain. More moaning and cussing.

"Looks like I owe you a new van," Bill shouted. "At least the repair cost, if it's worth fixing."

"I don't even want to think about it."

"Only one person around here that can be trusted to determine that."

I stood up and began limping toward the living room. "The bastard better work fast and cheap," I said. "That turd cozy needs to be roadworthy in five days. I don't see that happening."

"You could just buy a new van."

"It's not that simple, Bill."

He steadied himself on the armrest of the couch and stood slowly. "Knowing Rhonda, she'll probably just charge you admission to watch her."

It was a shock that the van started, and a minor miracle that it was still drivable. The steering wheel required significant counterclockwise tension to keep the van headed straight, and the suspension system sounded like the drumline of a marching band of the hearing-impaired. We approached downtown, my arm dangling out the window and my business finger tapping against the door in feeble response to everyone's staring and pointing. It was no use. Like an unexpected visit from the Wienermobile, there's just no turning away from a dented beer can on wheels.

Bill treated me to breakfast at Flo's Diner—one of several local businesses he owned—before directing me to Rhonda's place on the southwest edge of town. Bill had spoken of her in passing before, but I'd never paid much attention. I let my prejudices have their way, imagining a dumpy, meth-eroded, menthol cigarette smoker with a firm mullet and a five-o-clock shadow.

"Is this Rhonda gal another one of your fantasy broads?" I asked.

He laughed. "She's the best there is. Divorced nine years, but she's still got plenty of good miles left in her. I've always thought you two might make a good pair."

This was the first I'd heard of it. I pushed myself away from the steering wheel and nickered. "See here, Bill. This is what you do," I began, equally irritated and amused by his perseverance. "You get it in your head that I'm in some desperate place—and, like you're doing God's work—"

He extended his index finger toward me. "Dit dit dit dit."

"I'm not finished," I said, the wag of my index finger matching his. "You try and save me from the Eternal Fire by slapping me together with whatever local gal has been dancing through your dreams."

He tried to laugh it off.

"It's true, old timer. I've become a conduit for your codgerly fantasies."

"Let me tell you something, Carl. Trying to find an attractive, available woman your age around these parts is like hunting farts in a hurricane."

The fortress surrounding Rhonda's junkyard appeared to be constructed with panels of metal siding peeled from old semi trailers; each a different texture, but all painted barn red. At the very least, it had the makings of some hot post-apocalypse real estate. I'd driven past it dozens of times. But, since I've never been much of a gearhead, I hadn't given the place a close look. I did like the name of the business: RAYNOLDS DOWN-HOME WRECKING. It had a nice bite to it—a premise for a campy Nashville-grade song, if not something better.

We drove through the main entrance and I was struck by how well-organized and tended-to the place was. This was something I'd never seen, or even imagined before—a junkyard with a woman's touch. The place had an order to it that seemed at odds with its own nature. All of the dead vehicles were arranged in tight, evenly-spaced rows according to make and model. More remarkably, the access paths were all grated and graveled, and appeared to be free of any Canada thistle, cheatgrass, or bindweed. Either birds were afraid to crap there, or Rhonda had found a deal on Agent Orange at an estate sale.

"I've known her since she was just a little thing," Bill said, his hands rising as though he were about to play a toy accordion. "She's got the gift. An artist, like yourself."

"I feel sorry for her already."

We parked at the mouth of the larger of her two garages. The doors were high enough to accommodate a combine or big rig with several feet to spare. She walked out onto the gravel to greet us, wiping her hands with a greasy red rag. She wasn't the grotesque caricature I'd drawn in my mind. Quite the opposite. I'd noticed her around town a few times, at gas stations, the video store, or Wal-Mart.

She smiled a big Pepsodent smile once she recognized Bill. She looked about my age, with long, full, straight red hair streaked with a few strands of gray. She'd soaked in her share of ultraviolet, and appeared fit for the most part, but moved with the limited flexibility of someone who'd spent a lot of years bent over engines.

Bill introduced us, and I felt one of my knuckles pop as we shook hands. Our eyes met level to the ground, both of us in sunglasses.

"I've heard about you," she said, loud and confident. "You wrote that song a few years back." The song she was probably referring to is one that I've never been too fond of, though it added a zero to my royalty checks. "You sound like you know what you're talking about."

I thanked her, surprised and delighted that she'd spoken that particular phrase. Most songwriters of my ilk will agree that *you sound like you know what you're talking about* may well be the holiest of compliments, especially when spoken from the mouths of haggard coal miners, old ranchers, and other salt-of-the-earth types free of all the bullshit that passes for critical vocabulary these days. I found myself wanting to tell her all of this right then, and I struggled to keep those valves shut so as not to sound too anxious. It made me wonder if she'd done some homework, maybe at Bill's suggestion.

She began a slow walk around the rear half of the van, and I began to feel self-conscious about the wreckage she was inspecting, as though she might judge it as a reflection of my own condition.

"I've already guessed why you're here," she said, walking through a large oil-swirled puddle left over from the storm. There was a pessimism and heaviness to her tone, and I prepared myself for the worst. Sure, I could afford another van. I could afford and justify a brand new tour bus, in fact, but Percy was irreplaceable. Rhonda stopped in the center of the puddle and rubbed her chin. "Your average person would probably junk this, but it's fixable."

This was exactly what I needed to hear. I liked her already, but this elevated her to sainthood.

"Do you think it'd be worth it?" I asked. It was a dumb question that I should've kept to myself. I'd already decided to go forward with the repair, though I felt compelled to downplay my concern for Percy's welfare.

"That's your call," she said, before sharing a quick chuckle with Bill. "We're obviously dealing with sentimental value issues here."

Bill pulled a toothpick from his shirt pocket and placed it in his mouth. "I'll pay for it, whatever it comes to."

"That won't be necessary," I said, not wanting Rhonda to think I was a charity case.

"No, sir," Bill said. "I have money tucked away for these situations. Senility insurance. I should've cut that damned tree down fifteen years ago."

I thought to push my point further, but the issue seemed to have already been settled, as though Bill and Rhonda had their own secret language of negotiation.

"It all depends on how pretty you want it to be," Rhonda said, gathering her hair into a bun and skewering it into place with a short length of wire. "You're looking at maybe a week to get this thing back to the way it was, assuming there isn't significant damage to the chassis, axles, etcetera."

I told her I needed it back by Wednesday night, and that I had a trip to leave for on Thursday morning. This seemed to excite her. She asked where I was going and I gave her the general idea.

"I can put a rush on it. There might not be time for paint—and who knows about these doors—but I can get the big dents out," she said, still standing in the water. "Don't ask me how, but I'll think of something."

"I'm sure you will," Bill said. "You're the best there is, and that's the facts."

"Oh, Bill. Stop being so damned cute," Rhonda said, walking out of the puddle. Her coy manner with Bill made me wonder if they hadn't had some brief, age-gap-defying fling at some point.

She pulled a set of keys from her jeans pocket, removed one from the ring, and tossed it to me. "You can use Helga in the meantime."

"Helga?"

She gestured toward a motley lineup of bastards and mutts parked adjacent to the entrance.

"The black stationwagon," she said. "Just don't get pulled over. She doesn't have papers."

I assured her that I'd be careful.

She removed her sunglasses and wiped the lenses with her peach-colored tank top, exposing her vertically-scarred navel. Was it a C-section scar, or some other surgery? Bill hadn't mentioned her having any children. Then again, he probably assumed it'd scare me off. She looked me in the eyes and smiled. "The temptation will be there," she said. "Let that be a warning."

I thanked her again, and she waved it away. She said she'd probably get to working on the van the next morning. "I'll need at least one night to dream up a strategy—for starters."

Bill and I sauntered over to Helga, got inside, and fired her up. It growled and hopped like a muscle car and had that pre-catalytic-converter aroma that conjured memories of cruising around with my father in his '68 Dart. What'd inspired Rhonda to put the money and time into souping up a frumpy mid-seventies grocery getter? She'd gone so far as to install a manual transmission and a tachometer. I was intrigued.

"Hows about that?" Bill shouted over the engine noise.

"I could get used to a car like this."

"No, you fool. That," he said, red in the cheeks, extending his thumb in Rhonda's direction, his hand moving in a sort of jerk-off motion. "I think she could get interested, if it ain't already in the works."

"Enough," I said, rolling down my window. I'd gotten the same sense from Rhonda, and had decided that she was good for at least one night on the town, but I didn't want to stoke Bill's imagination and expectations.

"You're a strange one," he said, while attempting to remove his safety goggles before his visor. This created quite a tangle of elastic, to which he reacted by spitting into the goggles as though there were snorkeling to be done. "But I suppose you've heard that before."

I shifted the transmission into first and tried to accelerate without kicking up gravel. The stationwagon had more power than anyone who's ever driven one would reasonably antici-pate. The tires lost traction, spraying rocks against the metal fortress walls, sounding like the opening shots of a Civil War battle reenactment. I saw Rhonda smile and shake her head as we tried in vain to leave quietly.

"Redheads are dynamite in the sack," Bill said, with the slow, straightforwardness of a tractor salesman.

"For chrissakes, Bill."

"My wife was a redhead—before she went gray," he continued. "But I still see her that way. She's still a redhead as far as I'm concerned."

We turned out onto the road, and I floored the accelerator.

"There's probably a song in that," he said, before the roar of the engine drowned him out. When we hit 100 mph, I looked over at him. He had his hands tucked under his thighs, shoulders hunched, looking like an eight-year-old version of himself if not for the loafers, khakis, and faded yellow shirt. The safety goggles and visor lay twisted in his lap.

We took the long way home, just to see what Helga was capable of. Rhonda knew. The temptation was there.

Mere days before this, a box of 500 compact disc copies of *The Essential Carl Mahogany* arrived at my door—the album I was expected to sell during the tour. Someone at the record label had sent along a handwritten note that read:

> We never heard back form u on this. Hope all the liner notes etc is correct. To late to change things now, unfortunately. Best luck with the tour. Gods speed.

Things got worse.

I removed one of the CDs from the box and gave the artwork a quick once-over, expecting to see a familiar photo of myself on the cover, taken 10 to 20 years previous. It would be generally un-fucked-with, just a plain, straight-on, lightly-stylized pic. I'd be wearing a cowboy hat and other articles of clothing the publicist or photographer forced me into that day. There'd be a rural backdrop. This is what I'd become accustomed to, and what would've been fine. I'm not fussy.

Not so with this one.

Yes, the photo had been taken probably 15 years before, during a professional shoot at a well-known old-town Nashville bar. The snap is from the bartender's perspective. Members of my touring band and road crew are strewn about the barroom, conversing with one another. I am sitting at the bar, in the center of the photo, looking as though I'm explaining something, or telling a joke to the only other person within arms-length.

This other person happens to be that former manager and friend I mentioned earlier—the one that skipped town with Sheila.

I turned the disc over. Almost the same photo, except I am no longer in it, as though I'd had to use the restroom, or maybe had never been there to begin with. The former manager remains, staring directly into the camera lens, wearing a crooked, self-satisfied grin.

There it was: all the pain, suffering, and associated bullshit of my previous 12 months set right there in my hands.

I scanned the song list on the back cover. Ten of them, ranked according to sales. I took a closer look. There were two typos—transpositions, to be precise.

This wasn't just a prank, it was a cruel joke. The photo concept was poignant enough, but taking a jab at my dyslexia was a brand new low.

Someone would pay dearly for this.

But, the asshole responsible for this juvenile effort wasn't there right then, so I went after the disc itself, attempting to break it in half using only my hands. This didn't work, so my kneecap got involved, and after a few more seconds of torque and twist, I was reminded of previous attempts, and what a futile and pathetic gesture it'd always proven to be.

I frisbee'd it across the room, and it left a dent in the wall by the temperature control.

I felt very bad about this.

So, I sat back and made an effort to calm myself, and to consider what it was exactly I had in front of me.

It'd been a year—almost to the day—since Sheila broke the news to me about her affair. So, it wasn't a stretch to interpret this as some sort of cruel anniversary message. But from whom? Sheila? My ex-manager? It seemed immediately obvious to suspect one, or both, of them, but I doubted it somehow. A stunt like this requires a good deal of planning and follow-through—two qualities that come to neither one of them naturally.

Maybe they'd hired someone else to do the work. A project like this could be done for around $700, I figured, using intern labor. But, even this seemed to require more effort than either one of them would be willing to put forth.

I hadn't communicated with either one of them since, nor had I received any updates as to their current whereabouts, or anything else. Maybe they were no longer a pair, and one of them was trying to get some sort of revenge on the other?

Good god.

A familiar sense of disgust came over me, enough to spring me off the couch. I paced the living room several times, and then began forcing the discs back into their shipping box, as though that might shift my focus. No such luck.

I dragged it all out to Bill's burn pile, which sits about 30 yards north of the guesthouse. The box was heavy and awkward enough that the physical effort served to help burn off some of my anger. There was no specific return address, but the box had been sent from Hendersonville, Tennessee, a suburb of Nashville. I thought to save the shipping label in case a number or bar code might help me solve the mystery.

Although the whole mess with Sheila had been no secret, I'd ruled out the label folks as either the instigator or perpetrator of this stunt, as it would've been a waste of their increasingly scarce resources. They had nothing to gain from it, and there were very few people still working there with whom I had even the slightest personal relationship or mutual history. However, there was a chance they might've heard something about it through the vines.

So, I decided to phone them under the pretense that I was inquiring about a proof copy of the real Essential album, and why I hadn't received one. The receptionist connected me to one of the A & R guys. We exchanged some introductory niceties, and I asked him about the proof.

"We don't typically send out proofs of our Essential series," he said.

This didn't sound right, and I let him know. "Shouldn't the artist be entitled to have some input on the final product?"

He laughed. "Carl, Carl. It's all recycled material anyway. Old photos, old songs. These Essential collections don't even matter in the grand scheme of things. They go straight to the discount stores, truck stops, and clearing houses."

I grumbled and cursed as he promised to have someone e-mail the album art to me.

"I'm not a big fan of this series myself," he continued. "But, come to think of it, I don't recall anyone else on our roster putting up any fuss about their Essential collections. So, we must be doing something right with these."

Nothing about his tone made me suspicious that he had any idea about the box of discs I'd received that day, and I had no reason to continue the conversation, so that was that.

Here's the thing: releasing a "Greatest Hits" collection is dangerous enough. An "Essential" collection is the end. Traditionally, when a label puts out some type of greatest hits album of an artist, this suggested that the artist still had many prime years ahead—at least in the eyes of the label.

On the other hand, an Essential album typically happens after one of three things: an artist's death, retirement, or when that artist's high water mark has been set—usually decades before—and there's no faith from the record label that it will ever be surpassed.

I'm not dead, and nowhere near retirement, as far as I know.

Fortunately, I'd be released from all obligations to the label once the upcoming tour was complete. They'd wanted me to do a minimum of sixty dates. I counter-offered with two, they said thirty, I said three, they said twenty, I said four, and so on. We settled on six: Kansas City, Saint Louis, Cedar Rapids, Davenport, Chicago, and Minneapolis. It was not that I didn't enjoy touring, just the fact that they expected me to hock their half-assed product as though the whole thing were my idea.

When the real artwork arrived via e-mail later that day, it was just as I'd expected—a black & white 20-year-old photo, and a song list that looked much like the one from the prank disc. I didn't care for it, and I might've called and bitched about it had I not received the prank disc first, but it now seemed pointless.

There were new labels on the horizon, and a much-needed second wind. I'd begun courting a few independents shortly after moving to Forsyth, and had gotten many positive responses, enough to get choosy, anyway. One Chicago-based label seemed like the best place to hang my hat. Their roster was loaded with rootsy artists without the typical Nashville veneers. I had at least one, and probably two parallel careers' worth of unreleased material that I'd pitched to them, which amounted to three bulging milk crates of spiral notebooks and cassette tape demos that I dumped into a box and mailed out. Their main man had allegedly listened to all of it, and sounded thrilled to bring me on board. We were to meet in person at the Chicago gig and discuss the next moves.

I called the post office in Hendersonville, where the prank discs had been shipped from. They were no help.

4

With Percy safe in Rhonda's hands, and the prognosis good, I got back to the tedious business of prepping for the tour. That afternoon brought more rain. I opened all the doors and windows to let the cool breeze through, brewed some coffee, and sat down at the computer. I had a few details to iron out with the Quad-Room in Davenport, Iowa, so I sent their promoter an e-mail, and then had a quick look at my junk e-mail folder.

I assume I get the same junk as anyone else—subject lines that read: "mE s000 horn333", "the experlence of a lifetime", "SHE'LL NEVER AGA:IN COMPLAIN ONCE ABOUT YOUR SIZE B=======D, and on and on. I noticed a message toward the bottom of the muck from a Karen Williams, Ph.D. I'd dated a girl with that name when I lived in Austin, Texas, over two decades before. In fact, she had a lot to do with my leaving Texas for Tennessee, and everything to do with my arrival in Nashville wearing a black eye and a small, J-shaped scar on my left cheek that still turns purple in cold weather.

The subject line read: Is this you?

It was vague enough that I almost passed it over. But, I had all day, so I chanced it.

Carlo!
I was hoping you were still alive! This is Karen from the old days in Austin. It took some extraordinary finagling to get your e-mail address. You must get a lot of crazed fans wanting a piece of the Hog!!!! Anyway, how are

things? I've got a proposal for you. I'm hoping we can talk. Please respond ASAP!

Sincerely,

Prof. Williams

I leaned back in my chair and glared at the ceiling, regretting having opened the message. It was definitely the same Karen. No one before or since has called me "Carlo."

The last time I'd seen her was the night she broadsided my head with a folding aluminum-frame lawn chair. It was late-summer. I was sitting alone in the backyard of my rental when I heard someone approaching from behind. I assumed it was one of my six housemates leaving for a night on the town. There were a string of expletives, and a brief commentary on my socio-economic background. I sat forward, turned to face her, and *whammo*.

Had the plastic armrest hit an inch higher, I would've lost my left eye. By the time I got reoriented and realized I was bleeding, she was slamming the back gate and charging down the alley without another word. My veterinary-technician trainee housemate stitched me up free of charge.

If I'd given Karen good cause for such violence, I couldn't remember it, aside from a few vague suggestions that I'd been thinking of leaving Austin. And, though I won't deny the likelihood that one, or several other potential causes existed, her zeal for alcohol and diet pills at the time deserves mention.

I reread the e-mail, looking for subtext and some sort of clue as to what her proposal might involve. I eliminated the worst possibilities. Our last sexual encounter happened long before the AIDS scare, and any lesser microbe or virus would've sprung years ago. I'd heard a validated story or two about old lovers, flings, and one-nighters coming forward with news of unplanned parenthood, but the chances of this were zero. If I'd gotten her pregnant, she would've been on my trail immediately. If not her, then her father, accompanied by a small, determined militia of West Texas vigilantes, blood-sporting dogs, and bible-wielding attorneys on ATVs.

These extremes aside, there were still possibilities for extortion and blackmail. Maybe she overestimated my real-world fame, and thought she had a tabloid threat to make. Maybe she'd committed to The Program and was pounding that trail of tears. I had no way of knowing, and I didn't have the patience for any games she might be trying to play, so I sent a brief, but polite reply e-mail suggesting she call me later that afternoon.

It was already 5:30, and about as later-in-the-afternoon as it was going to get. I knew I should've bought myself an extra hour, as it would take a few stiff warm-up drinks before I was ready to face that conversation. I fixed a tall glass of tequila and orange juice, sat on the couch, and began noodling on my mandolin.

The phone rang within a half-hour, and though it was right there next to my thigh, I waited for the fifth ring before answering it.

"I can't believe I'm talking to you again," she said, with more fire than my ears were tuned for. "Tell me, tell me, tell me!"

I told her the basics: where I was living, the tour, the crushed van. She sounded disappointed that I didn't have a more enchanting presentation prepared. I felt the same way.

I asked about her. She was soon to begin her twelfth year as a tenured professor at a college in St. Louis, teaching courses in Woman's Studies and World Literature. I mentioned that I'd be in St. Louis that Friday, but she already knew. Her lazy Texas twang was gone, replaced with some combination of anchorwoman clarity and post-game cheerleader hoarseness.

"Married and all that?" I asked.

"Nope, never went there. You?"

"Same deal."

"Wow. I figured you'd have married a model or an actress by now. They go for country singers it seems."

"Not this one, thank god." It wasn't the first time someone from my past had assumed that since I'd hobnobbed with famous beauties a time or two that I would've, or should've, made it my business to yoke one of them.

I could hear ice clinking on her end of the line, and I pictured her sitting on designer outdoor furniture, drinking a fruity cocktail, her bare feet up on a table, nose in the air, her long, straight brown hair parted down the middle like Emmylou Harris in the early seventies. She was still 20-years-old in my mind, radiant, beautiful, excitable, and spoiled rotten.

She suggested we meet up for a couple drinks when I passed through St. Louis. I agreed to it, not wanting her to think I still held any resentment toward her. Too many years had passed, and I probably owed her something for the serendipitous events that she initiated by assaulting me, and the few good songs I wrung out of the whole ordeal. I could always cancel if I had a change of heart. I could always cancel for any reason whatsoever.

"Actually, I have another idea," she said, before explaining that she had some leftover grant money from a previous academic project. "I'd like to start something new. I was hoping that maybe I could tag along with you on your tour and try to put something together."

No way in hell. This was against all current Mahogany policies, but an amusing idea. I'd had journalists and novelists ride with me before, but never a professor. "Some kind of magazine piece? An exposé?"

"No, no. Probably nothing even journalistic, really. More of a philosophy-oriented exploration. Memoir-ish, maybe. Too early to say. I'm of a hundred ideas all at once."

This was just vague enough to be useless. "Speaking from plenty of experience, I think you're picking the wrong subject."

She asked why I felt this way, and I explained to her the gist. "Wanting to write about a musician on tour is a rookie mistake."

"Really," she said.

"Yes. Nothing of any importance ever happens. A grind is all it really is. Not really conducive to interesting reading."

This didn't seem to faze her.

"I need to study an artist," she said. "Someone outside of academia, but established in their field. You're the first person that came to mind. You'd be perfect."

"Perfect?" I laughed. "You must have me confused with someone else!"

"I plan to pay my way. Hotels, food, gas," she said, sounding like I'd already agreed to her coming along. I was reminded of her peculiar way of moving on to the next issue as though the present one had already been settled in her favor.

Several potential complications came to mind if I agreed to her coming along. What would happen in Chicago, for instance, when my old friend came to the show expecting me to go home with her afterward to do all those naughty things we've grown accustomed to doing? What would I tell Karen? "Hey Karen, you'll have to go get yourself a room. Maria and I are going back to her place to perform naughties on her Sleep Number bed."

Or, how about in Cedar Rapids, when Bethany demands we go back to her place and do bong rips in her hot tub? What would I say to Karen then? "Professor, there's a reasonable motel down the street. Bethany and I are gonna go do bongs in her hot tub and later perform naughties in her purple gazebo amid the sandalwood."

Situations like these would be inevitable. I didn't need the hassle, nor did I need any hoity-toity, philosophy-oriented drivel taxing my conscience.

Yet, something was preventing me from saying no right then and there. Did I feel some obligation to allow her a chance to redeem herself? Maybe I wanted to see her fail in the pursuit. It seemed that the most I could do at that point was continue trying to talk her out of it.

"I don't usually get hotel rooms," I said.

"Where do you sleep?"

"In my van. At a friend's house on occasion."

"You sleep in your van?"

"Why not? I've got a pretty nice little set-up."

"What about showers?"

"They get taken."

She saw fit to remind me of my own name and the fact that I was an established singer and songwriter. "I'd expect your living conditions on the road would be more consistent with that."

"Luxury takes too much of the edge off."

"I guess I shouldn't be surprised."

"I live a pretty miserly existence out there."

"Huh, well that's interesting," she said, before humming some gibberish as though she were jotting something down. I decided I'd already given her too much material to work with.

"Every writer I've brought along with me for any period of time has not been anxious to do it again."

"And how can you be so sure of this?"

"They've told me. Or walked away in tears," I said. "No one's been subtle about it."

More gibberish and jotting from her end. "Is there an extra seat in this van of yours?"

This was audacious. I held the phone away from my ear, far enough to give it a brief, puzzled look.

"I really want to do this," she continued. "I promise not to be a pain in the neck. But, of course, it's entirely up to you."

"We're both aware of that. So, that's good."

"I'd like to see you again, either way. We have a lot to catch up on."

Her parting words were "bye, love."

I tossed the phone to the other end of the couch, feeling as though I'd just been shystered into some pyramidal financial commitment, even though I had yet to actually agree to anything beyond our meeting for a drink.

Aside from her vague description of her so-called project, she'd given me no other sense of what her motivations might be, and this was as good a reason as any to be suspicious. I gave the professor an F for clarity of message.

One thing was for certain: If I were to allow her to ride along with me for any period of time, I'd have to write up some terms and conditions for her to read and sign. I did want to see her again, if only for a drink or two, and the perverse, morbid pleasure of seeing what twenty years of gravity had done to her. We could compare notes.

5

The Forsyth State Bank sign flashed 7:59 —— 74° —— 8:00 as I drove Helga to work the next morning. This meant that I was late for another scorching day of rat fumigation.

The fact of my "other job" is a topic my publicist insists that I avoid discussing with interviewers. He finds the entire matter soul-wrenchingly offensive, and is relentless about reminding me that "all serial killers got their start killing small animals." I can't imagine how anyone could be so emotionally invested in the plight of rats, but I do appreciate his faith that I still have a learning curve, and may one day become something other than what I am currently.

As far as my income is concerned, I don't need another job. However, I discovered early on that I don't have the capacity, nor the gumption to sit at an instrument eight hours a day, five days a week, turning straw into gold, as many songwriters do. I tried it once, starting at 8:59 AM one Monday morning during my early Nashville days. By noon, my thoughts had become such a tangled existential mess that I worried I might've botched my entire future as a songwriter. I didn't have a mentor to help me unravel, and the experiment happened to segue into a months-long dry spell, so I slammed the door on that approach forever.

Truth is, nearly all of my song ideas come to me while I'm not thinking about music. They hit me while I'm driving, or work-ing—manual labor, if I can help it. It may be because my earliest songwriterly thoughts and ambitions sprouted while enduring the rhythms, repetitions, exertions, and frustrations of toiling on my uncle's farm that I find it difficult to write without these things.

I went to work for Lloyd Schumacher within days of settling in Forsyth. His ad in the *Forsyth Sentinel* read: PART-TIME HARD WORKER NEEDED FOR PEST CONTROL OPERATION—WILL TRAIN. It was the only ad that looked promising, so I called him, and he subjected me to a two-question phone interview. He hired me on the spot, on the sole basis of my claims to understand both the shit/Shinola differential, and the virtue of punctuality.

I'd made it to work on time, or early, every day until I parked Helga in front of Lloyd's house that morning—the remarkably least-maintained half of a dumpy beige brick duplex. He shuffled out to the work truck smoking one of his french vanilla-flavored gas station cigars, looking like he'd gotten one hour of tooth-grinding sleep. I expected a comment about my tardiness.

"What the fuck is this?" he asked, upon noticing Helga. He looked as though he'd just discovered himself to be the victim of a crime.

"One hell of a stationwagon, if there ever was such a thing," I said, before explaining what'd happened to my van, and who'd leant me the car.

"I know where you got it," he said, as though I should've already known that he knew. He lifted a case of fumigation pellets into the bed of the truck. "Did you tell her that you're working for me?"

"No. It never came up."

"What's funny is that car—" he extended his middle finger toward Helga, and then turned it on himself, "—used to be my car. Before she went and made a mockery out of the thing."

It was an odd coincidence, considering Forsyth proper had over 10,000 residents. Of the thousands of automobiles that'd come into her possession over the years, why had she chosen to fix up and keep Lloyd's stationwagon?

Lloyd was always cranky in the morning, but seemed especially bent by the presence of Helga. I could tell that he'd already made up his mind that Rhonda was up to something. I asked him what he knew about her.

"I've known her twenty-five years, sorry to say. Since high school. Before she became the town bicycle."

A light dimmed in me right then. Although I knew Lloyd to be a frothing misogynist, and an unreliable source for most things subjective, I was disheartened that there might be some kernel of truth in what he'd just told me.

We hopped into the cab of the truck, and he continued with his character assassination, accusing Rhonda of being a gold-digger, a neglectful mother, a drama queen, and a narcissist. He provided no supporting evidence for any of it. I'd heard him talk the same way about his ex-wife, but his opinion of Rhonda seemed to carry extra thunder.

"I'd advise you to steer clear," he said, inserting the keys into the ignition. "But I know how people are."

"And how are people?"

He looked over at me, a wince of disgust and disbelief etched deep in his gray, windblown face.

We left Forsyth, headed northeast on Interstate 76. Very little was said during the hour drive, and this was unusual. I managed to get a few words out of him about his nine-year-old son, Caleb, who lived with his mother in Denver all but one weekend a month. Caleb had asked me several times to give him guitar lessons, but we had yet to get around to it. I'd deduced from many conversations with Lloyd that his son's education would include minimal exposure to the arts, humanities, or the sciences, or anything else, for that matter.

Lloyd had never asked me anything about my music career. Not that I really cared to talk about it, but his marked lack of interest in the course of general conversation made it seem as though he resented the fact. He seemed to lack any ability to comprehend or acknowledge it as an upstanding, legitimate way of making a living. It'd become somewhat endearing to me, as just about everyone I'd grown up with—my parents, especially—shared this particular deficiency.

We took the Julesburg exit and drove north a half-mile or so, before turning right onto a gravel road running parallel to the river. Lloyd spotted the carcass of a pre-WWII pickup truck rotting in a break in the cottonwood trees. Its roof appeared to be slightly caved in, enough to inspire him to ask me more about what'd happened to Percy. I laid out the entire pitiful story. He got a good laugh out of the rodeo section.

"Fuckin' musicians," he said, shaking his head.

I knew how to handle the belittlement of my people. "Tell me, Lloyd—how many musicians have you known in your life?"

He thought a second. "My little brother plays some bass."

"That's great," I said. "Maybe he'd be interested in writing my next album."

"I'll bet he would be," he said, without the least hint at irony or sarcasm. "I'll bet he'd be way into that, actually."

We worked through the lunch hour preparing two forty-foot-tall REMEMBER 9-11-emblazoned grain silos for fumigation.

Lloyd used the farmer's backhoe to re-skirt the base of each silo with soil taken from the riverbank. He'd given me the death-defying task of scaling the sides of the large cylinders on a rickety ladder looking for and repairing cracks in the concrete. It was amid persistent spells of vertigo and fear for my life that I began churning over Karen's proposal.

The study aspect of it bewildered me the most. Of all things—social justice, glass ceilings, race relations, evil axes—nothing about what I did seemed all that significant or worthy of academic attention. Were the wellsprings of her chosen field of interest as overdrawn as mine? Was there nothing of real importance left for her and her kind to do? It occurred to me that she and I may have found ourselves in similar occupational and intellectual cul-de-sacs; unsatisfied, uninspired, and frustrated. It also occurred to me that the vague philosophical study/memoir-type-thing was nothing more than a workaholic's justification for taking a vacation.

And, what had she meant by saying she needed someone outside of academia? I was sure there was a dig on my lack of schooling hidden somewhere in there.

It seemed presumptuous to think that she'd want to rekindle something, but it wasn't a ridiculous stretch, after reviewing the few facts I had. Even if that wasn't to be the case, why not have her ride along for a day or two. If she didn't want to find that old spark again, it might be worthwhile to find out some reasons why.

Lloyd and I had the silos sealed and ready to gas by two o'clock. Four hours on an antique ladder had given me what I can only describe as a mild case of sea legs. We inserted the poison, and then moved Lloyd's truck into the shade of a cottonwood tree to take our lunch break.

It was our rite of bachelorhood to compare lunches, each of us trying to outdo the other in a contest to see who had the least-nutritious and least-appetizing meal. I poured the contents of my lunch sack onto my lap, initiating the contest by holding an apple up before me.

He hissed. "That's a perfectly good apple!"

I rotated the apple 180 degrees, revealing a bruise equivalent in topographical sprawl to all of Eurasia.

"Hmmf," he said.

I took a bite out of Central America, and then began telling him about the phone conversation I'd had with Karen the night before, giving him only the pertinent background information, including the origin of my facial scar.

"She wants to tag along on my trip," I said.

He removed a small sandwich from a plastic bag, and lifted the top piece of crust-free white bread to show me its contents: four medallions of crinkle-cut pickle atop a thick bed of margarine.

"She's a Woman's Studies professor," I added.

Lloyd shook his head. "Why don't they just call it home-ec? What was so wrong with that?" He took a bite from the sandwich.

"I think it has more to do with women's political issues and things of that nature."

"Jesus fuckin' christ, Mahogany." Bread debris flew about the cab as though an explosion had just occurred in his mouth. "You wanna spend a week driving across the country with a femi-nazi?"

This wasn't going anywhere that I cared to follow.

"I'll need to write up some terms," I said. "She might have to drive separate."

"I'll tell you what's gonna happen. She's gonna get in the way of you getting a shot at some split-tail," he began. "You don't need that. Unless you think you're gonna get hooked back up with this home-ec femi-nazi."

"I doubt she's looking for that, considering."

"Like that matters one bit." He shoved the rest of the sandwich into his mouth, thereby finishing the entirety of his lunch. "Whatever shit you pulled twenty-some years ago, she's obviously over it now."

"You'd hope so."

He dozed off for his usual 45-minute nap. I walked to the riverbank, sat on a slab of discarded concrete, and began writing a rough draft of the terms and conditions in my pocket notebook. I've read and signed enough contracts to know about the double-edged sword—get the first swing and dull the other's side while sharpening your own. As thousands of rodents were succumbing to phosphine gas poisoning in the silos behind me, I put this together:

> Upon my agreement to provide your transportation, you must adhere to the following:
>
> 1) Without prior approval from myself, you must not compromise the integrity of any performance by causing unnecessary stress (physical, mental, emotional, et. al.) on me or anyone else involved with production of any given performance. This includes, but is not limited to, venue owners and their employees, members of the press, members of the audience, and other individuals who may provide accommodations for one or both of us prior to, during, or following a performance.

2) It is not to be assumed by you that I will provide any other accommodations that our mode of transportation (one 1982 Ford Econoline cargo van) cannot be said to self-contain. Restroom breaks will occur during fuel stops, and in legitimate emergencies. The van may be used at all times for sleeping. Desired alternative sleeping arrangements must be made at locations in reasonable proximity to where the tour vehicle is parked for the given evening.

3) Prior approval will be necessary if the vehicle is to be used by you for any extraneous travel. This includes any use of the tour vehicle as a means of transport to or from a destination not along the most direct route to the next performance. Whimsical "tourist-y" stops and sojourns are discouraged, as they are not part of the monetary and temporal budget. Exceptions to this may be considered as the "spirit of the time" allows. I will have the final word in all of these instances.

4) Extra passengers or temporary "ride-alongs" must be pre-approved by me.

5) Your observation of me should not become a detriment to my overall sense of well being. If I feel it becomes so, I have the right to terminate your provided transportation.

6) I have the exclusive power to amend this list at any time.

It covered all the foreseeable concerns I could imagine. If she drove separately, then I figured the worst she could be was a nuisance, and I'd learned several techniques for stopping that sort of behavior.

I read the terms to Lloyd on our drive home, hoping that he might be able to apply his preternatural talent for getting shat upon to point out something I'd forgotten to address.

"That's all fine and good," he said. "But I'll bet she finds a way around all that mumbo jumbo."

"I'll need to work up a 'transgressing all of this mumbo jumbo' clause."

"And like I said, you're probably gonna miss out on some good Midwestern split-tail."

I nodded, pretending to make a note. "And I'll need a 'mediating a split-tail acquisition' clause too, I suppose."

The last scattering of sunlight sank into the horizon as we crested the final hill and began the long descent into Forsyth. The distractions of our day's work, his victory in the shitty lunch contest, and my apparent willingness to accept his advice about Karen's proposal—all of these seemed to have diffused his earlier frustration about Helga and Rhonda. We'd traded jokes and insults most of the drive home, but the slap-happy mood vanished as soon as the sparkle from Rhonda's stadium-grade junkyard lamps came into view.

I pretended to ignore the lights, but it was impossible. I knew Lloyd couldn't either, as they were in the line of sight for any westbound driver on that six-mile downhill stretch of highway. I attempted a shift into songwriter-mode, conjuring some rather boring, fairytale-esque descriptions of them. It wasn't until I imagined myself as Lloyd, viewing the lights as a symptom of an impending migraine, that I had anything worth hanging a song on.

When we arrived at Lloyd's, I was so enmeshed in sorting through metaphorical possibilities that I announced my intentions to swing by Rhonda's to check on the van.

"I could give a fuck," he said, snapping me out of my songwriterly stupor.

We stood beside the work truck, both looking at Helga and saying nothing. I was sure he could sense my enthusiasm. He knew as well as anyone that I'd been an undersexed hermit for the last year, and that I was likely to make a play.

The hesitation and silence became awkward; until I got the feeling that I'd made a corporeal shift from a meek employee to competing, alpha male wolverine. I grabbed my backpack and began walking to the car.

"Same time tomorrow?" I asked.

He'd already gone inside his house and closed the door.

It was after 9:45 by the time I'd cleaned myself of all the mud, grain dust, sweat, and rat shit of the day. With a slice of cold pizza in one hand and a beer in the other, I walked around the south side of Bill's house to see if Rhonda's lights were still shining across town. They were. I ran to Helga and sped off, hoping to make last call at the junkyard.

It must've been a new moon. The streets were bare and the town was quiet, as was usual for a Monday night. What I chose to do next could've prompted a call to the Forsyth police, but I took my chances, justifying and encouraging my actions in the name of research. I was already on a roll with the migraine song, and now the material for another was presenting itself—a junkyard owned and operated by an alleged gold-digging floozy with a penchant for melodrama. The gritty, off-color subject matter would keep it off the charts, but that was no reason not to forge a tune. The old self-righteousness came over me. It became my duty to the greater good to see where this situation would lead. I parked in the neighborhood north of the junkyard and snuck up on the place.

What I saw through a small gap in the metal fortress was alarming, and not knowing the first thing about auto body repair techniques didn't help. What Rhonda was about to do looked like it would tear the van right off its chassis.

She had the roof hanging from two hefty chains attached to the prongs of a giant Caterpillar forklift. Within minutes, the rear wheels of the van lifted off the ground. She rocked the forklift back and forth, using the weight of the van to pull out the dent. I imagine parents feel a similar gut-punch watching a doctor set their child's broken limb. I turned away, only to find the whole thing even worse to listen to—screeching metal, hydraulic gasps, springs being compressed and decompressed, the *beep beep beep* of the forklift's warning signal. I envisioned a pair of adulterers making scrap out of a box spring and mattress in a ghetto motel room, both of them ignoring cell phone calls from their spouses. One could say that the dent in my van was being fucked back into shape.

After a few minutes of this, the noise stopped, and the forklift shut down. My jaw and temples ached. I looked back and was surprised to see Percy in one piece. It didn't resemble beauty, but the majority of the dent was pulled out. Rhonda let the prongs down on the forklift and hopped from it onto the top of the van to undo the chains. I took a deep breath and finished my road beer.

I waited for her to get off the van, move the forklift to its parking space, and look like she was moving on to another project. She walked into the garage and shut down the big lights. I decided to make my move right then, before she closed up completely. Her red-eyed, red-haired border collie greeted me without a single bark or growl, nibbling at my ankles as I approached the garage.

Rhonda made a visor with her hand. "Who's there?"

"It's just Carl," I said, entering the penumbra of the fluorescent tube lights buzzing inside the garage. "Hope I didn't scare you."

"That's what I have Satan for," she said. It took me a second to realize she was referring to her dog. "She seems to think you're okay."

Satan wagged her tail, walking a figure eight around us.

"Don't tell me Helga already broke down on you."

"No, no. I was just in the neighborhood and thought I'd see how the van was coming along."

She asked how I'd gotten there, and I told her that I'd parked Helga up the street in case she wanted to lock up the main gate. She told me how unnecessary she thought that was before turning to face the van.

"It looks better," she said. "Not great, but better."

I took a closer look at it and agreed. "How do you go about fixing a huge dent like that?" I asked, just to see how she'd respond.

"I'm afraid that's proprietary information." She winked and smiled as she said it, and I started to think that Bill might've been right—she could get interested, if it wasn't already in the works.

She told me I needed another beer, and I didn't argue. How she'd determined that the can I'd arrived with was empty puzzled me. She turned and walked toward a small fridge in the garage. I slapped a mosquito that landed on my forearm.

"Yeah, unfortunately junkyards provide an ideal breeding ground for bloodsucking insects," she said, having only heard the slap. It'd been a quiet one at that.

She opened the fridge door and mumbled something at the very instant I complimented her on her acute perceptive abilities.

"Thank you, Carl. But it doesn't take much to recognize when a fridge is empty of beer," she said, before closing the door.

I was sure she'd misapplied my compliment in every way, and I thought to rewind and do another take, but it was no use, as she'd already excused herself to get beers from the house.

I poked around inside her garage, marveling at her arsenal of large red tool chests, greasy hydraulic lifts, engine hoists, and shelves packed with various lubricants, cleansers, paints, and other fluids. I noticed a large blaze-orange Pabst beer banner hanging from a girder that read "Welcome Hunters." The bust of a bull elk or deer was printed on it; the creature having gender-defying, voluptuous, anthropomorphous lips. I hoped Rhonda wouldn't resent me for being generally ignorant about things like hunting or the current stats of professional sports teams. I pledged not to allow those subjects to surface. We could talk about cars instead—not that I knew much about those either.

I discovered a slingshot hanging from a pegboard. I grabbed it and tried it on, wondering how long it'd been since I'd held one. I walked onto the driveway, picked up a rock and shot it over the fortress and across the road. Shortly after it cleared the wall, I heard a cow mooing.

"I use that to scare pigeons away," Rhonda said, carrying a twelver of Coors Light cans. "They love to crap all over my sign."

She gestured toward a stacked quartet of plastic chairs and asked me to grab a couple.

"What do you want to listen to?" she asked, stopping in front of her stereo. "I imagine you're somewhat picky."

Where'd she get that idea? I situated the two chairs to face the van. "I'll listen to anything at least once."

"I bought one of these one-hundred disc changers. I'm just going to hit 'random play' and we'll see what happens."

"Fantastic."

"I love the random play button. It takes the pressure off."

I agreed, thinking what she said could be mistaken for swinger talk, and weighing that against Lloyd's earlier allusion to bicycles. The moment was as ripe as any for complimentary innuendo, but my nerves were too jumpy to utter anything worthwhile.

She switched off the fluorescents in the garage, leaving only a small incandescent lamp glowing in a far corner. "There Goes Another Love Song" by the Outlaws began to play. I remembered sharing a bill with them at a state fair somewhere in the South, sometime in the mid-eighties. I was tempted to mention it, but didn't want to come across as being a name dropper. A year in Forsyth had cured me of that industry habit.

She handed me a beer, sat down, wove her fingers together, and thrust her palms toward the sky. The stars were dense and bright, and it appeared that the stage was setting itself for a romantic evening at the junkyard. I hoped that I hadn't made it obvious that I was looking for one by stopping over. Much of me was, but if things didn't work out that way, fine. Keeping the conversation focused on the van seemed like the wise thing to do.

"I've gotten almost 440,000 miles out of that ol' beast," I said.

"Course that's three engines and two trannys later. Not bad for a Ford."

She leaned back in her chair, looked up at the stars, and began performing air mathematics with her index finger. "That van has circled the globe between seventeen and eighteen times. Almost unheard of. You must be a careful driver."

"Luck of the German, I guess."

"I don't think your van would agree," she said, pulling a cigarette from the breast pocket of her T-shirt and lighting it. "*Carl*, sure. But, *Mahogany*—that doesn't sound very German to me."

Only one other person had ever cast doubt upon the authenticity of my surname, and that was Sheila's father—a prominent, bulbous, good ol' boy, Nashville divorce attorney. But, what'd taken him four years to get around to doing, Rhonda had already done within ten minutes.

"It was my grandfather's idea," I told her.

"And why's that?"

"Well, let's just say a very distant relative of his pretty much fucked things up in the Old Country."

A cricket chirped in the far corner of the garage.

She took a pull from her cigarette and exhaled. "Well, what can you do? Though, I have to ask, what brings you to this godforsaken town? I can't even imagine someone wanting to stop here to die."

"Had to get out of the rat race," I said, mostly out of habit.

"But are you still a rat—that's the question."

And so we'd arrived, much sooner than I'd anticipated, at the topic of rats. I'd hoped to avoid discussing certain realities. However, if I expected to get any answers to the questions I had about her, Lloyd, and Helga, she would have to know.

"What's the story behind that stationwagon?" I asked, hoping she might admit to sending Helga with me as a way of irritating Lloyd.

"Good question," she began. "It was supposed to be a demolition derby car, but I ended up putting too much time into it."

I bought this. She showed no signs of withholding anything. I wondered if Lloyd had ever been made aware of this detail, and whether Rhonda had intended to demolish the car before a crowd of bloodthirsty spectators as some sort of symbolic retribution.

"Do you like it?" she asked.

"I love it."

"She grows on you."

She almost had me convinced that she wasn't playing games with me, but I still needed more information. I could continue asking questions about the car, while avoiding the Lloyd issue, but I knew that doing so would eventually reveal me to be untrustworthy.

"I talked to someone today who seems to know quite a bit about the history of that vehicle," I said.

She gave me a suspicious look. "You must've run into Lloyd. That used to be his car."

"He mentioned that."

"Where'd you run into him?"

"I work for him part-time."

She laughed. "What is someone like you doing in the pest control business? I thought you were a country star."

"I need to get my hands dirty once in awhile. Songwriting is sissy work."

"I'll bet it is."

I was happy that she could see things my way with so much ease. We sat silent a moment. She leaned forward in her chair and shook her head. "What are the odds?"

I decided to take my chances and ask if she and Lloyd had had some sort of falling out in years past.

"He didn't tell you?"

"No details."

"We went to our senior prom together. He's been a problem ever since. Frankly, I've always been a little scared of the guy."

"Scared?"

"It's hard to explain. Something in that messed up head of his makes him think he owns me. I think most towns would have him locked up in a nuthouse."

This was a side of Lloyd that I'd been blissfully ignorant of. He might've come across as a little obsessive and short-tempered on the job from time to time, but I'd always assumed it was the ex-wife, attorney fees, and occasional hangover bearing down. Maybe Rhonda was exaggerating.

"You're already in trouble is the thing," she continued. "I wish I would've known you worked for him. I would've sent you with a different car."

"Dumb luck. What can you do?"

"You might not want to mention that you came over here tonight."

"Too late for that."

She let out a brief menacing laugh, while slapping a couple mosquitoes. "Oh boy. Maybe we should move inside."

I wasn't sure whether it was the proliferation of mosquitoes or the thought of Lloyd lurking outside the fortress that prompted her suggestion, but we were on the move either way.

I asked how she'd gotten involved in her line of work as she began closing down the garage.

"It's the family business," she said. "My brother ran it for a few years after my father passed, and then I took it over. I was twenty-three, so it's been about nineteen years."

"That's a career."

"Tell me about it. Turning wrenches is hard on the body."

"You could sell."

"I've thought about it, but the idea never sticks. And what else would I do, really?"

She locked the front gate, and I followed her into the house—a two-story Victorian, probably built in the early 1900s. It loosely resembled my childhood home. A large metal Standard Oil sign hung above her stove that someone had taken a couple shots at with a firearm in years past.

I asked about her daughter, and she told me that Shannon was in her second year of college in Greeley, working on a business degree.

"More interested in the party scene, I'm afraid," she said.

"Plenty to learn there. Though it won't pay the bills."

"What she needs to learn is that mommy's gonna stop sending checks if she doesn't get her act together."

Rhonda didn't look too convinced by my assurance that Shannon would get herself straightened around. Had my superego not kicked in right then, I might've said "look how I turned out."

I followed her into the living room. She asked if I'd ever been married or had any kids and I told her. Then she asked my age and I told her.

"So, either you're broken, too much of a burden, have mother issues, or a closeted homosexual," she said.

"That's quite a list."

"I'm just messin' with you," she said, gesturing toward her large, faux suede, blue couch. "Have a seat."

I sunk into the swollen cushions, taken aback by what she'd just said. Not that I took much pride in my extended bachelorhood, but her comment produced a certain sting that I wasn't prepared for. I became fixated on the fact that she'd listed four issues, rather than the more natural-sounding three. If she'd really just been teasing me, I would've expected only three. The extra effort required to add that awkward fourth item seemed to suggest that maybe she wasn't joking.

"I'm just dedicated to my work," I said, attempting to play it off.

"Amen," she said, kneeling to flip through a large wooden crate of LPs. "It took me way too long to figure that out about myself."

This was a comfort, and a welcome change from the sideways, suspicious looks of pity I'd come to expect from most people upon their learning of my zero and zero marital record. It was at this moment that I became convinced that Rhonda would be worth a go. To hell with Lloyd.

I was anxious to find out which LP she was going to put on the turntable, and I hoped she wouldn't ask for my approval. I wanted her to slap something down with authority. This is the behavior of a woman who knows her music, and herself.

She told me what we were going to hear before the music began. "The thing about Roy Orbison that I like is I don't really have any memories tied up in the songs," she said. "Know what I mean?"

"You're one of the few. He had special powers."

She sat down beside me and lifted her feet onto the boomerang-shaped, baby blue mother-of-toilet-seat coffee table. "I gave away four big crates of records just like that one after my divorce," she said, lighting another cigarette. "My friends thought it was a stupid thing to do. But, hey—when you need to start over, you need some different music."

"That's what keeps the wheels turning," I began. "Some say all of the great songs have already been written, but every time a song gets associated with a bad memory, then a new one has to be written to take its place." I felt a rare sensation that I'd just come up with some songwriterly insight for the ages.

"Job security for you."

"I wish that were the case."

"That's one thing I've got here. People come to me from hundreds of miles around."

"Are you the best there is, like Bill says?"

"I'll let him be stubborn about that," she said, inspecting the grease spots on her shirt and shorts. She asked if I wouldn't mind waiting while she took a shower. "Make yourself at home."

I decided to give myself the grand tour as soon as I heard the water flowing. I'd already noticed that she kept a clean house. The fact that she also managed to keep a clean junkyard—well, I had nothing in my experience to weigh against that. Her walls were dominated by old signage from the oil and auto industries. Many of her smaller pictures, posters, and signs hung at an angle, and she had lots of 50s and 60s kitsch strewn about like a Route 66-style diner that was trying too hard. I didn't really care for any of it. But, who was I to judge. It was her house, and I'd seen far worse collections in other women's homes—macramé, ferrets, black lacquer, Jim Morrison.

I did a strange thing while in the kitchen and wiped my finger along the top of the fridge. It was the spirit of my mother possessing me. "The true test of a clean home," mother would say. There was no dust on my fingertip, and I wasn't sure how to take this. If Rhonda lived this clean, what might she think of the top of my fridge, and the dusty crannies of my life?

After inspecting the bathroom/laundry, and two other storage-type rooms on the main floor, I decided to have a look at her LP collection. Most people buy the majority of their records between the ages of sixteen and twenty-four. A close inspection of such a collection can produce a fairly accurate anthropological reading of an individual. I was glad she'd told me that she'd gotten rid of most of her albums, because what remained were titles like Blackfoot's *Vertical Smiles*, The Amazing Rhythm Aces' *How the Hell Do You Spell Rhythum?*, and Nazareth's *The Fool Circle*—one- or two-star albums from bands on their way off the radar. She didn't have any of my records. Maybe she'd given those away with the rest of the good stuff.

Right.

Orbison reminded me of Sheila, so he had to go. I found a gem toward the back of the crate; Patsy Cline's *Sentimentally Yours*. If there was to be any romancing in my immediate future, I knew Patsy would help me out. Rhonda began descending the staircase just as the stylus caught the groove.

"Do I look better?" she asked, posing at the foot of the stairs in a tank top and cut-off jeans—just a cleaner, wetter version of what'd been before. I decided I preferred her sweaty and dirty, but didn't mention it.

"You look like you're ready for a night on the town," I said, thinking it might relieve some pressure to get out of her house and hit a bar or two.

"I haven't done a night out in Forsyth in . . . geez."

Something about that bit of information came as a surprise and a relief in light of Lloyd's allegations. I began to suspect that Lloyd really had no idea what Rhonda actually did with her time. "Shall we go out for a few?" I asked.

"No, no. Not tonight. There's nothing going on around here on a Monday night. You oughta know that by now," she said, returning to her earlier spot on the couch. "Let's open a bottle of wine." She said it as though I had no choice in the matter. I've never been accused of being a lily-liver, but I was already feeling a bit above the weather. Opening a bottle hinted at a contract of sorts. We would drink wine, and I would be too drunk to drive, and so I'd either stay there, or walk two miles home. An offer seemed to be making itself.

"Yes, let's do that," I said.

She set some glasses on the boomerang table, poured the wine, and then handed me the bottle to inspect—a 1995 Coniale Di Castellare something or other. I swirled it around in the glass and smelled the red wine-ness of it, then took a little of it into my mouth and tumbled it around.

"Uniquely Italian," I said, holding the glass up to the light.

She laughed. "You're not a connoisseur."

"Of wine? No."

"Of what then?"

"Emotional baggage, human wreckage. You?"

"Have we met before?"

The wine went down fast as we talked more about her daughter, music that we'd grown out of, the junkyard business, and Forsyth. She asked about life on the road, and I told her a version of the truth—that I'd grown tired of all the forced environments and endless hours spent on interstate highways.

"Maybe you should have someone else ride with you," she said. Karen passed through my mind.

"I prefer not to, really," I said, trying not to sound like an ass. "The more people you travel with on a tour, the more waiting there is to do. I'm not at the right age to enjoy that sort of thing."

"I think you should take me with you," she said, excited by her suggestion.

Why was I being faced with two women wanting to tag along on this tour without me having offered either of them the opportunity? My efforts to discourage and talk down the experience didn't seem to be working on Rhonda either. I needed to improvise. "It's a little late in the game," I said. "I'd have to make all new arrangements."

"I'll pitch in for gas," she said. "And who couldn't use an expert mechanic on a long trip? That van could break down any second."

I'd have to start telling lies in order to deflect this. I told her that I'd been planning on staying in Cedar Rapids for awhile after the tour to spend time with an old friend who'd just lost his wife to cancer. This came out sounding like breaking news to me.

"I'm sorry to hear that," she said, placing her hand on my thigh.

I took a sip of wine, ashamed that I'd instigated our first maybe-sexual contact with a lie. I had to redeem myself with a truth. "I could use a non-working vacation one of these days, though."

"We should take one. Drive up to the Badlands, or something."

"We should."

She rested her head on my shoulder without saying any more. I rested my head on her head. For reasons that I could only blame on the Italian red, a scene from the movie *Rain Man* came to mind.

I put my arm around her as she nudged closer to me. She twisted her hair with her long, callused fingers. I hesitated for a moment, asking myself if all this was happening too fast. Considering the glacial velocities at which my life had moved over the previous year, what authority did I have to say what was too fast or too slow? What frame of reference, and what credibility did I have to fairly judge that?

Soon enough, there was no good reason to fight it. We fell onto the floor at some point, as Patsy sang "Strange."

6

I woke alone in her bed—a waist-high, king-sized, dual box spring monster truck of comfort. There were no noises to indicate that she might still be in the house, just the faint whir of a refrigerator motor and the eerie burble of a pigeon perched within feet of the bedroom window. Judging by the cool air flowing through the room and the electric blue sky, I figured I had a good hour or more to get home and prepare for work.

After a few dumb minutes of glowing reflection on the previous night's events and the end of my dry spell, I stood from the bed and began gathering my clothes. Everything was accounted for except one sock that I assumed Satan had snagged sometime in the night. I got dressed and put my shoes on, walked downstairs into the kitchen, and looked out the window toward the garages. No sign of Rhonda there either. I discovered a note on the kitchen table informing me that she'd gotten called out on a tow and didn't expect to be back until after 9:00 AM. I patted myself down, searching for my phone, before realizing I'd left it in Helga. The clock on her microwave read 8:10.

When I reached Helga I was out of breath and in the early stages of a shin cramp. My cell phone was lying face-down near the gear shift. I flipped it open, only to discover its battery had drained. Two options presented themselves: I could race home and call Lloyd, or I could risk showing up at his place in his old stationwagon, trying to explain why I was late, minus a sock.

I knew Lloyd to be a varsity drinker, but not the type to be seven or eight drinks along by 8:30 AM on a Tuesday, which he no doubt was when he answered his phone. Before I even had a chance to speak, he'd made it obvious that work was out of the question. I should've hung up right then, but thought I'd better plant a few lies in his head.

"Brown bottle flu?" he asked.

"Nope. Power went off. I've got blinking clocks in every room."

"I've heard em all," he said, sounding amused by my excuse. He made a bunch of woo, hey, and whoa sounds as though a small circus had just invited itself into his house. "Well, alright. You sound pretty chipper this morning. Somebody musta gotten a piece last night."

I was sure I didn't sound any more chipper than any other morning, though my 100-yard dash from Rhonda's to Helga was probably working against me.

"Not me, if that's what you're implying."

"You still driving that stationwagon around?" he asked.

"Yep. Probably for a couple more days."

"We're not working today. Taking the day off."

"I figured as much."

There was a long pause. I could hear canned laughter from his television. It sounded as though Lloyd's attention had turned that direction, and so I told him that I planned to take Wednesday off to prepare for the trip. He seemed to have not heard me.

"What'd you do last night?" he asked. This was the first time he'd ever asked me such a question, that I could recall.

"Just worked on some shit here at the house."

"Just worked on some shit there at the house, huh?"

"That's about it. Couldn't sleep for shit."

"Thought I saw my old car parked over by Rhonda's."

He was onto me, but I figured I'd try to talk my way out of it. "Yeah. I went to look at a guitar to buy."

"And you stayed the night there?"

"No, the damn thing wouldn't start. The guy gave me a ride home."

"And then the car fixed itself?"

"Rhonda got it started this morning. Bad battery connection was all."

He laughed. "I liked the power outage better."

He had me. "Shit'll happen."

"I didn't take you for a lying sonofabitch, Carl. Shame on me."

And without another word, he hung up. The fact of his drunkenness had pretty much erased all credibility and accountability on his end, but it wasn't much comfort knowing I'd be able to use it against him in the future. It was reasonable to assume that some of the finer details of our conversation might not survive his next hangover, though I was sure whatever problem he had with Rhonda and me would persevere.

Rhonda was still out on her call when I returned to the junkyard. I parked Helga where she couldn't be seen from the road and decided to wait in the house. A brief search of likely canine hiding spots produced no missing sock, so I gave up, sat at the kitchen table, and began flipping through the June issue of *Motor Age*.

I'd never experienced Lloyd in a full-blast stupor before. From what little Rhonda had told me the previous night, I assumed she probably had a time or two. I hoped she could provide some perspective on his behavior over the long-term that might ease my concerns. It occurred to me that I might be making a big deal out of nothing, but I couldn't ignore the madness that I'd heard in his voice. It'd given me no reason not to worry that he might unravel and come after one or both of us in a booze-fueled rage. How that event might unfold was anyone's guess, though I imagined it'd probably involve him dropping by the junkyard, unannounced, with a few things to share.

Rhonda returned a little before 10:00, towing a recent-model American sedan. I walked outside and watched her as she put the tow truck in reverse and backed the sedan into the garage in one graceful stroke. She stepped out and away from the tow truck, allowing Satan to leap down from the bench seat and charge at me.

"Looks like you've made a new friend," Rhonda said, as she began lowering the front end of the sedan to the concrete floor. "I take it you've got the day off."

"Yeah," I said. Satan walked frantic circles around me as I approached Rhonda. "Lloyd's just not himself today."

She gave me an *uh oh* look, as though she knew I'd just made a generous understatement.

"Seems he was doing some snooping around the neighborhood last night," I said.

She shook her head, and her eyes opened wide, looking annoyed. I got the sense that she didn't care to hear any further details. "Don't you worry about him."

"You don't think he'd—"

"What, actually do something? He wouldn't dare. You can quote me on that."

I stood silent for a moment, not at all convinced.

"Though, I must say you do look pretty handsome standing there all worried about it," she said. "The one sock really helps."

I looked down at my ankles, each one entirely covered by the material of my jeans. There was no way anyone would've been able to tell by sight alone that I was one-socking it.

"It's probably still up on the seat," she said, pointing at the truck's cab. "I hope it wasn't your favorite sock or anything."

After a few minutes of loitering and watching Rhonda hook the sedan up to some sort of diagnostic gizmo, it dawned on me that I should leave her to concentrate on her work. I asked if she'd like to come over for dinner that night or the next.

"We can celebrate my one year anniversary," I said.

"Of what?"

"Living here."

She laughed. "Surely, with your imagination, you could brew up a better reason to celebrate."

"I'll work on it."

She suggested we wait a night so she could be sure to have the van ready. "As much as you love that monstrosity, love alone will not heal it."

"Whatever you have to do." We had a brief kiss and then I started for Helga. "Bring a few bottles of that wine. That seemed to do the trick."

"I agree," she said. "Is Satan invited?"

"Satan is always welcome."

I drove home, made some coffee, and began sorting through my song catalog, deciding which of them would be the least painful to perform. Three hours later, I'd settled on my list of twenty, which included only two from the *Essential* compilation. Half of them I hadn't played in over a decade. A few I'd forgotten altogether, including a couple of my better ballads that the record label had thought "too evocative, in places, of unpleasant realities," thus making no effort to market them at the time of their release. At least one person liked one of these songs enough to steal the premise, give it the Hallmark Treatment, put his name on it, and sell it to Alan Jackson, who then went on to make a minor hit out of it.

By the time I took a break and checked my e-mails, I'd pretty much forgotten about Karen. A new message had arrived:

> C, Just wondering if you've come to a decision yet. I promise not to be a parasite! Put me to work selling CDs and shirts! No hurry. Just wanting to know if I should make other plans for the week. Love, K

Meeting her for a few drinks in St. Louis is all I'd agreed to. But, here again, she'd already decided—in her anxious entitlement-complex logic—that I'd already committed to much more than that, and now should be held accountable for it.

> K, We'll meet for a couple drinks in St. L. Lookin forward to it. C

Sundown came, and I was inspired to go watch it, so I took a walk around the north end of Bill's ominous windbreak of Russian olive trees. I brought my phone along in case Rhonda called, ignorant to the possibility that I might get a call from anyone else—Karen, in particular—but I answered anyway.

And, without a return greeting, the thrust began: "I'm sorry. I don't mean to sound so forward."

"This is Carl, how may I help you?"

She paused for a few seconds. "Are you okay?"

"Better than ever."

"Is this a bad time?" Her tone had an irritating sobriety to it, sounding like the voice of an artificially concerned, preoccupied shrink. It was enough to get me out of the negotiating mood.

"Yes," I said. "I was just about to enjoy the sunset."

"Have you thought about my proposal?"

"About meeting up for a drink? Yeah, I'm sure we can arrange that."

"Okay," she said, followed by much silence, as though she expected me to continue. "And what about all the other stuff?"

"I've thought about that."

"Well, what do you think?"

"I can meet up for a drink. That's all I can promise."

"You don't want me to ride with you then?"

Now she was trying to guilt me. "Haven't we been over this?"

"But you haven't really given me an answer. I'm confused."

"About what?"

She let out a condescending laugh. "If you don't want me to ride with you, just tell me."

"You talk like I've already said yes, is the thing."

"No."

"Then why do I feel like I'm trying to back out of an agreement I never made?"

"I don't know. I'm just hoping you'll let me ride along with you."

"Why?"

"Because I think it would be a good thing."

"Why?"

"Jeezus, Carl. Do you have to be so difficult? Is it really that big of a deal?"

"Tell me why you want to do this again?"

"I've already told you!"

"I've heard a lot of *ums, huhs,* and *not sures.*"

"Do you want me to write you an essay?"

It was a great idea that I should've thought of before. Maybe this was my out. "That would be wonderful."

Silence.

"You're not being serious."

I thought a moment. "I want a five-page outline. Due by 7 PM tomorrow."

"Wow," she said. "Really?"

"Yes."

"You want a five-page outline."

"And be sure to include a section entitled 'What's in it for Carl.'"

"Seriously?"

More sighs and grumbling from her end. It all sounded very adolescent to me, and not the reaction I'd expected from an exalted academic. Was a five-page outline really all that much to ask? Couldn't she do that in her sleep? I probably should've gone with her original idea and demanded an essay.

Before I hung up, I bastardized some useless words of wisdom I'd picked up at the one and only songwriter's workshop I ever attended, hoping it might irritate her as much as it had irritated me over the years: "Try to channel all these feelings of disbelief into the body of the outline."

7

I don't know much about Forsyth's history, but I do know what I like. I liked Bill's explanation that the only thing I needed to know about the town was that it sits at the intersection of the South Platte River and the center of the primary southern migration route of the North American tumbleweed.

He shared this bit of knowledge with me the first time we met. I was at the end of my second day driving away from Nashville and the Sheila disaster when I stopped in Forsyth for dinner and a room. At the recommendation of a truck stop cashier, I drove two miles out of the way to a place called Jim's Steakhouse. They had a "famous" dish—self-proclaimed, I assumed—called "Beef Charlemagne" that I ordered solely on the coincidence of the entrée's Steely Dan-sounding name.

Bill sat alone two barstools away, drinking a scotch. He initiated our conversation by asking where I was from. This led to an abridged version of what'd spat me out of Music City. He asked what I did for a living, and it turned out he was familiar with some of my songs.

The matter of where I planned to go next soon followed. I told him I was looking to find a place in the Rocky Mountains, though I had no specific area in mind. After a few more drinks, he offered to spare me the hotel expense and put me up in his guest house for the night. He seemed like a trustworthy, upstanding, community-oriented old man, so I took him up on his offer.

He'd failed to mention the extent of his wealth during our conversation at the steakhouse. What he'd referred to as his guest house was a 1,500 square-foot, fully furnished, all-brick ranch style number that sat in the center of 320 acres. The next morning, he treated me to breakfast at Flo's and offered the house to me for $400 a month.

"You're not going to get a deal like that anywhere near the mountains," he told me. "We're right on the edge here. After this it's all hippies, Mormons, radioactive fallout, and then the whole California problem."

I figured it couldn't hurt to try it out for awhile.

And then awhile turned into a year.

Bill helped kick off my 365th day in Forsyth by joining me for a walk around the inside perimeter of his property—a challenging three mile journey alongside sagging, rusted barbed wire fence smothered by thistle, tumbleweeds, and prairie trash. We talked a little about the tour, and I told him about Karen and her proposal.

"That sounds fishy," he said.

"No doubt. But, I think I talked her out of it."

"You think?"

"Well, I didn't say no, but it was the very next thing."

"Have you told Rhonda about this?"

"Why would she need to know about it?"

He took a whack at a rotted wood fence post with his walking stick. "Here I thought you and her were making time."

I laughed. "What would give you that idea?"

"Where did you sleep the other night?"

I didn't respond fast enough, and he swatted my shoulder

with the back of his hand. "You can't fool ol' Bill. How dare you even try?"

"She knows nothing about it, and there's no reason she should."

He whistled a few random notes. "Loose lips sink ships."

"Exactly. All this will probably amount to is a couple of drinks before a show. I'd like to see how the years have treated her."

"Whatever you say, Carl."

"That's right."

I hoped the walk would inspire me to think up an impressive dish to prepare for Rhonda that night, and this was all I could think about while Bill rambled on about the aesthetics of wind turbines and the future of wind farming. I had nothing to go on. Was Rhonda a vegetarian? Did she have any food allergies? All of the guessing and worry could've been taken care of with a simple phone call, but I didn't want to disrupt any anticipation she might've been feeling. I was feeling it, and had learned to appreciate and coddle the rare, precious, and fleeting anxieties of a new relationship while they lasted.

Unfortunately, I had no desire to remain in Forsyth for any reason, new relationship or no. Exactly when I was going to act on my impulse to leave was uncertain, as was even the most general idea of where I might want to go next. All I knew for sure was that it was time to move on to something else, and soon. It soured my mood to think I'd have to tell Rhonda, and that I should probably do it that night. I thought I'd better tell Bill while I was thinking about it.

"Move? You just got here for cryin' out loud," he said.

"Well, old timer, I think I've accomplished what I set out to accomplish by deciding to live here."

"And what was that?"

"I guess you might say I needed to subject myself to the healing hands of time."

He stopped, and then I stopped a few steps beyond. I looked over my shoulder at him. He had a thumb hooked around a belt loop.

"Good lord, Carl. That's dumber than a fish in shit."

I continued my walk. "Well, I didn't come here for the action."

"Baloney," he said, jogging a little to catch up with me. "There's all sorts of fun to be had around here. The rabbit hunting is excellent. We've got the biggest bowling alley between Denver and Omaha. Cabella's is only forty-five minutes away."

"Maybe you're right. What am I thinking?"

"You'll miss out on the new fun park. And what about the county fair? All the big names come through eventually." On and on he went, naming as many of the area's recreational opportunities and annual events as he could think of. I listened to his list as it began to gasp, putter, and cough, hoping he might've gotten my point by the time it was exhausted. Not a chance. "See, Carl. Plenty to do around here."

We weren't a half mile along before Bill had to stop for air. He bent over and placed his hands on his knees.

"Whew, I'm out of shape" he said. "Too much waiting around to die, I guess."

Although it was said in good humor, it struck me as the saddest thing I'd heard in a long while. "Shall we head back to the homestead?"

"It'll be less carrying for you to do later."

We walked back in fifty-yard increments, Bill assuring me at each resting point that he was only short of air and not experiencing any other tell-tale symptoms of imminent death. He grew frustrated by my repeated questions regarding his well-being.

"If you're gonna move, then what the hell are you going to do about Rhonda?" he asked.

"She's bringing the van by tonight," I said. "I'll talk to her about it over dinner and let you know."

"She's cooking you dinner?"

"Other way around."

He nickered, as though he were insulted by the idea. "Don't go putting ideas in her head."

"What's wrong with a little gesture of gratitude? She's saving Percy's life."

He stepped aside to kick a dirt clod. "I don't know. Maybe I'm too old and out of touch, but I never knew a man who wasn't a fruitcake to cook dinner for a woman unless he had carnal designs."

"Call me a fruitcake, then. I've endured worse."

He began puckering and relaxing his lips as though he were preparing a lecture. I asked him, in partial jest, what he thought I should make for Rhonda that night.

"I don't know the first thing about cooking. That's why I bought a restaurant."

"She's not a vegetarian or anything like that, is she? Do you know?"

"Are you kidding?" He stopped again to catch his breath. "Rhonda could eat a live alligator."

I returned Bill to his mansion, still at a loss as to what I was going to cook for Rhonda. A drive to the grocery store to scan the shelves and freezers for inspiration seemed like my best bet, so I fired up Helga and headed for town, scanning the radio for something tolerable. What I ended up with was a plan—thanks to the classic rock radio format and its odd inclination to dip a toe into the Steely Dan catalog.

I charged into Jim's Steakhouse as though I owned the place, demanding the recipe for Beef Charlemagne from the teenaged hostess. My forwardness appeared to have instigated an explosive bowel movement within her black slacks. She recoiled in fear, probably assuming I was cresting a meth high.

"It's something of an emergency," I said. "Bring me your chef, if you would."

I knew it was an affront to culinary ethics to ask a professional cook for his recipe, even in a dedicated meat-and-potatoes town like Forsyth. Bill didn't own the place, or else I might've been able to play that card. A man about my age emerged from the swinging doors of the kitchen and approached me, looking inconvenienced and short on patience.

"Can I help you?" he asked.

"Are you the kitchen manager?"

He sighed. "I've been the head chef here for eight years."

I got straight to the point. His head shifted an inch or two to the side, as though it were part of a dance routine. He was someone Bill would probably describe as a fruitcake. "We haven't offered that since last December."

"Why'd you take it off the menu? It was dreamy."

"No one was ordering it. I think we sold ten in a year."

"I'm just looking for the recipe."

He leaned against the hostess' podium and began massaging his brow. "I don't know where you're from, but it's really not appropriate to walk into a restaurant asking for something like that."

"Was it a recipe that you created?"

"No."

"Somebody else that works here?"

"No."

"Then what does it matter?"

He shuffled his feet and arched his back. "Listen, sir. We've got a lunch rush to prepare for. I don't have time for this."

"I don't either," I said, before telling him I was a recovering Nashville songwriter, and familiar with any fourth wall he could ever hope to put up between us. "Just tell me what was in the magic sauce. I can figure out the rest."

He looked over at the clock behind the bar and sighed again. "Sir."

"The sauce."

Another sigh. "Hollandaise and wasabi. That's all I will tell you."

"You won't regret it."

I left the steakhouse and drove to the public library in search of cookbooks. It'd been three years since Sheila's step-mother had demonstrated the finer points of preparing hollandaise to me, and I couldn't seem to remember anything about it aside from how easily fuckupable it was. However, I was determined to make the dish for Rhonda, and no sauce was going to intimidate me, especially one that Sheila's wine-saturated step-mom could whip up in a matter of minutes while balancing on one high heel.

It's generally known that all female librarians over a certain age are also knowledgeable cooks, so I found one and told her my situation. She gave me the reverse-smile, baring most of her bottom teeth.

"You've never made it before?" she asked.

"No, I haven't. You look terrified."

"Oh boy," she said, gesturing for me to follow her. She led me to the cookbook section and began scanning the shelves. "You're starting with several handicaps."

"And what might those be?"

"You're male, for one," she began, as she handed me the first of three books. "You probably aren't the type to read through all of the directions before you start something. That'll be the key to your success with this capricious little sauce." She spoke at an unusually loud volume for a sixty-some-year-old librarian in her natural habitat. It occurred to me that we were possibly the only two people in the small building.

"I would plan on doing a few test runs first," she said, opening a thinner, sauce-specific book, and flipping through the pages. "This is one of those things you won't get right the first time no matter how closely you follow directions."

"I've got all afternoon."

"At least you're planning ahead," she said, handing me another book. "Those should do the trick. It's always good to have at least three different perspectives on how to do something."

I followed her to the circulation desk, and she advised me to buy enough extra ingredients to allow for at least two botched attempts. "I have to say that in almost thirty years of working here, no man has ever come in asking for a hollandaise recipe. I think I can retire now."

I didn't have a library card, so she took my information and began entering it into the computer. After a moment, she looked over the top rim of her glasses. "Any relation?"

"To who?" I asked, figuring she might be aware of a more

genealogically authentic, historically significant Mahogany.

"To whom," she corrected me. "You're the country singer, right?"

"Afraid so."

She handed my driver's license back, and I was glad that she wanted no further information or conversation along those lines. I asked where I might be able to get wasabi in Forsyth.

"Geez," she smiled, still typing. "You are one demanding patron."

"I am?"

"I'd say so, yes. Not that I mind."

After giving me a brief lecture about real versus imitation wasabi, she asked what it was, exactly, that I was making, and I told her. She picked up the copy of *Mastering the Art of French Cooking* that she'd just checked out to me and flipped to its index. After running her finger down the page a couple times, she looked up at me, stumped.

"You'd think something like that would be in here, considering. Logic fails again. You'll have to let me know how this turns out."

I told her I would and thanked her before grabbing the books and turning toward the double doors.

"This is going to be on my mind until you do," she said. "I'm curious."

"You and me both."

I emerged from Wal-Mart a half hour later, chin aloft, ready for any and all culinary contingencies: one small stainless steel bowl, two large New York strip steaks, a bottle of wasabi powder, two large potatoes, four lemons, one pound of unsalted butter, and two dozen eggs.

I noticed a Forsyth police officer leaning against his prowler, which he'd parked in the space next to Helga. We made eye contact while I was still six or seven automobiles away. This was somehow enough to indicate that the car was in my possession. A smarmy grin emerged from beneath his walrus mustache as I slowed and dug in my pocket for the keys.

"Any reason you think you can drive this thing around without plates?" He said it as though he'd had several minutes of prep time.

"What?" I looked at the rear bumper and noticed there was no license plate where I was slightly less than half sure there'd been one before. I inserted the key in the hatch. "This is not my car."

"That's what I was afraid of."

"My van's in the shop. This is a loaner."

"I'm aware of that. This is one of Rhonda Raynolds' cars."

After much encouragement, the hatch lifted, and I set my groceries in the back of the wagon. "Why, yes it is." I closed the hatch and took a couple steps back. The entire tail end of the stationwagon was covered in a thin layer of dust—all of it except for a license plate-sized rectangle. I alerted the cop to this detail. "It appears we've got a license plate thief on the loose."

"I'm going to have to search the vehicle," he said.

I doubted his legal right to do such a thing, and asked him what he had for probable cause.

He looked at me as though I were the first idiot he'd seen that day. "No license plate."

I looked at the pair of keys for a moment, wondering which papers Helga didn't have, and how much of a fine I could expect. "If this isn't my vehicle, then am I even authorized to allow you to search it?"

He was not impressed. "We can do this the easy way or the hard way."

"Have at it. The doors don't lock." I figured this little fact might help me weasel out of any lack-of-papers issue.

I stood behind him and watched as he looked in the ashtray and glove box, and under the seats. He didn't appear to be looking for paperwork of any kind, and I had no reason to worry that he might find something. A dispatcher's voice blasted out of the walkie-talkie attached to his belt, reciting a series of numbers and a street name I didn't recognize. This signaled the end of his search. He brushed some dirt from the knees of his pants.

"Tell Rhonda she's got until Monday to get some new plates on this."

"Will do."

"You might suggest to her that she oughta be more careful about what she leaves in that ashtray. We've got some new guys on the force that aren't gonna know to turn a blind eye."

And so I was free to go.

I took the liberty of finishing off the joint the cop had been referring to as soon as I arrived home. In keeping with the spirit of the day, I dug out the one Steely Dan album I'd acquired over the years, *Countdown to Ecstasy,* and blasted it while I began my quest for hollandaise perfection.

By the time the last song on the album faded, I was transfixed by the ease in which my second failed attempt oozed in clumps through the black rubber sphincter-like passage into the garbage disposal. It will never be known how long I stood there, head in hands, leaning over the sink. All I know is that the familiar bleat of Percy's horn was enough to snap me out of it. I slapped myself on the face a few times and hurried out the front door.

Rhonda already had the hood up and was checking fluids. My eyes were drawn to her and not the van.

"You're going to find a few insects stuck in the paint," she said. "And the new paint isn't an exact match, but it'll look better once it dries."

"It looks great," I said, not yet having looked close enough to notice the color difference.

She listed everything else she'd had time to fix—the alignment, a brake line, a strut. This was dwarfed by the list of other things that'd have to wait, including the sliding side door and one of the rear doors. "All I can say is that it's drivable."

"That's all I needed to hear."

Her shoulders dropped, relieved. "Good."

"You don't know how to make hollandaise sauce, do you?"

"Don't push your luck."

She followed me through the front room into the kitchen, carrying two bottles of wine in a brown paper sack. "Boy, did I have a shitty afternoon," she said. "We'll need to open one of these immediately."

I fetched a corkscrew from a sparsely populated drawer of kitchen utensils and went to work on the first bottle. She began telling me how she'd driven to Julesburg on a tow dispatch that she suspected had been a prank. Once she'd arrived at the Texaco station and discovered that no one was there in need of a tow, she called the number back and got the station's payphone. No one at the station claimed to have noticed anyone using the phone that day, or anyone complaining of car trouble. She began blaming herself for neglecting to get any other information from the caller other than his location.

"Who would think to do something like that," I said, filling her wine glass.

"I know. This is the first time in almost twenty years."

I suspected Lloyd right away. He had a reason to be in Jules-burg, possibly following up on the job we'd done a couple days earlier. I didn't want to mention it until I had more evidence, figuring Rhonda'd probably just laugh it off and accuse me of having "Lloyd anxiety." I asked what the guy sounded like.

"I don't know. Frustrated"

"You didn't recognize the voice?"

"Why would I?"

I mentioned the license plate incident, and she had the same questions I had: why would someone steal a license plate in a busy parking lot in the middle of the day, and who would think they could get away with it? She asked me what the cop planned to do about it.

"Not a thing," I said. "But he suggested you might want to stop keeping your jazz cigarettes in your ashtray."

She looked at me with every muscle of her face contracted, as though she'd just bitten into one of the lemons that were sitting on the counter. "What?"

"There was half a joint resting in there."

"I don't even smoke pot."

I thought a moment. "Maybe the license plate thief planted it there."

She didn't appear to take my suggestion seriously—not enough to build on it anyway. "Doesn't Wal-Mart have surveillance cameras in their parking lots?" she asked. "I know they do."

"I'm sure they charge a hefty fee to look at their footage. More than a license plate is worth, anyway."

"It's sad that you're probably right about that."

It turned out that Rhonda did know how to whip up a batch of hollandaise. She sent me out to the back deck to grill the steaks while she performed her hocus pocus. I watched Satan frolic amongst the brush, chasing rabbits and prairie dogs. When the sauce was finished, I insisted Rhonda leave the kitchen while I added the secret ingredient, thinking she might not be able to guess what it was.

"Wasabi and hollandaise," she said, after swallowing her first bite. "Interesting combo."

"Charlemagne sauce," I said. "This is the first meal I ate in Forsyth." I told her what I'd gone through that day in preparation for our meal—the pretenses of the steakhouse chef, the sexist taunting of the librarian, and the imminent terror of falling prices amid the aisles of Wal-Mart.

"I'm charmed," she said. "No one's cooked for me in a very long time."

"You did the skilled labor."

"Nah."

"What's the secret?"

"Why should I tell you? Then you'd have one less reason to invite me back."

We caught the sunset from the other side of the Russian olive wall, and ran out of wine in the meantime. I suggested we walk the mile to the liquor store, but we couldn't make it on foot before closing time, so we took Helga, and I bought two more bottles. When we returned, I prepared a small bonfire off the back deck with wood from the elm branch that'd crushed Percy.

She requested that I play a few songs for her, and so I went inside to grab my guitar. Satan was sleeping on the couch.

"How about some old cowboy songs," she said. "Some Gene Autry or Roy Rogers."

I remembered only one cowboy song, and so began singing a

rendition of "Happy Trails." She was quick to interrupt with a laugh. "Don't tell me you learned that off a Van Halen record."

"It's Hollywood either way."

I sang a couple of my own, watching her as she gazed into the fire, her face aglow with contentment. It was a look I hadn't seen in the flesh for longer than I could remember, and probably not since the first few months I'd dated Karen; before I faced the reality that every dude in Nashville—from panhandler to plastic surgeon to politician—was also an above-average singer and instrumentalist on the make in one way or another. For the first time in over two decades I was singing to a woman who seemed thrilled to listen, and not just suffering another fool's musical ambitions.

Satan began barking in the front room as my final song of the evening came to an end. She ran to the front door and gave it a scratch before noticing us on the back deck and running toward us. I opened the sliding screen door and she charged out and around the side of the house.

"What's gotten into her?" I asked, returning to my chair. Rhonda sat silent, staring at the fire. I asked if something was the matter.

"I'm sad," she said.

"What is it? Was it my song selection?"

"No, no." She sat forward and grabbed a twig that was lying at her feet. "I get the sense that you don't plan on sticking around here very much longer."

"What makes you say that?" I hadn't mentioned anything about my future plans beyond the tour, other than the lie about visiting the friend in Cedar Rapids. "Do you know something that I don't?"

"I doubt that," she said, using the twig to poke at some

embers. "I don't even know you well enough to be sure of what I do know."

"I've been considering a move."

"I figured as much."

"No idea where to, though."

"Not back to Nashville?"

"No way."

"You must've left quite a mess back there."

I hadn't mentioned anything to her about the true nature of my leaving Music City. However, I was not the least bit surprised that she'd guessed correctly on her first attempt.

"I've been thinking about it a lot," she said. "There's just no other explanation for you being here, really. Am I wrong?"

I tossed another chunk of elm onto the fire. "It was a mess alright."

"We don't have to talk about it."

"I'll tell you anything you want to know."

She thought a moment. "Well, if it's a story of lies, back-stabbing, and betrayal, then I guess I don't really need the details. I've lived it."

"That's the gist."

We heard a whimper just then, and Satan emerged from around the corner of the house. Her front leg looked to have suffered an injury of some kind. My first thought was that she stepped into a prairie dog hole and sprained something. Rhonda helped her into the kitchen to get a better look at the leg.

"It doesn't appear to be broken," she said, combing through Satan's fur, looking for sign of other injuries. "Looks like she took a bite out of something, though." She pointed to a small patch of blood drying on Satan's lower jaw. I thought to call Lloyd and ask how his leg was doing, convinced that he'd been out there lurking behind one of Bill's outbuildings or amongst the small grove of evergreens. The thought made me laugh. Rhonda asked what was so funny.

"I just can't help thinking that Lloyd's been behind all the shit that's happened today," I said.

"Really," she said, humorless, sitting and swinging her feet up onto the couch. She didn't seem interested in entertaining the notion any further.

I sat beside her and began establishing a timeline: the license plate incident happened sometime around noon, She'd gotten the call from Julesburg around 3:00. Lloyd often bought his lunches at Wal-Mart. "It's not impossible."

She shook her head. "Enough. You're suffering from an abundance of paranoia. Please don't spread the wealth."

I decided not to press the issue further, though I was more convinced than ever that Lloyd had something to do with at least one of the day's problems. I grabbed my wine glass and lifted my feet onto the coffee table. Satan walked in after awhile and curled up on the floor beside the couch. Her limp seemed to have improved a little.

The hour was getting late, and we were halfway through bottle number four. Rhonda lamented over having to wait two weeks to see me again.

"It might be sooner," I said, softening up the lie I'd told her about visiting Cedar Rapids. "I'm not sure how long I'll stay. Not even sure my friend will want me there more than a couple days."

She nudged my thigh with her foot. "It probably will be sooner," she said, as though it were something more than a roundabout suggestion or request that I hurry home.

"Oh yeah?"

"Yeah. I'm thinking I'll fly out to see one of your shows."

"You'd do that? That'd be a pricey little vacation."

"I need one."

I was fairly sure that I'd deterred Karen from following through on her project, but not completely sure. If she hadn't yet sent her five-page outline, it was now overdue, and I could use that as a reason not to let her come along. I stood from the couch and went for the computer to check my inbox.

"Would you even want me to?" Rhonda asked.

My inbox opened. Karen had not turned in her outline.

"Of course. I'd like that," I said, returning to the couch. "Which show?"

"Hmm. Maybe I'll let that be a surprise."

I assumed KC and St. Louis were out. Too soon. The Iowa gigs—well, why would she want to fly to Iowa? Chicago or Minneapolis seemed more likely. Flights would be cheaper, at least.

"Are you sure it would be okay?" she asked.

"I'll be disappointed if you don't."

Side two of *Meet the Beatles!* played out. Rhonda yawned and blamed me for keeping her up late again.

"All I'm good for at this time of the night is sex," she said.

8

An aggressive wind blew from the east as I loaded my gear into the van the next morning. I packed a couple hundred copies of my earlier CDs to sell. Karen's outline still hadn't arrived as of 7 AM, but I stuffed my terms and conditions in the glove box just to be safe.

Bill walked out in his lime-green bathrobe, carrying a paper grocery sack rolled at the top. His thin wisps of hair swirled above his head as if caught in a dust devil.

"What'd I tell ya," he shouted over the gusts. "She's a prairie magician."

"She did a fine job." I assumed he was aware that she'd spent the night, and I expected a smart-ass remark about it.

"Here are some things to take the edge off," he said, handing me the sack. He began a slow walk around the van, rapping his knuckles on the metal. I opened the sack and looked inside. He'd prepared an assortment of oranges, apples, candy bars, and a bag of Corn Nuts. There were a handful of CD cases in there as well. I pulled out the discs: *My Life* as read by William Jefferson Clinton.

He came around the rear of the van and saw me looking at one of the disc cases. "Books on CD ," he said. "Six-and-a-half hours on six CDs. That oughta get you most of the way to Kansas City at least."

I read the title aloud, laughing. "The guy isn't even dead yet." It was something Clinton and I had in common—we'd both been *essentialized*, though I hadn't chosen to be.

"You might be surprised," he said. "I actually started to like the guy after awhile."

I don't know why he assumed that I had some prior beef with Clinton, but it wasn't the time to get into that discussion. I dropped the discs back into the bag and thanked him for the care package. A powerful, sandblasting gust brought on a long pause in conversation. When it died down, we both began to talk at the same instant. I insisted Bill go ahead.

"Heard any more from the professor?" he asked.

"She missed the deadline I gave her," I said, scraping a grain of sand from the corner of my eye. "Looks like I'm in the clear, far as that's concerned."

He looked at his feet, nodding. "I'm glad to hear it."

I slammed the passenger door against the wind and told him that I needed to get moving. "I've got one hell of a voyage in front of me if this wind keeps up."

"Well, give ol' Bill a hug," he said. I gave him a quick one. "Don't hesitate to call if you get into trouble. And if you get down in the dumps, toss some of that Clinton into the stereo."

"Sure thing."

Bill stood his ground, smiling and waving as I drove away. That would be the last living image I'd have of him.

I stopped at the Sinclair station to top off the gas tank and my coffee thermos. The wind had sped up another dozen MPH. Trash and tumbleweeds blew across the streets and parking lots. The strip of pennants lining the Hyundai dealership had broken away from its fastenings and was causing some traffic congestion as it whipped and wavered across the main drag. The soon-to-open fun park Bill had mentioned sat directly across the street from the gas station. The wind had robbed a couple blades from a windmill rising from the center of their mini-golf course.

I heard a train's airhorn as I left the gas station. After a year of working for Lloyd, I knew to take sidestreets if I hoped to outrun the train. Those same sidestreets led me past his house, and as I drove by I could see the crossing signals flash and the gates lowering a few blocks ahead. The morning trains always slowed to a crawl as they passed through town, and each one averaged a mile long. I had at least a ten minute wait, so I stopped the van, put it in reverse, and backed up into Lloyd's driveway.

I left the van running to facilitate a speedy getaway, should one be necessary. He answered the door wearing only a pair of gray sweatpants. There was pizza sauce forming an equals sign below his left nipple. He leaned against the doorjamb, almost as though he were trying to keep weight off his right leg.

"What the fuck you doin here?" he asked. I caught a whiff of booze.

"On my way out of town. Waitin' on the train. Thought I'd stop by."

He caught me looking past him at his mess of pizza boxes, beer cans, and assorted bottles. He looked over his shoulder, and then back at me.

"The fuck," he said. "We're not working in this wind, are you kidding me?"

"No, Lloyd. I'm driving to Kansas City today. Remember?" It was pretty clear that he'd been up all night drinking, so I casually backed off his concrete step onto his dead lawn. "Well, I'll give you a call when I get back into town."

He held up his index finger. "Wait a minute," he said. "I've got your check. Let me go get it."

I was sure that Satan's teeth were the cause of his limp as I watched him stumble down the hallway and disappear around a corner. I waited, watching the train pass in the distance. It occurred to me that payday was still a week away and he'd never cut me an early check—not that I'd ever asked for one. Was this to be my severance pay?

I turned to look down the hall, and saw Lloyd leaning against the wall holding a compound bow, struggling to get an arrow set. I ran around the front of the van, opened the door, hopped up, shifted into drive, and stepped on the gas. Bill's care package spilled on the floor, and I heard a loud pop coming from the rear of the van, sounding like it might've backfired. Once I had the van headed straight I looked at the sideview mirror. There was Lloyd, standing in the middle of the street 30 yards behind holding the bow above his head like the letter D.

The train had stopped, so I hung a left, heading back toward Main. I was out of harm's way, and would be for the next week at least, but I worried about Rhonda. I called her as I approached the east edge of town.

"Don't tell me the van broke down already," she said.

"Lloyd just shot at my van with bow and arrow."

She laughed. "You're kidding."

"I'm telling you, he's out of his mind. Maybe you should start worrying."

"Oh, Carl. He wouldn't dare try anything."

Highway 61 cuts south a few miles past city limits. Although I was no longer driving headlong into the wind, it was still blowing against me, as though the gods were trying to turn me back.

9

The wind didn't let up until after I'd connected with I-70 and put a hundred miles of Kansas prairie behind me. It was a long overdue kick in the ass to be back out on the road again; a return to form, and the feeling that I was doing something useful again after a year of general idleness.

My fellow eastbound travelers had seemed especially cheery and prone to waving throughout the morning. It wasn't until I stopped to refuel and walked around the back of the van that I discovered why.

Lloyd's arrow was protruding from the driver's side rear door.

I gave it a few pulls and twists, but it wouldn't budge. Removing it would require surgery, so I decided to leave it, hoping it would survive the tour for novelty's sake. If nothing else, it would be hard evidence for Lloyd's crumbling sanity that Rhonda couldn't ignore.

I was immersed in the fifth disc of *My Life* by the time I passed the midpoint of the drive. An outline for a country rock opera had begun to take shape, and former-Doob Michael McDonald playing the lead role seemed predestined. I had a song in the works, one in which the hero addresses the spirit of his deceased father. With the windshield wipers keeping time, and the rubbery *brrump* sound of the rumble bars serving as a brass section, I sang:

> *If only you could've faced life,*
> *Brrrrrrrrummmmp*

With the courage you faced death,
Brrrmp, brrrrrmp,
You would've been quite a guy.

Clinton's story struck a chord with me, particularly the sections where he discussed his late father. My father didn't die of cancer. He flipped a speed boat on Lake of the Ozarks in the summer of 1990, taking my mother with him.

I imagine her last words went something like *slow down, Jim!* and my father's went something like *here we go!* According to eyewitnesses, they were traveling at a speed that renders life preservers irrelevant.

My father flew bombers in the Air Force until I came along, after which my mother insisted he find a more family-friendly line of work. This course of things eventually backfired for my mother. Dad got a secret vasectomy and began a lifelong commitment to the American Legion and Old Style beer, while mom—a Lutheran—devoted herself to volunteering at St. Mary's Catholic Church.

For reasons seemingly unknown to everyone but them, they became oddly adventurous and unpredictable in their later years, almost as though they'd been turned on to some miracle drug or guru. I don't expect I'll ever know what triggered their change in behavior. But, in my bluest moments, imagining myself dying cold and alone in the dark, I think of their final years together and all of their fooling around, and that gives me some hope.

Thinking about them, and listening to Clinton review all of his grand achievements began to depress me. I had to remove the CD . His life was beginning to defeat mine, coincidentally, only a few miles southeast of Russell, Kansas—the birthplace of Senator Bob Dole.

I arrived at the venue in Kansas City a little after six, set up my guitars and amplifiers, soundchecked, and sat down at the bar. It was still early and the room was empty. I alerted the bartender to my aching hip joints and she served me two aspirin with a glass of beer.

After a few failed attempts at small talk with the bartender, I reached for a copy of the *Kansas City Star.* Their entertainment section had a one-paragraph write-up of the show under the heading of "recommended." The photograph they used was fifteen years out of date. The blurb got the facts right, but the other more subjective, poetic license of the writing was the usual slop, most likely paraphrased from something my publicist had provided to them, referring to my "road-worn, edgy explorations of the human condition…masterfully crafted tales of woe and redemption, rolled out like a red carpet, welcoming passage by anyone with the emotional wherewithal to endure the journey…Mahogany is the real deal."

I tore out the blurb, stuffed it in my shirtpocket, tossed the paper aside, and looked up at the television where Homer Simpson was also sitting at a bar, sipping a beer, and watching television. At the very moment I got the existential joke, a woman walked in from the street, hefting a large army surplus duffel bag. I barely gave her a glance, but she looked several years beyond her punk rock glory days.

"Is the entertainment here yet?" she asked. The bartender pointed at me. I did a double-take, and by the time the woman was approaching me, a triple-take. It was Karen. I hadn't expected to see her until the next night, if at all, but there she was, and

I had nowhere to hide, so I swung around to face her.

"What is this?" I asked.

"I had the itch. Hope you don't mind."

"I didn't get my five-pager."

"I've been so busy." She dropped the duffel bag and lifted her arms toward me. "How are you, you old dog?" We hugged and she made the mm-mmm sound one might make sitting down for a thanksgiving meal. She felt much thinner than I remembered, almost brittle. She ordered a double whiskey sour.

"You lost the Emmylou look," I said.

"Probably about the same time she did."

She wore tight, tattered jeans and a plain black t-shirt, torn a couple inches at the trough of the neck. "This is more of a Patti Smith-Chrissie Hynde presentation."

"I just spent five hours in a grad student's Ford Festiva. Cut me some slack." She stepped back and sized me up. "Now you— you haven't changed a bit."

I sat down on the barstool and slapped my hand on my belly. "I've put on about ten pounds of liver and onions. Other than that, just the usual wear and tear."

"Well, I'm impressed."

I took a closer look at her as she dug through her purse. She'd taken pretty good care of herself over the years. Definitely less sun time than Rhonda. The Karen I remembered still had some baby fat on her. The new one looked either over-exercised, undernourished, or both. She pulled a jewel-encrusted cigarette case from her purse, flipped it open, and offered me one. Fancy brown cigarettes. She lit mine, and then hers, before sighing one of those sighs that always seems to precede the question, "where do we begin?"

"Let's talk about you," she said.

"No way. Too close to showtime."

"I get it. This is some sort of pre-show superstition ritual."

"Nope, just the rules. Anything to do with my past, or plans for the future—off limits two hours before any show."

She reached for her drink. "And why's that?"

"It's just the rules. Handed down from on high."

She set her drink down and began twisting the maraschino stem. "Are you always this difficult?"

I pulled the *Kansas City Star* blurb from my pocket and recited it in the style of William F. Buckley, Jr. "I'd say that about sums it up. What do you have to say for yourself?"

After a short preamble, she went on at length about the project she'd spent the last couple years working on, and had just recently finished—something to do with 19th century female proto-environmentalists. The topic seemed interesting enough, but her presentation sounded like a stuffy recitation of an unreadable essay. I nodded my way through it, saying things like *okay* and *I see*. Frankly, her spiel bored the hell out of me, and I wasn't convinced that she was all that enthused about it either. She noticed my wandering eyes and stopped. "Are you understanding anything I'm telling you?"

"Sure!"

In my own defense, I was getting anxious as the room began to populate. Certain reputable music critics have accused me of writing "literate" lyrics—an allegation that's had some rather annoying side-effects. It was only a matter of time before a fan approached, trying to engage me in a deep conversation about the intended meaning of this or that lyric of mine, or a guitar tone I'd gotten on a recording from 1983. They'll do this. Time was they'd only expect a handshake, an autograph, or a photo, but now it's become a battle of the aesthetic sensibilities. I swore long ago that I'd never become one of those entertainers that hide on their tour bus or in the dressing room before and after a show, but that day has long since passed.

Karen pointed out a cluster of people who looked like they were mustering the courage to come talk to me. It was time to make a run for it. She finished her drink and we went for the green room. On a small folding table sat the most pathetic attempt at fulfilling the "nutritional requirements" section of my rider that I'd ever seen. I mentioned this to her, and after a moment's consideration, she said, as though reciting a poem: "So much depends upon a bag of baby carrots, bathed in fluorescent light, beside an already opened bottle of ranch."

I suggested we go somewhere else, so we snuck out the venue's back door, and eventually settled in a windowless tavern a few blocks away. Karen claimed us a booth as I went for the restroom to wash the Missouri humidity from my face. The paper-towel dispenser was empty, so I drip-dried, and had a quick look in the mirror. There was no sleep in my eyes, no ambitious nose hairs, and my default coiffure was in order. I figured I looked the best I could without bringing in consultants.

A round of drinks had arrived before I sat down. Mel Torme's rendition of "Stardust" wafted out of the jukebox, giving the wood-paneled room an almost elegant recess from its own bleakness. Karen looked around at the cluttered walls. "So, this is where bowling trophies and fish mounts come to die."

"Welcome to the Western Missouri Museum of Un-Pawnable Wonders."

"The Not Quite Ready for Antiques Roadshow Players."

I lifted a red glass bulb that sat at the center of our table and lit the candle inside. "So, when do you plan on telling me about this project of yours? I can appreciate improvisation, but—"

"You're in luck."

"I am?"

"Yes. I discussed it with a protégée all the way from St. Louis. I think we came up with something workable."

"Uh huh."

"I'd like to explore how dominant Middle-American values work to oppress the creative drive."

"That sounds like more hassle than it's worth."

"Fundamentalist modes of thinking—what we know as good ol' protestant common sense—cripples creativity. The artist or thinker trapped within this notion of common sense is held back from their creative potential."

"I suppose this can wait."

"And yet, people like you manage to break out of that to some extent."

I imagined my list of terms and conditions floating through the ether. "People like me—okay."

"So, what must one do in order to escape this?"

"You want me to answer that?"

"You don't have to do anything. It'll take care of itself."

I asked where this protégée of her's was. She said he was having dinner with his family and then possibly coming to the show.

"Possibly," I said.

"He has social anxiety issues, so we'll see."

This had all the makings of a classic Karen move. She'd given this protégée some kind of personality flaw, which she could then use at the end of the night to explain why he'd abandoned her, thereby creating ideal conditions for her to guilt me into giving her a ride back to St. Louis.

"Isn't he your ride home?" I asked.

"I can take care of myself."

We each took a sip and let the awkwardness dissipate. I asked if she knew any cruel jokes. "You should know that I prefer a light conversation before a performance."

She looked toward the ceiling. "Let's see. You want something that exposes my inner racist or sexist. Is that it?"

"For starters! Get it all out here on the table." I moved the candle toward the wall. "There."

"Huh." She went for her pack of cigarettes, fumbled with it, eventually setting it aside. Her shoulders dropped, and she looked me in the eyes. "I can't think of anything," she said. "Though, I did meet the 'Strongest Woman in the World' at a roller derby match last weekend."

"Okay."

She flicked her thumb as though she were flipping a coin. "She can stick her thumb up her butt and hold herself out at arms length."

I got a good ten or fifteen-second laugh out of it, which is a great run for any joke. Not that her delivery was so remarkable, just that the Karen I used to know would've been too uptight to speak such a thing without a cascade of qualifiers.

"I thought you might like to know," she added.

Maybe twenty years had mellowed her out a little, and I didn't have so much to worry about after all.

We riffed awhile about our old haunts back in Austin, and people we'd known. She spoke of her old college buddies and sorority sisters as though I should've remembered them. I pretended to try for awhile, but the fact was that I'd never spent any time with those people. She dropped another half-dozen names before I decided to say something about it.

"You didn't want your blue-blooded friends to know you were dating some schmoe who washed dishes at your sorority kitchen," I said.

"That wasn't it at all."

I laughed. "I'll give you a moment to re-think that."

"Okay," she said. "Maybe that was part of it."

At least she'd given an honest answer—enough to buy her some credibility, however temporary.

Show time was approaching, so we finished our drinks and moved out onto the sidewalk. The briny stink of a hot dog vendor across the street made me mildly nauseous.

"I'd like to get a room tonight, if that won't be too much of a problem. I'm buying," she said. "I could really go for a soak in a hot tub. Ford Festivas were not designed with human comfort in mind."

We stopped at a crosswalk and I looked at the blinking red hand across the street. It was official. She'd invited herself along for the ride, and was already beginning to make herself comfortable.

The idea of soaking in a hot tub was enticing, but I wasn't sure about sharing a room with her. She was already three drinks along, and considering her past behavior, I felt uneasy about how the end of the evening might unfold. I could always get my own room, or just sleep in the van. I didn't feel like it was worth bickering about, so I caved. "Fine by me, as long as we get out of the city first."

Despite feeling manipulated, I spent a good part of the

performance imagining her in and out of a bathing suit. This added some energy to the show that I'd have to thank her for in some way. I made my first public announcement of my ambitions to write the Clinton opera. The audience seemed to like the idea, though I doubt any of them thought it might amount to anything more than a joke.

I signed a few CDs and old LPs afterwards, and one boob. It was a freckly handful, and something I hadn't been asked to do in many years. I suspected a dare or lost bet was involved, as the woman seemed very shy, and she reeked of peppermint schnapps. The Sharpie I used was low on ink, so I had to apply increasing pressure in order to make my mark. I was able to get my first name down, but had to end it with a faint M. Her friend took a picture. I asked the woman if she'd had her boob signed before.

"Once. Don Dokken, Santa Monica, 1989," she said, revealing her right breast, where Mr. Dokken's signature had been tattooed in place.

At least I got the spot over her heart, Donald.

I was paid and loaded out by midnight, pleased that the first show had gone well. Almost a sellout.

As expected, the protégée never materialized, and Karen didn't seem the least bit concerned about it. We found our way to the interstate and stopped for lodging at a Best Western some twenty miles east of the city. I waited in the van while she went inside to make arrangements.

We'd gotten their last available room, according to Karen. It had two queen-sized beds. She made no comment about it as we entered the room, which led me to believe that she was at least entertaining the idea of avoiding end-of-the-night foolishness.

She sat at the foot of the bed nearest the window and began to undress, showing no apparent concern that I was right there to watch her. I walked to the window to avoid the awkwardness. There wasn't much to see other than the blue, UFO-like glow of the outdoor pool and hot tub—just miles of darkness and the slow-blinking red lights of distant radio towers. I turned around to find Karen removing her shirt. Her breasts looked familiar, but there were a few ribs that I couldn't remember. She'd obviously been cutting carbs. She caught me mid-gaze.

"Nothing you haven't seen before," she said, looking down at them. "They've held up pretty well, I'd say."

I agreed, reminded of her nudist tendencies, and all the day trips to Lake Travis years before, when she'd insist on going topless until some crotchety tourist or park ranger made a complaint.

She tossed the shirt onto the table next to the television and went for her duffel bag, pulling a white tank top from it. I mentioned the late hour and asked if we should even bother trying to access the hot tub.

"Of course," she said, jogging to the bathroom, grabbing a towel, and moving into the hallway. "Meet you down there."

I hurried into a pair of cut-off jean shorts and headed out to the van to grab beers from the cooler. Karen was already soaking by the time I made it around back. A sign on the chain link fence said the pool and hot tub closed at ten. I looked around for hotel personnel as I carefully opened the gate.

"Don't mind that sign," she said, in a forceful whisper. "The world's full of general guidelines."

I moved into the water, opposite from her. Her breasts were half-submerged, and I found it difficult not to gawk, as she was making every effort not to conceal them. I handed her a beer.

She opened it and let out a sigh.

"I can't believe this is actually happening. We're going to have a lot of fun." She stretched her arms upward. "I sure need it right now."

I'd already begun to suspect that her reasons for wanting to tag along extended beyond whatever academic ambitions she claimed to have. I dipped my head under the water, and pulled my hair back away from my face as I sat up. "Would you call this research, what you're doing here?"

She appeared to give it some serious thought. "Yes. Very much so."

I opened a beer and sipped the suds from the rim of the can. "I've had to tolerate music journalists, but it's hard for me to imagine myself as a subject for academic research."

"Then don't. It would be much better if you didn't, actually."

I wasn't going to be taken for a fool. "I know how you writers change things by observing them."

This seemed to catch her off guard. "Heisenberg, right?"

"Hell if I know."

"That's something any researcher has to consider," she said. "But you can't let it stop you from doing something."

I couldn't argue with that. It occurred to me to remind her that I'd probably be sleeping in my van at a truck stop had she not embedded herself in my life that day, but I didn't want to sound either too grateful, or ungrateful. Still, I needed more convincing that she actually had a story to chase, and wasn't just hanging on for the fun of it.

"Maybe I'm all trapped in Midwestern common sense, but how are you going to dress my bullshit up to look even slightly relevant? You scholarly types must be running out of crap to get serious about."

She laughed. "It's the era of cultural studies, Carl. Anything goes."

"Anything, huh?"

"Yes. Pretty much everything."

I guess us songwriters had to wait until everything was fair game before we were allowed our place in the academic sun. "What an honor," I said.

Her legs floated to the surface. We both watched her stretch and wiggle her toes. I wanted to touch them, but I shoved my hands under my thighs.

We talked about the great tunesmiths of the pre-rock and roll era—the Cole Porters, Harold Arlens, Johnny Mercers—geniuses that never get the serious nods that the Hindemiths and Coplands do. I was impressed with her knowledge of these artists and their work, but it was a conversation I'd had so many times that I no longer felt I had any investment in it. I wanted her feet and everything above, but we were talking about geniuses.

"Does that frustrate you?" she asked.

"What."

"That songwriters aren't held in as high regard as classical composers?"

"I couldn't care less."

"You sound a little worked up over it," she said.

"No. There are more pressing things."

She wiggled her toes again, as though she knew exactly what I wanted. "What might those be?"

I grabbed her feet. "Give 'em to me."

They weren't rough old hippie dogs, stained and callused from running barefoot through inner-city nature preserves. This set had been kept out of the elements, cared for like sacred ivory sculptures. She leaned her head back and closed her eyes. "I haven't had a decent foot rub in ages."

A light turned on near the lobby of the hotel, and seconds later, an elderly woman wearing a bathrobe walked out the back entrance. She stopped at the pool gate and explained to us how we were violating Best Western's hot tub use policy.

"Stay here. I'll take care of this," I whispered to Karen. I climbed out of the tub, wrapped myself in a towel, and went to negotiate with the lady. There was no way I was going to let some arbitrary rules get in the way of a good soak with a beautiful woman who had intelligent things to say, so I had to come up with something fail-proof.

"Ma'am," I said quietly. "My wife and I recently lost our daughter. We're having difficulty sleeping."

The woman touched her fingers to her lips. "Oh, that's terrible. Just terrible. I'm very sorry for you." She looked down at her slippers. "I know what you're going through. I lost a child."

"I'm sorry to hear that." I swallowed hard. "We're a mess. We were hoping a soak would help us relax."

"I understand. Oh, you poor things. Please, please take your time. I am so very sorry. You're in my prayers."

I thanked the woman, my head hung low. "We appreciate it very much."

Karen stood up as I walked back to the hot tub. "We're fine," I whispered. "We've got all night if we want it."

"What did she say?"

"That we're in her prayers." I dropped my towel, and slid back into my earlier position.

"What a bizarre thing to say. What did you tell her?"

"I don't know, but it was powerful, whatever it was."

Karen's feet resurfaced and I resumed the massage. She let out some quiet oohs and aahs, while I sat silent, disturbed by the performance I'd just given the hotel lady. I'd clearly upset her, and I hoped it hadn't been enough to ruin the rest of her evening. What a low, songwriterly thing to do. Hindemith and Copland would never have done such a thing.

"I need to be honest with you, if I may," Karen began. "I'm not going into this with any plans on getting back together or anything like that."

It sounded contrary to all the evidence, and I wanted to call her bluff.

"It's just a foot rub," I said.

"I know, but I'm liking it more that I expected."

"Should I stop?"

"Don't you dare."

She had a shower when we got back to the room, and fell asleep while I took one. I stood in the gap between the two beds for a moment, watching her, wanting to climb in with her, but decided that if we were to go any further than foot rubs, it would be up to her to instigate.

I turned on the television and zoned out to a PBS documentary on Alexandre-Gustave Eiffel. The night had gone well, and I was thrilled to be away from Forsyth. Maybe it was time to get serious about moving. Rhonda walked through my mind as my eyes began to close. She stopped and glared at me for a moment, fist on hip.

I woke tummy-up, having neglected to get under the covers. Karen was styling her hair, wearing only a bra and thin, lacy white panties. I fixed my eyes on them like I used to do as a kid looking for Mary Tyler Moore's face through the relentless static of my parents' black and white television. The gazing strained my eyes, and made me aware of my slight beer headache.

"Good morning," she said, eyeing me in a large mirror. "What were you dreaming about?"

It took me a second to realize that I had a visible erection. I reacted as though a black widow had set up shop down there. Karen laughed and tossed her towel at me.

"Let's go find something to eat."

We made it down to the lobby in time for the dregs of Best Western's complimentary continental breakfast. I had a cup of coffee, a bowl of Raisin Bran, and a banana with a bad case of liver spots. Karen had a cup of orange juice and the last bagel in the plexiglass case, which she discovered to have a single blueberry hidden inside. "Like a neglected old pearl," she said.

We were about to stand from our table when the lady from the night before approached us.

"It looks like you two were able to get some rest," she said, placing her hand on Karen's shoulder. "I'm so sorry for your loss."

Karen looked at me with her brow raised, waiting for me to intervene.

"We appreciate it," I said. "The hot tub helped a great deal."

I hoped our chat would end there, but the lady decided to grab a chair and join us. She turned to Karen. "Like I told your husband last night, I too lost a child."

Karen's face went pale. The toe of her Chuck Taylors struck my shin.

"It's just not natural," I said, shifting in my chair in an attempt to cover up the sharp pain.

The hotel lady began rearranging the salt and pepper shakers.

"No, it's not. There aren't even words for it."

"Excuse me," Karen said, standing from the table and heading for the hallway.

The lady rose from her chair. "I shouldn't have imposed. I apologize."

"It's okay, ma'am. We're both struggling. The littlest things can set us off."

"You will be in my prayers."

I thanked her before she turned and walked away. The local morning news was on the TV. I sipped my coffee, anticipating Karen's return. After a couple minutes, she zipped past the dining area hefting her army bag, out the double doors, and across the parking lot. The van was locked, and I had the keys. She charged back into the lobby.

"Keys," she said, her hand held out.

We'd done five miles of interstate before she spoke her mind.

"Wow. That really takes the cake," she said.

I'd been in songwriter mode since we left the hotel, adding branches and silk to my outline for the Clinton opera. "What?"

"That's a lie you just don't tell."

"It worked, didn't it?"

She sighed. "It was in poor taste, if not downright cruel."

"How was I supposed to know?"

She pulled a small notebook out of her bag. "Is that all you have to say for yourself?"

"Sometimes you have to take the controversial position in order to get what you want. Maybe you've heard of the Suffragettes."

"Whatever," she said, searching for something in the notebook. "Oh, and by the way, I'm hosting a party tonight, after the show."

I began cranking on the window handle. "Afraid I'll have to pass. My body's only good for one night of partying in a row."

"My friends and colleagues are anxious to meet you."

Great. Just what I needed, a night of forced schmoozing with academic types.

"Nah. Think I'll opt for a hotel."

"But you're the guest of honor."

"How long have you been planning this? A bit more notice might've been a good idea."

"If it helps any, there'll be twenty-five or thirty ticket holders there that wouldn't have paid to see the show otherwise."

I adjusted the sideview mirror. The all-engulfing stench of a nearby pig farm filled the van. "Are you guilting me? That's not how we get things done around here, Karen. Get to know that."

This shut her up for awhile, and she began writing in her notebook. We had five hours of driving ahead of us, and I didn't feel like discussing the matter any further.

Within a dozen miles or so, the onslaught of garish billboards and exit signs for Lake of the Ozarks began. I'd mentioned my parents' accident to Karen the night before, but had evaded most of the details. She set her notebook aside and asked if I'd ever atoned with them.

"Meaning what?"

"Did you ever settle your differences?"

"Hard to say. If we did, it wasn't the result of diligent effort from either side."

She suggested that *atonement* might not be the appropriate word, as it implied something proactive. We discussed the need for a term describing something positive that results from decades of apathy, repression, willful ignorance, and avoidance. We made a few attempts at coining such a term, but the idea became so counter-intuitive that we gave up.

"We'd have to consult a former Soviet," Karen said.

She told me her father died of a heart attack while playing racquetball at a health club a few years previous. Her mom re-married within months—a man Karen described as looking like a wax figure of himself, and someone worth several million dollars more than her own father.

"No surprise there," she said, of her mother. "From almost any angle, you can see dollar signs in the twinkle of her eye."

"You haven't followed in her footsteps, apparently."

"Luckily, I've been able to afford not to. It was never my thing."

I asked her what her thing was.

"Being a nerd, I guess. My heroes have always been nerds."

"And what's wrong with that?"

"It's been rewarding from time to time."

I asked her more about her personal life; questions that weren't even all that personal, in my opinion, and certainly nothing I'd hesitate to answer myself. She'd speak at length about her academic career, but when it came to discussing relationships she'd had over the last twenty years she either changed the subject or deflected with a "you don't want to know" or "if you only knew." I felt like I was getting everything but the central stuff. Facts without ideas. What was she keeping from me beyond the usual heartbreak and turmoil? I began to suspect that she'd endured some traumatic event that she wasn't ready to share.

Of all her insufficient responses, my favorite was: "Maybe I'd tell you more if you'd promise to come to the party."

10

The soundman shook me awake a half-hour before show time. My neck ached, and my left arm was completely numb from shoulder to fingertip. I stood up, hit the dead weight against the wall, and then windmilled it until the painful tingling began. Time was I could sleep on nearly any flat surface, but anymore there's a pea under most anything that looks promising.

I snuck out the back door of the venue to avoid meeting Karen's friends before the show. Good coffee and fresh air was in order before I'd be worth the price of admission. Neither was to be found in that part of the city. The thick, warm atmosphere smelled of rancid meat and diesel exhaust. A convenience store a few blocks away sold me a cup of gritty, burned hazelnut-flavored joe. I took a leap of faith and bought a blister pack of "Iron Man" performance-enhancing supplements. The cashier recited the opening line of the Black Sabbath song, and laughed as I walked out the door.

Some people that I rightly assumed were with Karen's crew made bizarre requests for songs I hadn't played in fifteen years or more. Those clever academics had done their research. One of them shouted: "Inscribe a ballad on our docile bodies." Another shouted: "Play something that demonstrates Nietzsche's priestly inversion."

I had no idea what any of that meant, but I did play what I could remember of Jack Nitzsche's "Needles and Pins."

The supplements were a bust and I ran out of steam, cutting the set short at an hour-and-twenty minutes, plus one encore.

Karen helped load the van afterwards, showing no regard for the welfare of my guitar cases. A door shut on one of them and I heard a slight cracking noise. I told her to go easy, but instead of apologizing, she insisted we hurry to her place where guests were waiting. I reminded her that keeping my gear in working order was a higher priority than timely arrival at her house party, and I pressed the issue until she finally sighed an apology.

We drove a web of poorly lit, narrow streets, eventually parking in the driveway of her small stone house. The front porch was lit up like a Chinese holiday, and the guests appeared to have already made themselves at home.

"Oh, good. Johnnie must've let them in," Karen said.

I asked who Johnnie was.

"Just a friend. You'll meet him soon enough, believe me." She hadn't yet mentioned anything about the guy. I tried to play along like he was nothing to worry about, though I wondered why he had the key to her house.

"He didn't come to the show?"

"No."

"Why not?"

"You should ask him."

We walked together onto her porch where people that I recognized from earlier were drinking wine. The buttery stylings of Johnny Mathis wafted out the front door and window. Karen introduced me to everyone, and I quickly forgot all of their names. They said things like "I enjoyed the show" and "very good" before turning back to their conversations.

The collective education level of her guests was already beginning to stifle me, as I'd never even done junior college. It occurred to me that this would've been a perfect time and place to wear the silk screened T-shirt I made in high school art class that read: SOME KIDS JUST AREN'T COLLEGE MATERIAL.

I followed Karen into the house and made a quick survey. One wall of the front room was obscured by four fully-stocked, ceiling-to-floor antique bookshelves with glass doors. I made a bet with myself that she hadn't read all the thousands of books, as I looked for and failed to find any Kinky Friedman novels—the only classics I'd ever read. A large painting of a reclining nude female with her back turned hung from the opposite wall. The model was obviously Karen. But, the artist—Taylor, I saw from the signature—got the shoulder blades all wrong.

"What would you like to drink?" Karen asked, entering the kitchen.

"Whatever's on the bottom shelf." After saying this, I noticed a man rolling his eyes, as though my passing low-brow remark had offended his sensibilities. He stood in the doorway between the living room and kitchen snapping his fingers lightly to Mathis. He looked like a mutt of several ethnicities, resulting in an unfortunate sort of amphibious, salamander-like appearance.

Karen returned from the kitchen with a bottle of Miller High Life.

"The champagne of beers," she said, handing me the bottle.

She introduced me to the man standing in the doorway. "This is Johnnie."

I extended the glad hand to him, and after some hesitation he extended his.

"Call me Don Johnnie," he said, avoiding eye contact, his voice a breathy tenor, and his handshake so limp that I felt like washing my hand immediately.

"We don't really know what John does," Karen said. "He has a tendency to lurk. Don't ya, John?"

"Puh-leeze," he said, his eyes rolling again.

"What do you do?" I asked.

He took a sip of his wine. "Philanthropy."

I stood there waiting for him to expand on that, but it was no use. He looked away as though he were expecting someone more glamorous to arrive, someone who might discover his bountiful hidden talents and elevate him into stardom. "Okay. No need to say more," I said, turning away, hoping to avoid him the rest of the night.

I followed Karen out to the back yard. We approached a white-haired man smoking a pipe with an ivory bowl. Behind him were two young ladies sitting cross-legged at the edge of a koi pond, pointing at fish and smoking cigarettes. I was introduced to a few others flanking the pipe-smoker, all students or colleagues of Karen's.

"I really enjoyed the performance," the pipe-smoker remarked. "You do some very interesting, playful things with form that at once seem conventional, but come off as wildly unpredictable, fresh, and a real treat to the ear."

I thanked him, holding back laughter. I thought to ask him if he'd ever tried his hand writing entertainment blurbs for the local paper.

Karen placed her hand on the old man's shoulder, and introduced him as Doctor Cohen. "The doctor plays seventeen different instruments."

"Only the ones I can lift," the doctor said, visibly pleased with himself, flexing the bicep of his left arm as though he had the world in a headlock.

Karen introduced me to a woman who resembled a young Mia Farrow. She was the most attractive of the guests I'd seen thus far, until she opened her mouth: "I didn't even realize this until about halfway through your show, Carl. But I was dating a guy—this was years ago—who listened to your records a lot. It's strange, but I feel like you and I have already slept together in some disembodied sort of way. Does that make sense?"

My eyes opened wide, and I looked around at the others standing in the circle, hoping for some guidance as to how to interpret her statement. It either sounded like the most abrupt and strange come-on I'd ever heard, or the most ridiculous confession I'd never asked for. The conversation quickly spiraled away into more outlandish territory before I had a chance to honor her question.

Woman number two: "I can't have an orgasm within five days after hearing Christopher Cross. I really have to be careful where I shop."

Woman number three: "Gary went through this period where he insisted we listen to Stravinsky's "Rites of Spring" while we performed the act. He'd whisper a bunch of nonsense about 'spheres.' He'd say 'let our spheres pass through one another. Invite other spheres to do the same.' I can't get off in the same room as anything spherical."

Woman number four said her cousin slept with Huey Lewis back in the 80s.

They were no longer addressing me at this point, though I was clearly right there to hear all of it. Were these women always so open about their sex lives? I drew the conclusion that even literature professors couldn't keep their book club discussions on track.

Afraid I'd be prompted to contribute an equally intimate story of my own, I moseyed away, eavesdropping and gathering a loose compliment here and there. I stopped at the edge of the koi pond and looked down into the water. I heard a young man standing behind me tell another to "quit thinking about strata as layers of rock, and think of it as the dual set of pincers on a lobster; each pincer having a double nature in itself." I looked back at him and he was doing hand puppets. "Double articulation, you see," he added.

It was a freak show. I turned back to face the pond, watching the fish swim in and out of view, and listening in on conversations. I was reminded of the Lou Reed song, "Kicks," with the short bits of dialogue rising up and out of the mix too quickly to get any bearing on what's being said. I was nowhere near my element. Other than Don Johnnie, everybody seemed friendly enough, but nothing anyone was talking about seemed to make any sense, or seemed worth talking about to begin with. I'd never spent any time around academics before, and so I was probably listening for the wrong things, being made to feel stupid by the very machinery of my own ignorance.

"Do you partake?" a waifish, bespectacled young man with tight black curls asked. He'd been sitting alone on a bench on the opposite side of the pond.

"Who, me?" I pointed at my chest.

"I'm gonna go burn one in the garage," he said. "You're more than welcome to join."

"Why not," I said, against my better judgment, knowing I had a tendency toward paranoia when on the grass. I followed him around the clusters of people into the old wooden one-car garage. The structure had an obvious lean to it, like the right gust of wind could topple it, and pick it back up again just as easily. The kid began rolling a joint on the top of a dusty file cabinet. He said his name was Blaine.

"It's Old English," he began. "Meant to suggest that I'm the source of a river. What does 'Carl' mean?"

"It means my parents were German and lacked creativity."

He smiled. "You share the name of many great men. Marx, Jung, Sagan. While I'm pretty much on my own over here."

"Even more reason to become great," I said. He seemed like a kid I could talk to for awhile—at least someone who could help save me from being the quiet loser in the corner. "Some party, eh?"

He twisted the ends of the joint. "You're kidding, right?"

"Not at all," I said, looking up into the trestles. It was pretty clear that Karen spent little or no time in there. I noticed a couple stacks of water-damaged cardboard boxes with the name *Taylor* written on them in black marker.

"I'd assume that after all the rock star parties you've been to, this would seem like an ice cream social."

It occurred to me that most industry parties were just that— record company execs overstating the talent and future significance of their latest artists, like parents talking up their average kids.

He handed the joint to me. "You must've partied with some big-time cats."

"Sure." I lit the joint and took a short puff.

He asked me to name some of the rock stars I'd partied with.

I held the smoke in while trying to talk. "I'm not much of a name dropper." I blew the smoke out and coughed a few times. "But if someone else drops one, I'm not afraid to pick it up and run with it."

"How about Elvis?"

"Nope. Before my time. Some of his old band, though."

"Dylan?"

"No. I rode in an elevator with him once, though." I passed the joint back.

"Any of the Beatles?"

"Never." I took a drink of my beer, and brought out my old trusty clincher to put an end to the hero worship. "You ever heard of Johnny Cash?" I asked.

His eyes lit up. "No shit? You partied with Johnny Cash?"

"Nope. Can't say that I have."

He looked down at his buckled shoes and shook his head. "Ah, forget it," he said, looking disappointed that I'd led him on.

I noticed a few more of the mysterious boxes as I poked around the garage. "Who is this 'Taylor' person?" I asked.

"I couldn't tell you."

"You don't know, or you can't tell?"

"One or the other."

I asked what his relationship with Karen was, and he told me he'd had a few seminars with her.

"It's pretty amazing to see her again after twenty-some years. We used to date, you know." I immediately regretted having said this, as it was none of his business.

"Then the rumors are true," he said, passing the joint to me. I waved it away. The paranoia was already taking hold. I shoved my hands in my pockets and began sweating in unusual places.

"Rumors?" I asked, my voice cracking. I coughed. "What sort of rumors?"

He looked amused as he took a long drag from the joint. It seemed that he was going to take his time revealing the content of the rumors. I browsed a fleeting catalogue of possibilities, figuring they were probably sexual, as most rumors tend to be.

"You won't hear any gossip coming from me," he said. "I like to think of myself as above that sort of thing."

I felt a strong need to press him on the issue, but it felt juvenile. "I'll have to see what she has to say. Does she know about these?"

"My lips are sealed."

He deserved some respect for that. "You're all right, Blaine," I said. He attempted to pass the joint back to me, but I refused it.

"It's the best red-string you can get around here."

"I wouldn't even know."

I left the garage and wandered through the crowd toward the house, deciding that I'd allow myself one more beer before turning in for the night. As I entered the kitchen, I realized that I hadn't thanked Blaine for sharing his grass with me. I thought to bring him a drink, so I opened the fridge and looked at the options. I heard Mathis drifting through the house like cotton-wood seeds on a breezy summer afternoon.

"Shut the door, Mahogany. You're letting all the cold air out," someone shouted from the front room—a genderless, grumpy, low-level bureaucratic voice. I stepped back and looked into the front room to see who it might be. There was Don Johnnie sitting on a sofa, alone, flipping through a hardback. Maybe he'd finally warmed up to me and was kidding around.

"I'm having a hard time deciding here," I said, scanning the shelves.

"That's certainly not my problem," he replied, almost under his breath.

"Excuse me?" I stepped back again.

"You didn't shut the back door all the way either," he added. "You're going to let all the bugs in."

Indeed, I'd failed to shut the back door all the way, and so I walked through the laundry room and closed it firmly, sure that I'd never have done that if I wasn't stoned. When I returned to the kitchen, Don Johnnie was holding the refrigerator door open, glaring at me. Without breaking eye-contact he shut the door, opened it, and then shut it again, like a frustrated *Price is Right* stage manager re-explaining the fundamentals to one of his appliance bimbos.

"Don't you understand that when you leave the door open for too long, you allow all the cold air to escape?"

"Oh, for chrissakes."

He moved aside as I opened the fridge again, grabbed two Millers, and promptly shut it.

"Well," he said, arms crossed, his head moving side to side. "Now you're getting sassy."

I turned and began walking toward the back door.

"You're a selfish, inconsiderate, and immoral man," he said.

I turned to face him. "How the hell would you know that?" I asked.

"I've known Karen a long time," he said, leaning against the doorjamb. "She confides in me."

"Did she tell you I was all of these things?"

"I can read between the lines."

"Good for you."

"I don't want to see her get hurt again."

"And why would you assume I'd want to do something like that?"

"You tell me, you tell me," he said, returning to the front room, humming along to the chorus of Mathis and Deniece Williams singing "Too Much, Too Little, Too Late."

How had I become the bad guy? What information could

Karen have possibly given him that wasn't two decades old and irrelevant? That's all she really had on me. If she still had hard feelings, she was hiding them well. I walked out to the back yard leaving the door wide open. Karen caught my eye as I wandered with the two beers, looking for Blaine.

"There you are," she said, reaching her arm around my waist, drawing me in, and asking where I'd been.

"Getting my ass chewed by your dandy friend."

"Johnnie? Oh, don't mind him."

A few of the other women in the circle looked like they were holding back laughter.

"What's so funny?"

"What's with the two beers?" Karen asked.

"I was bringing one to Blaine."

"He just apologized to me for some odd reason, and left through the alley," she said, taking one of the beers from me.

"I think I may have upset him."

Karen's friends laughed. One of them began to share a story about Blaine, until she was interrupted by a disturbance near the koi pond. Everyone turned to see what'd happened. Karen hurried over to help the young woman out of the water.

"Oh, I can feel the fish all around me. Yuck, yuck, yuck!" the young woman shouted. She was thoroughly soaked, but didn't appear to be injured. The event seemed to signal the beginning of the end of the party. The Christopher Cross woman ran inside the house to grab some towels for Koi Pond Girl, while everyone else looked around for a flat surface to rid themselves of their drinks. The party was over—for me anyway.

I grabbed my bag from the van and walked through the house to Karen's bedroom, turning off the Mathis on the way. Don

Johnnie remained on the sofa flipping through a magazine. I told him the party was over. "Some girl just fell in the drink."

"Yes, but is the party ever really over?" he asked.

I wanted to stomp and clap my hands like one has to do in order to motivate confused livestock.

"For you it is." I stood outside the bedroom door waiting for him to make a move.

"What, are you kicking me out?" he laughed. "You act as though this is your house."

"It isn't yours, now is it?"

I shut myself in Karen's bedroom and went for her private shower. I took my time, hoping everyone would be gone before I finished. This was not to be. I could hear her talking quiet and serious with someone—probably Johnnie—in the front room as I dried and dressed.

Her bedroom suffered from the clutter of a typical flea market booth. I poked around, looking at all of her knickknacks and bric-a-brac. She had a small army of female superhero action figures standing in formation along the top of an antique roll-top desk. There were two framed portraits atop her dresser; one of her with her parents, and one of her standing beside a young man in a graduation gown. I began looking for other photographs, and found two baby photos elsewhere in the room.

I sat on the edge of her bed and turned on her clock radio. Some Native-American-inspired, breezy flute music played. The reverb and echo effects should've made me sleepy, but I had questions to ask, and felt the need to apologize for being a lousy guest of honor.

Karen entered the room minutes later. "Are you okay?" she asked.

"I'm out of my element," I said, still antsy.

"You're high."

"That's no excuse," I said, turning the radio dial.

She pulled her kelly-green sundress over her head and tossed it into the closet. "Did you have any fun?"

"I think so."

She laughed. "Don't sound so sure of yourself."

"I thought musicians were strange."

"That crowd can get pretty ethereal," she said, sitting on the bed, rolling her black panty hose down her legs.

I asked if Don Johnnie had returned to the Black Lagoon. "Not since the beginning of time have I beheld terror like that."

"You're awful."

"Why does he have keys to your house?"

"He's my house sitter," she said, standing and walking to her dresser. "I'm afraid that's his only marketable skill. I try to help him out."

She paused for a moment after she opened one of the drawers, looking at one or both of the framed photographs.

I blamed Blaine for getting me high, adding that I thought he seemed like an alright kid. "He said there were some rumors floating about." I swung my legs up onto the bed and lay back, gazing at the ceiling, anxious for her response.

"Oh yeah?" She hopped onto the bed next to me with a young girl's enthusiasm.

"I was hoping you might have some insight. He wouldn't tell me anything more."

"What? About us?"

"It seemed that way."

A few seconds passed as she looked like she was thinking through some possibilities.

"Who is this 'Taylor' you've got stored out in your shed?" I asked. "I'm assuming this is the same one who also does large paintings of nude professors."

Her eyes lit up and her cheeks flushed, but it was not a look of embarrassment. I expected some witty response or excuse, but was not getting one. Her expression grew solemn and she looked away from me. I apologized for prying into her personal business.

"It's your business." She sat up and took my hand into hers. "I don't know how you're going to take this."

Oh shit. I already had a pretty good idea what was coming.

"After you left Austin…" She broke eye-contact.

"Go on," I said.

"I have a son, Carl. I found out about two weeks after you left."

I shifted my weight up onto my elbows, and the buzz I'd developed cowered behind my organs.

"Uh huh. And you mean to tell me—"

"I was waiting for the right time."

I stood up from the bed and began pacing the room, searching my memory for clues and hints that I might've missed. "Well, shit. I'd say about twenty years ago might've been the right time."

"Listen to me, Carl. I know this is weird. Please don't get angry. I'm not angry with you. It was my decision."

I sat at the foot of the bed and held my head in my hands for a moment, my thoughts racing like a cartoon animation of an atom. She repeated my name as though she were trying to bring me back into consciousness.

"What a lovely surprise this is," I said, amidst a fury of hot flashes. I wanted to hit something, but decided to grab my bag and go for the door.

"What are you doing?" She sat cross-legged, holding her bare feet. "Don't tell me you're leaving."

I cursed her and her project as I charged through the front room, out the door, across the porch, and down the steps. I could hear her calling me back as I stamped across the lawn toward the van.

"Carl, I'm not asking you for anything. I just needed to tell you. Please don't leave." She stood at the edge of the porch, wearing only a T-shirt and underwear.

"I'll be in touch," I said, rolling up the van window.

"Carl, please."

I backed the van onto the street, the rear bumper scraping the blacktop. I saw Karen sit down and cover her face with her hands as I began driving away. If she could keep a secret like that from me for twenty years, then I could come and go anytime I pleased.

I'd considered turning back within a few miles of leaving Karen's, but I didn't wish to reward her by giving her another chance. Not right then. She'd forced her way back into my life under false pretenses, and so she could think about that for awhile.

As for the big news: Why hadn't Taylor taken any initiative to contact me? Did he not know who I was? How bad was his information? I couldn't imagine why he wouldn't have made some attempt. Sure, it was possible he wanted nothing to do with me, but this didn't feel right, unless his mother had made me out to be a monster. Regardless, if I were in Taylor's position, I'd still want to meet my father.

All I had were guesses, and it disgusted me to think I'd eventually have to contact her for answers. What was her excuse? There isn't a person on earth that can't be reached via a competent attorney, so she couldn't play that card. She'd obviously decided early on that I wasn't suitable father material, but I didn't need to beat myself up thinking about that. Whatever her reasons and excuses were, I felt the vertigo of learning twenty years of possibility had just been yanked out from under me.

There'd be little to no sleep that night, so I drove to Cedar Rapids.

11

I woke in the van, parked on the street in front of Clay and Marnie Jameson's house. My bladder was in critical condition. A pulsing pain shot up and down my right leg like a section of electrified fence. It couldn't wait, so I made sweet relief in the gutter, pretending to talk on my cell phone, hoping the passenger door and Jameson's oak tree would be enough to shield me from onlookers.

I hadn't gotten more than two or three hours of sleep. My thoughts immediately turned to the events of the night before, my morning-after instincts telling me that I should've stayed in St. Louis, rather than storming off like an outraged teenager. My father would not have been proud.

I peed, and peed. When it finally began to let up, I noticed a warm itch radiating from my groin. I looked down to investigate. A sprawl of large red bumps had developed, and my lymph nodes were tender and swollen. I soon noticed similar sensations coming from both armpits. I'd gotten rashes before, from certain detergents, but this one looked exotic and imperialist. I was convinced that I had the plague.

The Jameson's big front window curtain moved when I turned to look at the house. One of them had witnessed the whole thing.

Clay answered the door in a garish Japanese-style robe, holding an open half-gallon carton of milk, his John Lennon eyeglasses sagging a bit to the right. He'd passed a certain milestone since I'd last seen him, one particular to former rock and rollers. His hair had thinned enough on top that he'd finally made the decision to crop the rest.

"Holy shit, Carl," he began, scanning me from toe-to-head. "How the mighty have fallen."

"We have a bathroom, you know," a female voice shouted from deep inside the house. I couldn't see who it was, but I assumed it was Clay's teenaged daughter, Vanessa.

"It's a wild world," I said, scratching at my left armpit.

"Are you okay? Do we need to get you to the hospital? Rehab? Should I call the cops?"

"I'd just like some water. May I come in?"

"Just this once," he said.

I followed him to the kitchen. Vanessa sat at the table eating cereal, barely raising an eyebrow as I sat down across from her. She smelled like a dozen different hair products, lotions, and perfumes.

"Can we maybe open some windows?" I asked.

Vanessa could sense that this had something to do with her multiple fragrances. "Can you not ever urinate in the gutter in front of our house again?"

Clay laughed. I assured Vanessa that it was a once-in-a-life-time kind of thing.

"You look like a shell-shocked Korean War vet," Clay said. "After only a couple days out. You should see your hair. I'd offer to make you some breakfast, but you don't want to eat what Marnie's got me on these days."

I asked about Marnie. She was at work—the Nurse Manager at the free clinic where Clay had met her seventeen years before. It's one of his central stories. He walked in for a routine VD test, passed her physical exam, and the rest is history.

"I need to talk to her," I said. "I've got this rash."

Vanessa let out a protracted groan. "I'm trying to eat my breakfast here."

"Sweetie," Clay said, filling his coffee mug. "Rockers at Carl's level get rashes sometimes. It comes with the job—like your mom has to wear those special leggings."

Vanessa looked at me as though she needed some reassurance that she would never, ever turn into her father someday. I didn't know what to do other than shrug.

"I just hope it's not the plague," I said, thinking a flea may have bitten me as I tiptoed across Bill's prairie dog-infested pasture the previous weekend.

"Don't worry, ol' buddy. Even if it is, I'm sure we've got something that can wipe that out," Clay said, handing me a pint glass of water and a mug of coffee. "We've got the best medicine chest in Eastern Iowa."

I didn't doubt his claim, and it was enough of a comfort to allow my thoughts to turn to Taylor for awhile as Vanessa bickered with her dad over what she was and was not allowed to do that day. I felt some fleeting relief that I'd been spared Taylor's adolescent years, as I knew I'd been an especially defiant and ungrateful shit at that age, and that it was probably the product of a dominant gene in the Mahogany line.

Their argument eventually reached an impasse, and it seemed as good a time as any to tell them about Taylor. "I've got some news to share with you."

Clay smiled and pointed his index finger at the ceiling. "Wait. Shush. Let me guess. You're out of the closet."

"Dad!" Vanessa shouted, either offended or amused, or both.

"Nice try. But, no." I took a sip of coffee. "I had a baby."

Clay asked me to repeat myself, and I did.

"Twenty years ago. I just found out last night."

They demanded a full explanation, so I told the abridged, PG-rated version, starting in Austin and running through the events of the previous night. Clay laughed.

And laughed. Even Vanessa began to snicker, until I told them both to knock it off.

"You're a born entertainer," Clay said, removing his glasses and wiping tears from his eyes. "Man oh man."

"Jeezus. Do you think I'm making this up?"

He put his glasses back on. "Absolutely not. Do you think I'd be laughing like this if you were?"

My eyes darted around the kitchen as Clay let out a few more laughs. Vanessa told him to calm down.

"You're just not ready to see the humor in your situation," Clay said.

"No, I'm not. I'm still pretty pissed off about it."

He removed his glasses and wiped his eyes again. "Sorry, ol' buddy," he said. "I guess I haven't heard the whole story."

"No, you haven't."

I'd known Clay too long not to give him the benefit of the doubt, so I waited for him to gather himself.

"I guess the question is what are you going to do now?"

While Clay wasn't the first person I'd think to consult regarding a matter like this, we'd known each other most of our lives, and he deserved some credit for being a dedicated family man, despite his wealth of backward attitudes and unrefined behaviors.

"I should probably head back to St. Louis."

"When?"

"Sometime today."

"What? You'll never get down there and back in time for the gig."

"Who cares about the gig."

"Don't be ridiculous," he said, sitting down at the table. "Looky here. A person like you makes his career by taking and keeping blood oaths—to the music, to the road, to the life. That's why you've made it so far."

"I could care less about the gig!"

"I, unfortunately, did not see through on mine," he continued, having forgotten that his daughter was still sitting at the table listening. "What was someone of my abilities supposed to do when the nineties hit? You can't just forget how to play well…then again, it's all about being in the right place at the right time, as you know…"

Vanessa and I looked at one another, both aware that her father was in the midst of trying to hustle his failed rocker complex back into the bag.

Clay eventually caught himself. "But, don't get me wrong, I'm happy with my situation now. I love my wife and my daughter. Life is good."

"I'm sure it is."

Clay continued his gratuitous backpedaling. "Fatherhood is a magical thing. Marnie and I would've had a kid earlier if we'd known it was going to be such a kick."

Vanessa stood from the table, tossed her bowl in the sink, and headed for the staircase. "Whatever, dad," she said.

Clay stamped his foot on the linoleum. "Go on. Get! We've got grown-up business here."

"You wish," she shouted.

I put a toothpick to my lips and let Clay continue.

"She can drive her lyin' ass up here if she's so inclined," he said, in a forced whisper. "You've got a career to worry about. You need to finish the tour and worry about this other shit later. End of story."

I took a sip of coffee and ruminated.

"You know I'm right. I always am about these things."

He was. The situation with Karen could wait, though I'd have to contact her. I needed to know how to get in touch with Taylor, and I needed to put a few other things to rest.

I needed some rest more than anything. So, I napped a few hours on their basement couch, which didn't seem to help much. Whatever dream I had caused me to wake feeling as though I'd just slept through that night's gig. I hopped up shouting for Clay, and looking for a clock.

It was 1:30 in the afternoon, and the house was empty. With nothing better to do, I grabbed a beer from their fridge and took a walk across their back lawn down to the bank of the Cedar River.

After a few minutes of sitting at the end of Clay's boat dock, trying to get my thoughts and priorities in order, I decided to make the call and get it over with. My chest tightened with each dial tone. Here was a moment of truth waiting to happen. Karen answered, and I apologized.

"Oh, it's okay," she said. Her tone seemed flippant. "It was probably the natural thing."

"It was rude. I feel like an ass."

"You had a very natural reaction, considering."

Was she letting me off the hook? Did she even care? "I guess we have some things to talk about," I said.

"Yes, we do."

"How and when do you propose we do this?"

"I'm on my way up there right now."

I wasn't expecting this, and wasn't sure I liked the idea. If she did make the drive, then what? Would she plan on returning to St. Louis the next day? Doubtful. I got the feeling she was putting me into another situation. She'd have leverage to guilt her way back into the van after going so far out of the way.

"It's no problem," she said. "It's only five hours. I can do that in four-and-a-half."

"Maybe that's not such a good idea." I imagined taking a bong rip in Bethany's hot tub.

"Then what do you propose?"

I had no alternatives prepared. St. Louis wasn't exactly on the way home from Minneapolis, or else I might've considered passing through after the tour was over. "I don't know," I said. "I'll have to get back to you on that."

She thought a moment. "I'll just see you tonight. Don't worry. I'll stay out of your way."

I tried to take comfort in the fact that it was a long drive, and that she'd have ample time to change her mind about going through with it. But, considering the shit she'd already pulled, I knew there was no way of predicting what she might do.

Before we hung up, I asked her where Taylor was.

"He's in Mexico." She sounded as though she disapproved.

"Doing what?"

"I don't want to go into it," she said. I tried for more, but she hesitated. "It's complicated."

"Is he in trouble?"

"Not like that," she said. "We'll have plenty of time to go over the details."

Clay and I spent the late afternoon racing up and down the river on his pontoon boat, drinking beer to temper the effects of the pill we'd split. "You don't want to take a whole one," was all he'd tell me, evading any questions as to the name of the drug, as though my asking defeated the purpose.

He cycled through a stack of CDs, playing the first minute or so of any given song before changing it out for another. He greeted passing boat captains and shoreside fishermen with the horned hand gesture, showing off the alleged $3000 stereo system he'd installed himself. His tastes in music hadn't evolved any—early Van Halen, Kiss, Led Zeppelin. I suggested he just turn on a classic rock station to save himself the hassle.

We grew up together in Dodgeville, a town of a few thousand that sits an hour north of Cedar Rapids. He was the only other kid I knew that had musical ambitions and whose folks allowed him to have an electric guitar. He got good at it quickly, far surpassing my skill level. Had he been more open to playing any type of music besides 80s butt rock, he might've gone further with it. Instead, he retired from playing in bands around '93 and set out to make a name for himself in the business community as the owner of a chain of discount cigarette stores scattered around the city.

He turned the motor off several miles upriver and let the current take us. I told him about Rhonda, mostly to make him jealous. It'd always been a dream of his to own a junkyard.

"That's bullshit," he said. "You're making this chick up."

"Over twenty acres of classics," I said. "With minimal rust."

He informed me that starting a new junkyard business is nearly impossible in most states because of environmental laws, and that a person would have to buy an existing junkyard, inherit one, or marry into one. "The last of the great American junkyards are out your way."

"Huh," I said, looking off into the thick woods lining the riverbank. My indifference seemed to irritate him. He asked me what all she had out in the yard. "Where do I start? You'll have to be more specific."

He named off various classic makes, models, and years. I told him Rhonda had at least two and probably three of everything he mentioned, which may well have been true, but I really had no idea.

"No offense, but I cannot think of a single person more unworthy than you of scoring a chick like that," he said.

I reminded him of how he'd met his wife.

"What's your point?"

The boat had spun around a few times and was now floating backwards. I mentioned that Rhonda had brought up selling the place and he pestered me until I got my phone out and gave him her number.

"Way to fuck things up," he said. "You find yourself a solid woman that owns her own junkyard, then you go blow it twenty years earlier on some trust funder hippie. Funny how time works, isn't it?"

"Yep."

"Now I suppose you're going to go back after this chair-wielding Karen gal."

"What makes you think I'd want to do that?"

"You're banging her, aren't you?"

"No, I'm not banging her. I gave her a foot massage the other night is all."

He laughed and tossed his empty can overboard. "The only difference between a foot massage and a fuck at our age is a couple of formalities." He reached into the cooler, grabbed a couple beers, and pitched one to me. "And you know that."

"She's out of my league anyway."

He asked me to explain, and I told him about Karen's friends from the after-show party. "I can't even speak these people's language. You ask one of them a simple yes or no question and you get a description of a Salvador Dali painting."

He moved to the captain's chair and began straightening the boat around. "Think of it this way, Carl. You're in an ideal spot in many ways. The kid's grown. Your genes are out there to be passed on, so you don't have to worry about that. The life force is taken care of, more or less. You can pretty much do whatever you want at this point."

"I've been doing that since we graduated high school."

"You've gotta be careful with women our age, though. They don't want to face their later years without a husband."

"What does that have to do with me?"

"You don't want to get talked into doing something hasty."

"Tell me, Clay. What would you have done without Marnie and Vanessa holding you up? You'd have died face-down in a porn arcade along the interstate."

"There are worse places."

The day devolved along those lines, on into the night as we set up our gear at Howlin' Wolff's. We'd arrived at the club a little later than some people on the staff had hoped, but there was still plenty of time to get set and start on the mark. The young, hotheaded manager was short with me as I adjusted the volume levels of my amps.

"You can't just show up whenever you feel like it, man. This is showbiz."

I laughed. "Since when did playing a dump like this qualify as showbiz? The Hog arrives when Hog wants to arrive."

This shook up the cocky ex-jock. He folded his arms and thrust his chest out. "I can see to it that you never play here again, if that's the way you want it."

I turned to Clay. "Is this guy for real?" I turned back to the manager and asked him where the owner was.

"He's not here yet."

This bit of information gave me a little room to maneuver. I told him that the owner happened to be a long-time friend of mine, and had insisted that I not start the show until he arrived. "That's showbiz, buddy."

I did an hour's worth of tunes by myself before taking a break. There was no sign of Karen, and I had no way of reaching her or fetching her number since I'd let my phone battery run out. Maybe she'd changed her mind.

Bethany hadn't shown up either, for the first time in a dozen years. That saddened me, although it was some relief knowing the end of the night wouldn't get complicated, should Karen eventually appear.

Clay joined me with his guitar for the second set. Marnie arrived a few songs into it. I could hear her voice over our music, so I guessed she'd started in on the bottle immediately after work. She approached the stage between songs and gave me the come-hither finger. I walked to the edge of the stage and leaned down, expecting to hear something that would make it difficult for me to get through the next song without laughing. This was something Marnie loved to do. She whispered in my ear: "I'm gonna rape the shit out of you later."

We finished our last song a little after 11:30. It'd been a long day of intoxication. Our motor skills were failing and the crumbling integrity of our sound produced a tinge of nostalgia in me for the old high school glory days of our first band, Flesh Toothbrush. We'd come full circle in terms of musicianship by the time our last song fizzled out, and we sounded like beginners again.

Bethany emerged from the crowd and approached me as I hopped down from the stage. We embraced for a moment before she introduced me to her NFL lineman-sized husband, Pete. I imagined an orange soda machine falling over on a porcelain vase.

"I didn't know," I said, shaking Pete's banana hands. "Congrats."

"And we've got a nine-month old girl. It all happened pretty fast. We met over the internet."

That almost sounded familiar.

"I wish we could hang around and talk, but we've got to get home to the babysitter," she said, looking up at Pete with that twinkle in her eyes.

We said our goodbyes and she promised to send some pictures of the baby. I sauntered into the restroom, relieved myself, and thought about Bethany and her new life. Though I hadn't had any contact with her in over a year, I felt a sense of loss, a connection, a possibility that I'd been putting off for a day that probably wouldn't have come anyway. She'd always been a woman I thought might be there if I ever had the itch to settle down and make good on a promise. Not that I ever told her that. But, that book was shut now. I would miss the bong rips in the hot tub, the purple gazebo, and the naughties.

Karen and the Jamesons had made each other's acquaintance by the time I found them. This was odd, since they'd never seen each other before that night. Karen looked stressed and overstimulated by whatever story Clay was barking at her. I suggested we find a booth, and as we wandered the room looking for one, I asked Clay if he'd said anything to Marnie about Taylor. He assured me that the subject hadn't come up yet.

"I've got some news for you," I told Marnie, once we'd settled in the booth. "Or, rather, we have some news for you." I put my arm around Karen, who stiffened a bit.

Marnie's eyes lit up. "You're getting married," she said, sounding as though she'd just set down a 100-pound sack of oats. "Well, I'll say it's about time you came around, Mahogany."

Karen and I looked at each other.

"Not exactly," I said.

"What is it then?" Marnie asked, looking straight at me as though she wasn't about to tolerate any bullshit. The rest of her head slowly twisted to the right—the way she's always looked at me when suspecting mischief.

"Karen and I have a twenty-year-old son. His name is Taylor."

Marnie shifted her weight, nodded slightly, and tightened her lips as though she were about to laugh. Karen and I took simultaneous drinks of water as we watched the news sink in. I got the sense that Marnie was going to need some more information before her official response would be released. "You mean... you just found this out?" she asked, looking at me, then Karen, then back at me.

"It's the best news I've heard in a long time," I said, in an attempt to cut through the awkwardness.

Marnie let out a sigh. "That's great, Carl. You're a daddy now. In a very unconventional, Mahogany-esque way, naturally. Congratulations."

"It's a long, very complicated series of events," Karen added.

I could tell Clay was biting his tongue.

"We don't need to go into it now," Marnie said. "We've got all day tomorrow."

Marnie continued asking questions about Taylor, and Karen answered them without much detail. I learned nothing I didn't already know. Within a couple minutes, the conversation began to dwindle, yawns began to happen, and we soon agreed that it was time to leave. Clay and I packed our gear and loaded it into our respective vehicles. The manager had loosened up a little since our earlier encounter. He paid me in full and thanked me before mentioning that the owner never showed up.

"Yeah, that's too bad," I said to him, even though I wouldn't have recognized the owner anyhow. "That's showbiz."

I was far too drunk to drive, so I talked Karen into leaving her car behind and driving the van. We followed the Jamesons at a distance. Marnie was behind the wheel of their Jeep and had no apparent concern about getting pulled over. She failed to turn her lights on, and whizzed through three stop signs.

"Do we really have to spend all day tomorrow with those two?" Karen asked.

"That's the plan."

She sighed.

"They're good folks," I said. "You'll learn to like them."

Another sigh. I became annoyed.

"If you wish to continue this trip, then you'd better remind yourself who's running the show," I said.

"I drove up here to spend time with you, not you and your friends. I thought you might want to discuss some things."

"They'll get discussed, trust me."

"I'd expect you'd be a little more anxious to know."

I was, but the contrarian in me needed to assert itself. "It's been twenty years. A few extra hours aren't going to kill me."

Karen parked, turned off the ignition, and sat for a moment. We could hear Clay berating Marnie about her reckless driving as they walked from their garage to their house.

"Don't try to make me feel worse about having waited. I don't need to feel more like I've done something wrong. It's always already there."

"Sure thing, boss," I said, stepping out of the van. I had the presence of mind to know that my BAC wasn't conducive to any further conversation about the matter.

"How did you end up finding those two anyway?" I asked, as we approached the Jameson's front door. "Must've been two hundred people in there to choose from."

"Clay hit on me while I was ordering a drink at the bar."

"Mom!" Vanessa shouted, from the bathroom across the hall. "I need a ride to church."

"Ride your bike," Marnie shouted from the kitchen.

"But I'll get all gross."

I covered my head with a pillow, reminded of the joys of living alone. The end of the previous night had been a blackout. I hoped that I'd been able to make it up the stairs and to the bed on my own, at least. Karen wasn't lying next to me when I woke, but the pillow beside mine still had a head print in it. It could've been Clay's for all I knew.

Karen and Marnie were chatting away in the kitchen over the television noise and clanging cookery. I waited a few minutes for Vanessa to finish in the bathroom, and then I made a bee-line for the shower. The situation in my armpits and groin hadn't improved. Cold water helped, but I would have to consult with Marnie and dip into that medicine chest before too long.

I walked down the steep staircase into the kitchen, sat at the table, and put on a pair of sunglasses that were sitting there. Bacon sizzled on the stove top.

"How's your rash?" Karen asked me.

"And good morning to you," I said.

"I've got it too."

Marnie handed me a glass of water and an orange prescription container. "You've been soaking in hot tubs when you shouldn't have been. Always mind a hotel's hot tub rules."

Karen felt it appropriate to brief me on how they'd come to the conclusion that the untreated hot tub water had caused the rash and not something else. "I knew it couldn't be venereal," she said. "Considering."

I imagined the Best Western lady leaning back in her easy chair, cackling herself into a gassy heart-attack.

Clay walked into the kitchen, rubbing his eyes. "See what I have to put up with, Carl?" He pulled the sunglasses off of my face and placed them on his, then sat down at the table opposite from me. "That's the problem with having a nurse for a wife. Your whole body and medical history becomes public domain."

Vanessa was on the phone in the next room, trying to hustle a ride to church. Karen and I looked at each other as we listened to her pleas.

"Your daughter goes to church by herself?" I asked. "That's about the last thing I'd expect."

"She goes with her friends," Marnie said.

"Teenagers choosing to attend church. What will they think of next?" I said.

"It's fine with me if she wants to spend her Sundays at church,"

Clay said. "Better that than giving hand jobs in the Quaker Oats employee lot."

"Clayton!" Marnie shouted.

Karen looked at me wide-eyed as though she'd had enough of the Jamesons. "I'll have you know that Taylor is a churchie."

This was the first tangible information I'd gotten about Taylor, other than his age, and the Mexico trip. My son—a Christian soldier. It was an amusing thought.

Karen continued: "And, in his case, I'm against it one hundred percent."

"It's been a great thing for Vanessa," Marnie said, flipping a fried egg. "The more I think about what I was getting into when I was her age—makes me sick now. I'm sure it's nothing to worry about. You know how kids are. Their friends start doing something and they fall in line. It's probably just a phase."

"Taylor has gone way beyond that, I'm afraid," Karen said, shaking her head. "When does a phase end and a way of life begin?"

"Let's try not to get too worked up over it," I said.

Karen looked at me like she'd heard this one too many times. "You have no idea. You haven't had to deal with it for the last five years."

"And whose fault is that?" I asked.

A long silence ensued. Marnie offered to whip up some Bloody Marys, but there were no takers. She then began listing all the people she planned to invite over for the barbeque that afternoon.

This seemed to put Karen over the edge. She excused herself and headed for the stairs. I let a minute pass before following her, dreading the tongue lashing I was sure to get as I entered the guest room. She had her duffel bag hanging from her shoulder, looking as though she were ready to leave that instant.

"What's your deal?" I asked.

She spoke quietly, but not without force. "I'm sorry, but I'm not going to spend my day at a redneck barbeque. Not after driving all this way. No thanks."

"You're gonna stand there and insult these people after what they've done for you? They just saved both of us a trip to the doctor's office."

"I'll just meet you in Davenport."

"Oh, come on now."

"We can go together, right now, or I'll see you there."

She charged past me and down to the kitchen. I gathered my few things and followed her. She managed to muster up enough courtesy to thank the Jamesons for their hospitality and the antibiotics. She mentioned something about meeting a friend for lunch in Iowa City. This was news to me.

I returned to the kitchen, where Marnie was explaining the importance of taking one antibiotic pill a day until they were all gone.

"Same goes for you, Carl, especially," she said. "I know how your attention span likes to wane."

Karen walked out the front door and looked at the sky.

"Will you give me a ride? I think it's going to rain."

I tossed her the van keys. "I'll meet you out there."

The Jamesons and I stood silent, each taking turns looking out the front window, waiting for Karen to be out of earshot.

"Did we say something to upset her?" Marnie asked.

"Why have you brought this person into our world?" Clay asked, as though he were auditioning for the community theater.

"I don't know what we're dealing with here exactly." I half expected a follow-up lecture about blood oaths from Clay, but he just stood there in his sunglasses, arms folded, smiling.

I must've given off the impression that I was planning to leave for good, because Marnie asked if I was. "We were really hoping you'd stick around."

"Who knows what'll happen," I said. "I guess I'll see you if I see you." I shook Clay's hand and gave Marnie a hug, thanking them just in case I didn't make it back.

"Hold on a sec," Clay said, opening two large cabinet doors above the sink. This was the medicine chest he'd boasted of—an army of orange bottles three feet across, and several bottles deep. He grabbed one of them and tossed it to me. I noticed the label had been removed. "Welcome to the real world," he said. "You're going to need those."

Before we drove away, I removed my list of terms and conditions from the glove box and handed it to Karen. "Read and sign, please."

She'd finished looking it over just as we pulled into the Howlin' Wolff's parking lot.

"Lovely," she said, refolding and tossing it onto the dashboard.

I pulled up next to her car and kept the engine running. "If you want to continue this project of yours, then I'm gonna need to see some ink."

"You actually expect me to sign that?"

"Up to you. You're not riding one more mile with me if you don't. I've got a business to run."

She grabbed the list from the dashboard and had another look. "You know this thing is virtually useless, right?"

"Do you want to try me?"

I lit a cigarette and waited. Ted Nugent's "Cat Scratch Fever" started playing on the radio. I turned the volume up until Percy's stock speakers began to distort, thinking it might speed up negotiations.

It worked. She fetched a pen from her army surplus bag, flattened the page on the dashboard, and signed.

12

We left Karen's car parked on a residential street, and then got on I-380 headed north. Her pride had taken a hit by signing my contract, and I was absorbed in the luxury of silently gloating over it. I'd had my fill of the Jamesons as well, but I wasn't about to let her know this. We were several miles out of Cedar Rapids before either of us spoke.

"We're not even going in the right direction," she said, having found our location in my road atlas. "Should you even be driving?"

"I'm taking you to see my old stamping grounds," I said, opening the pill container Clay had given me. The pills were different from what Clay and I had shared the day before, but I took one anyway, and washed it down with flat 7-Up. Karen asked what I'd just swallowed.

"Allergy pills," I said, placing the container back in my shirt pocket. "It's the corn pollen."

"I'm sure."

A few miles passed. It seemed as though she wasn't going to volunteer any information about Taylor, so I asked what he was doing in Mexico.

"You're pathetic. You asked me about this last night. Don't you remember?"

"I just need a reminder."

After a minute of silent treatment, she was kind enough to repeat herself. Taylor was on a "team-building vacation" with the state representative whom he interned for.

"Doesn't sound like a bad gig to me," I said.

She went on at length about the politician, whom she called a "fire and brimstone, religious right anachronism." She gave a detailed overview of the guy's voting record, his various affiliations, and personal history. She seemed to know more about this guy than I knew about Clinton.

"Big whoop," I said. "It's just an internship."

"Taylor really looks up to him. I'm afraid he's become something of a father figure."

"Ha! So you want me to intervene. Is that what this is all about?"

"It's probably too late for that." She lit a cigarette and then rolled her window down. "He's bought into the worldview that humanity is moving ever closer to the circle of hell. The whole cast will be there: the four horsemen, various beasts, the Whore of Babylon. There will be wailing and gnashing of teeth. He believes this very deeply."

"There are better ways to face the day, I suppose."

"It's depressing."

"When am I going to meet him?"

"He's planning on contacting you when he returns from the trip."

"Why now?"

"He's ready, I guess. You'll have to ask him. I thought I should prepare you for what you're likely to encounter."

I laughed. "Is he gonna come at me with the cross?"

"No. Nothing like that," she said. "Though he does have a knack for expressing rather strong opinions. It can get a bit tedious."

"I wonder where he got that."

"Oh, please." She looked at me, disgusted. "Just try to understand that seeing my child—"

I interrupted. "Our child."

This seemed to annoy her, but she continued. "Taylor go in this direction has been difficult for me. I know it's not drug addiction, or general apathy, but it is in its own way."

She went on about the college he was attending—a Christian liberal arts school, which she enclosed in finger quotes. He'd graduated high school as valedictorian, and had been especially adept at entrance exams, leading to a full tuition scholarship to the school. I was happy to learn that he hadn't inherited the shroud of my learning disabilities.

"It was the only school he even looked at," she added. "He could've gone anywhere."

She mentioned that she didn't have the leverage of paying his tuition, and how that had made it impossible for her to have much say in his decision to attend the college. This cleared up any doubts as to Karen possibly having some control issues.

"It's a factory for right-wing politicians and Stepford wives," she continued. "The 'cream of the crop,' they tell themselves. They have curfews and demerit systems for crying out loud. What intelligent young adult would submit to that?"

It occurred to me that she'd let her imagination run too far in the wrong direction. "They're doing the same things other kids do. They just get started a little earlier in the evening." I asked if Taylor had a girlfriend, and Karen told me he'd brought the young lady to St. Louis the previous Christmas.

"A very pretty, petite little thing," she began. "She's obviously taken some advanced courses at the Martha Stewart School for Competitive Homemaking. I eventually had to smoke a joint and let her do all the 'woman's work'—as she so affectionately called it—and then she feigned a marijuana allergy for chrissakes."

I felt a tightness develop in my throat as the Dodgeville water tower began to come into view. It's one of the first images imprinted on my mind as a child: returning home from a day-trip to Cedar Rapids, mom driving, dad complaining about something, old country music playing quietly on the AM radio. I hadn't been back since my parents' funeral. A rush of old memories began to resurface as I drove past the familiar scenery on the outskirts—farms I used to work on, country churches, sites of legendary auto accidents, and the radio transmission towers my friends and I used to climb.

Karen had headphones on and appeared to be sleeping. I slammed on the brakes just enough to scare her out of her slumber. She looked around, as though she were expecting carnage, or something else worthy of urgency.

"What was that all about?" she asked, removing her headphones.

"Raccoons."

The southern edge of town was unrecognizable to me. A Super Wal-Mart had gone up, along with a new bank, and a couple chain restaurants. The WELCOME TO DODGEVILLE sign that used to mark the far southern edge of town now sat a half mile in, still flanked by weather-worn F.F.A., B.P.O.E., Knights of Columbus, and Mason's insignia. The sign listing Dodgeville High School's athletic triumphs hadn't been added to in over a decade.

Karen asked why there wasn't a sign that read BIRTHPLACE OF CARL MAHOGANY.

"You obviously aren't from this part of the country."

She hissed, and went for her pack of cigarettes. "You don't have to give me this holier-than-thou, more-country-than-thou crap."

She'd missed my point entirely, as only astronauts get their names on the type of sign she was referring to, but I decided to go her path. I thought of the most brutal, real-life, generations-old farm chore that I could recall. "But have you ever drowned a pillowcase full of barn kittens?"

She froze, and gave me a look of fright and disbelief. While I'd never personally drowned a pillowcase full of barn kittens, I chose to leave things open-ended.

"Oh, my god, Carl," she said, beginning to squirm. "You did that?"

I pointed out some of my old haunts as we drove along the main drag. Nearly all of them had been turned into something else, or were boarded up. The hardware store where my mother used to work was still in business, but other than that, nothing.

My parents' old house looked as though it had gone the way of a junky den. A swarm of unsupervised children loitered on the porch, their faces messy with candy and dirt. One of the boys wielded a garden hose between his legs, squirting a notice-ably younger kid in the face. Piles of yellow foam insulation were strewn across the front lawn, replacing my mother's once-meticulous landscaping. I stopped the van in the street and shouted to the kids, asking them who lived there.

"Ain't nobody lives here, yo," one of them said.

"Where'd you get that ugly van?" another asked. The kids laughed.

I turned to Karen. "There you go."

I whipped around and headed back toward the highway.

"I thought you grew up on a farm," she said, as though she'd caught me in a lie.

"That's next."

The radio reported 105° heat indices across most of the state as we left Dodgeville. I'd determined some years before, while driving through Illinois, that the reported heat index generally corresponds to Percy's interior temperature, while moving at 55 mph or more with both windows down. Karen had been complaining about the heat every 20 minutes or so, and was down to only her sports bra and shorts.

My uncle's old farm sits about three miles east of town, just south of the highway. Two full-sized school busses were blocking the driveway. This meant it was seed corn detasseling season, and the farm was being overrun by dozens of teenagers laboring miserably. I parked along the roadside and looked for a crew supervisor or someone who could move the busses and let us drive up to the house, but there was no one in sight. I looked out over the field, trying to find the outlines of the house and outbuildings. I thought maybe the corn was too tall, so I climbed atop Percy to get a better look.

"Well, sonofabitch," I said. "It's all gone!"

As soon as I said it, Percy's roof caved in. Not much, but enough to knock me off balance and send me falling seven feet to the ground. I tweaked my right ankle on first impact, and then slid to the bottom of the bar ditch, leaving a pretty good scrape on my right forearm. Both palms were scratched and dented from gravel.

Karen asked if I was okay repeatedly as I took a moment to gather myself and get back on my feet. I was pretty banged up, but mostly just embarrassed. I took great comfort in the fact that the school busses weren't full of laughing adolescents. I climbed up out of the ditch and brushed myself off.

"Well, that could've gone in a completely different direction," I said, before limping back to the driver's seat. Karen offered to drive, and after some hesitation, I took her up on it.

I guess Clay's pill kicked in, because I have no memory of the next few hours.

Karen woke me at a stoplight as we rolled into Davenport, and asked where we were going.

"The QuadRoom," I said, not yet fully alert. I handed her a sheet of paper with directions.

"Charming name," she said, in a condescending tone that was becoming too familiar. "I wouldn't be surprised if the owners were old friends of yours."

"I'm just waking up here," I said. "Do you have to start right in with the fussing?"

I had no idea what she was talking about. We were in the "Quad Cities" area after all, and it seemed like a fitting, though perhaps unimaginative, name for a venue. She uttered a few associations that explained her concern about the name, and I conceded that, yes, I too wouldn't be surprised if the owners turned out to be people I used to know.

She parked the van across the street from the venue. It not only looked closed, but condemned. I walked to their main entrance. A piece of cardboard had been taped to the inside that read: Closed due to fire. Sorry for the inconvenience.

I called the promoter immediately. He didn't answer, nor was I given the opportunity to leave a message. I walked to the Kum & Go at the end of the block and asked the cashier what she knew about it.

"Burnt last Wensdee," she said. "Arson, they're sayin."

"That place sucked anyway," said someone from behind me. His British accent struck me as completely out of context, so I turned to face him. The thin, slight man, with shoulder-length black hair wore sunglasses and a brightly-colored bandanna across his forehead that read MAGIC. He pointed toward the door. "Ride, my friend," he said. "Ride like the wind."

Perhaps I'd been hallucinating, but I did run, as much as I was able with a bum ankle. I double-checked the messages on my phone before I got to Percy, and discovered what I already suspected, that no one from the venue had bothered to inform me of anything.

Karen got an earful as I drove us across the Centennial Bridge into Illinois—mostly about the canceled gig and the general state of the music biz. I went off about my parents' old house, my uncle's farm. It was all of this, plus the heat, the pill, the wasted time, Karen's agenda. I didn't even mention the prank CD , Lloyd, and all the other weirdness I'd left in Forsyth.

I was approaching critical mass. While I hadn't been making any effort whatsoever to impress Karen up to this point, I now felt like nothing more than an official, low-rent, inconsequential dude driving across the Midwest in a shitty van. It seemed unlikely that there'd be any opportunity to rectify, or even blow off the situation any time soon. She made several attempts at bringing balance to our dialogue with platitudinous comfort phrases like "shit happens" or "maybe it's for the best." This just made things worse, and it went on for miles, until I began littering, of all things.

"You need to calm down before you get us both killed," she said, before offering to drive.

I adjusted the rear view mirror for some reason, and it detached from the windshield. I threw it out the window, not out of any attempt at grand symbolic gesture, but because it was right there to be done. Karen shouted at me repeatedly to pull over, but it just wasn't going to happen that way.

The van overheated not thirty miles into the state. Luckily, it happened in a town, and a stone's throw from a tavern. I parked under a shade tree, popped the hood, and attempted to kick the bumper, but ended up putting a crack in the grille. Karen grabbed my arm and spun me to face her before slapping me on the cheek.

"Get a grip, Carl."

I touched my face where she'd hit me. "For fuckssake!"

"Do you want to get yourself arrested?"

"Do you want to take a bus home?"

She stormed off. Toward what, I don't know. There was a Pizza Hut, a Casey's General Store, and a vinyl siding business ahead of her. While I'd managed to have the last word of that particular exchange, I still wasn't satisfied. "You've physically assaulted me two of the last five days that I've been in your presence," I shouted. "I'd say that's pretty goddamned remarkable!"

The air-conditioning in the tavern hit me like a shot of morphine. I sat at the bar and ordered a pitcher of Coors from the barkeep. She looked about 25 going on 45, having gone the way of too much methamphetamine and soft drinks.

"How many glasses?" she asked, setting the pitcher before me.

"One."

I pulled a fifty dollar bill out of my wallet and set it on the bar. She looked hesitant to reach for it.

"I'm gonna take one of those booths over there, drink whatever I can of this, and then get some shut-eye," I said, standing from the barstool.

"I can't have you sleeping here, mister."

I glared at the fifty dollar bill, and then back at her, until I was sure she understood me. "Whatever happens, make sure I'm back in that van by sundown."

13

It was night, Karen was driving, and we were on an interstate when I finally came to; the muggy evening illuminated by the distant light pollution of what could only be Chicago. Karen tapped her fingers on the steering wheel to the "Pina Colada Song" as I pushed myself upright from a deep slouch, my shirt and shorts sweat-grafted to my skin. She began to hum along with the radio. My index finger extended cocksure toward the SEEK button before the chorus was allowed another go around. She took the next exit, and hung a right into a hotel parking lot. The hotel had a bar and grill attached. Their marquee promised SUN AUTHENTIC KARAO E W DAR EL SAN.

"I know what we're doing tonight," Karen said.

"Forget it."

"You owe me one," she said. "Having to drag your ass out of that tavern."

I felt horrible about it—what I could remember of it, anyway.

"I took the liberty of throwing those pills away that Clay gave you," she said. "You obviously aren't meant to be together."

Within an hour, she had me following her into the dim lounge, after repeated reminders that I was there solely to watch from the darkest possible corner, and maybe have a drink or two.

The expected scenery was in place—beer banners fighting for wall space, pleather upholstery, arcade games, pool tables, foosball. We settled in a corner booth by a pair of electronic-score dartboards. A waiter approached us, and tossed coasters onto our table like a card dealer, asking what he could do us for. I asked him when the karaoke was to begin. "So we know how much of a window we have."

"Mr. San always runs late," he said, sounding as though Darrel had become something of a nuisance or a liability. "Let's just say he's got a few problems. If you stick around, you'll hear all about 'em."

This sparked my curiosity. What sort of problems do karaoke hosts have to deal with, and when did they start incorporating them into their act?

Karen asked me which song I'd sing for her. I reminded her that I didn't do karaoke.

"No one's above karaoke," she said. "It's built into the philosophy."

I explained to her my version of the caste system of musical showbiz. In a slow, hand-jive motion I began: "At the bottom are the wedding DJs. Above them, the karaoke hosts. Then you have commercial radio DJs . . ."

"No one's above karaoke," she repeated. "Especially you, after your behavior this afternoon—the last couple days, really. Consider this your penance."

I continued. "Karaoke singers, cover bands, jingle writers . . ."

"These are all people who love music but aren't fortunate enough to have the gifts that you have."

She was right, though she was taking me too seriously. "Yeah, but who cares who I step on, on the way down."

She waved it away. "You've lost all touch with reality."

"I don't think so. I'll admit I'm a wash-up."

"I've noticed."

"Oh, you have?" I said, not expecting her to be so frank about it. I knew where I was—or thought I had a pretty solid idea. I didn't need to hear it from someone else with so much more certainty. What business did she have reinforcing that?

"I'm not going to lie to you," she said.

"Oh, you'd never do that."

This gave her pause. "Let's just say that I agree that you're not in the greatest of places. Nor am I, to be honest."

"Maybe you should elaborate. You don't seem to like to talk about anything unless there's already some other drama going on."

"You agree to sing, and I'll elaborate. I'll tell you anything you want to know."

Just then, a fifty-something, bald, pasty, mustachioed white man in a wrinkled suit forced his way through the lounge's front door carrying a large suitcase. He and the bartender exchanged curt greetings, and the man apologized for being late, mentioning something about kids slashing his tires and having to beg a ride from his now-former mother-in-law. He wiped sweat from his forehead as he continued bowlegged across the dance floor to a large folding table set up in the corner. Darrel-San had arrived, and there was nothing remotely east-Asian about him.

I watched with great interest and curiosity as he began setting up his karaoke gear. Karen approached him to ask for song lists and he spooked, nervously dropping the tangled mess of audio cables he'd pulled from his suitcase. Some part of my mind thought to laugh, and the muscles in my face were about to follow, but I ended up just feeling bad for him.

Karen returned, carrying two thick three-ring binders. She slapped one of them down on the table before me.

"Anything worth singing," she said, pointing and staring at it, as though it were a child being disciplined. "Right there."

"You've already got your hopes up, is the sad thing," I said, pushing the binder away.

"You need to reinvent yourself, Carl," she began. "I can't think of a more perfect time and place." She told me I could pick my own song to sing, or else she'd gladly do it for me.

I made one quick flip through the binder before pushing it away again. "Sometimes a person's just not in the mood for certain things at certain times."

The lounge began to fill with girls-night-outers, middle-aged couples, and assorted stag deadbeats, all sitting as equidistant as possible from one another. Darrel-San spoke gibberish into the microphone, adjusting the volume levels and mix of the PA system. I checked my phone for the time of day. It was not late enough to convince Karen it was time to leave. I sipped my Irish coffee, knowing my naps that day had ruined any chance I had of getting a decent night's rest.

Welcome, ladies and gentleman, to authentic karaoke. I am your host, Darrel-San. Still working as a shift manager at Cargill. Four ten's, which is nice . . .

Karen settled on a song to sing and wrote her vitals on a slip of paper. I asked her what song she'd chosen, and she said it wasn't appropriate to ask. Where had all these rules come from? Japan? The west suburbs of Chicago? Was she making them up as she went?

My wife, as some of you may remember, has left me and moved back to Duluth. But my mother-in-law seems to think its okay to continue to stay with me. But enough about that . . . Let's get Shelly up here . . .

Again, I thought to laugh, but no one else was laughing, or

seemed to be paying any attention to Darrel. His stage presence wasn't one of a stand-up comic. The faux-confidence wasn't there, nor did he seem to have any regard for the art of timing. He seemed to be talking to himself—a self that was tired of listening. I felt some kinship with him there, and I felt sorry for him if he was telling the truth about the inert mother-in-law. I thought to buy him a sympathy drink. I imagined he drank manhattans or something named after a dead golfer.

"Johnnie and I do karaoke every Thursday night," Karen said. The reminder of Don Johnnie sent a shiver through me. "He studied musical theater. He's a pretty amazing singer, actually."

"Good for him."

"As for me, this is my only musical outlet anymore."

I was reminded of the open mics that we used to frequent in Austin. I'd clock out from working the Kappa Kappa Gamma kitchen, and she'd be waiting for me out back in her '65 Mustang convertible. We'd take the long way to wherever the open mic was that night, sipping whiskey and smoking from my pipe with Billy Carter's mug engraved in the bowl. She always had the newest, most intricately ornamented acoustic guitars, but they were never beautiful enough to compensate for her tone-deaf renderings of Linda Ronstadt or Emmylou tunes. At some point, she began fantasizing aloud about a musical partnership between us. We would move to Los Angeles and perform as a duo in all the seedy Hollywood nightclubs we'd read about, where many of the artists we liked had cut their teeth—Tom Waits, Ricky Lee Jones, Randy Newman.

Shelly, the karaoke queen of the moment, sang: *Here's your one chance, Fancy, don't let me dow-ooo-own.*

Karen stubbed out her half-smoked cigarette. "Telling me how awful I was, was probably the best thing you could've done for me," she said.

"When did I ever do that?" I asked. "I don't remember wording it that way."

"I do," she said. "I remember every word. You told me I oughta think seriously about plan B and beyond."

This was a phrase I'd inherited from my father. What, exactly, had possessed me to say such harsh things? She must've brought it on with an insult of her own. I couldn't remember.

"I know we were probably three sheets to the wind, but it really crushed me at the time."

I took a sip. "I'm truly sorry about that. That wasn't my place."

The audience applauded for Shelly, as she blew a pair of kisses around the smoky lounge. An odd sense of community had begun to develop amongst the crowd of singers, none of whom appeared likely to communicate with one another outside the barroom.

"I knew I wasn't a good singer," Karen continued. "I just liked doing those open mics with you. That was the most fun I'd ever had. And I recognized it then, amazingly enough. How many times do you feel like you know how much fun you're having at the time you're having it?"

"I can't say I've ever experienced that. Probably a personality flaw."

"It can be a powerful thing. I guess that's why it hurt so much when you told me that. It sounded like the end of something great, you know?"

The time to apologize was right there, but nothing I had at the tip of my tongue felt adequate. I knew rejection, but not the personalized, cruel sort she was accusing me of. No wonder she'd wanted nothing to do with me.

"I didn't really think we'd ever perform together in a serious way," she continued. "I wasn't about to get in the way of what you were doing. I just wanted to go along for the ride."

This was a shocker. It saddened me, as this hadn't been my impression at the time, or the one I'd settled on and left behind. She'd always been an ambitious, forceful person, and not prone to fits of relaxation and letting things happen. I considered the possibility that her perspective had become muddled by hindsight, the product of some urge to reconfigure bad memories into some useful, productive arrangement. *Okay, Carl, you crushed my hopes and dreams, but look at all that it did for me.*

"You're along for the ride now," I said, anxious to hear how she'd respond. Did that sound too trivial? Was I was blowing off the gravity of what she'd just told me?

"I like it," she said, grabbing my hand, squeezing it gently, cooling my nerves.

Darrel-San told the crowd about how his insurance company dropped him after making a claim on slashed tires. *And the neighborhood kids did it again today . . .*

He had me hooked, enough to begin imagining myself in competition with him for low man on the pole. There he was up on stage, the ringleader of this bizarre coming together, and I didn't even have a room to play to. Maybe I was a wash-up, but at least I'd had the opportunity to reach the heights of that particular low.

A white kid in oversized shorts and a paltry moustache wielded finger pistols and rapped something about closets and cleaning. Karen told me Taylor had gone through a hip hop phase, before turning to religion and renouncing all music that wasn't strictly instrumental or Christian-themed. I'd failed him for sure. The least I could've done was instill a sense of taste in the kid.

Darrel sang Rick Nelson's "Garden Party" without looking at the teleprompter.

My father died in a V.A. hospital. He told the nurse he wanted that song played at his funeral, but none of us got around to doing it, I guess...

Here was Charlie Brown in the flesh—a man who understood and embodied bad luck in ways I could never imagine.

Karen sang Loretta Lynn's "You Ain't Woman Enough to Take My Man," twirling the mic cord around her thin fingers, affecting melodramatic facial expressions wholly inappropriate for the material, moving about the stage as though she'd learned her moves from Miss America talent competitions. I suspected she had some statement to make in her choice of song, even though she had no idea that she might be meeting Rhonda within a couple days.

My honest opinion of her performance would have to remain in the hole. No more insults out of me. Her voice sounded pretty good, though—within a few semitones of being on pitch. Maybe she'd just needed a couple decades to calm down a bit. Hormonal shifts, perhaps.

The crowd applauded as her song ended. I expected her to place the microphone back on its stand, but this was not to be.

"We've got a special treat tonight," Karen said, gesturing for me to come to the stage. "All the way from Nashville, by way of Forsyth, Colorado, my dear friend..."

There was no escaping it at this point. The entire crowd of thirty or forty had their eyes fixed on me, in varying states of disbelief. I stood and made the move, putting on my game face out of habit.

"You owe me one," I told Karen. Darrel handed me his wireless microphone, and then clapped his hands together and bowed toward me. I had no clue what song we were about to sing. I asked Karen. She said it wasn't appropriate to ask.

"You know it. Don't fuck it up," she said. "These people expect a little more out of you."

I looked at the teleprompter. A day-glow illustration of a desert island appeared—a lone coconut tree, a Rip Van Winkle type sleeping against it.

"Islands in the Stream."

We gazed into each other's eyes as we traded verses. Her voice sounded angelic, and though she was obviously going for theatrical gas, there were a few moments when I was sure we were in love in some parallel existence, feeling that wringing-out of adrenaline as we harmonized the choruses.

Sail away with me, to another world . . .

It was a sensation I couldn't remember having during any other musical performance. Maybe I got carried away, but I had the wireless microphone, and so I began walking through the crowd as I sang. I stopped at a table of ladies that were obviously taking the night off from their husbands and kids. I knelt and put my arm around the one who looked the most lifeless and embarrassable and tried to get her to harmonize with me.

"I don't know the words! I don't know the words!" she said, blushing as she grabbed her drink and looked down into it.

I made it back up to the stage in time for the last chorus. As the final chord faded and Darrel told everyone to put their hands together for us, I grabbed Karen and planted a kiss on her cheek.

Whatever she was attempting to do for me felt pretty good.

"See, that wasn't so bad," she said as we returned to our booth. Several people in the crowd shouted for more. We'd barely gotten settled when a round of whiskey shots arrived, accompanied by a couple of cowboy types and their ladyfriends. They wanted autographs, so I indulged them. Karen sat back, amused by it all, as though she'd written and directed the whole thing. One of the cowboys asked me to sing a tune with him. I hesitated, and as I did, Karen grabbed my business underneath the table, which provoked a yes out of me. Now she was playing dirty—and after no more than two drinks. Where was this going to lead? I hoped she'd want to leave right then, and that the duet with the cowboy wouldn't happen, but it did, almost immediately. The cowboy had gotten us on Mr. San's fast track, and we sang Waylon & Willie's "Good Hearted Woman."

After another round of free drinks I got suckered into a quick photo shoot in the parking lot with the cowboys.

"I didn't figure big-shots like yourself sang karaoke," one of them said.

"No one's above karaoke," I said, looking over at Karen. The cowboys laughed, agreeing with me. The cowboy I'd sung with handed me a CD of songs he'd written.

"Do whatever you want with 'em," he said.

"I will."

I hoped to avoid a prolonged meet-and-greet with the rest of the karaoke crowd, so I jogged around the side of the hotel, telling Karen in a shout-whisper to hurry up and follow me. Her smile and strut had a smug air of accomplishment to it. So she'd tricked me into singing karaoke for the first time—big deal. Had I reinvented myself? No. Did I feel better? Sure.

"They were howling for us out there," I said, as I rinsed off in the shower. I heard her spit toothpaste and knock the toothbrush against the sink.

"You could use some work," she said. "But you've got potential. Karaoke is a whole different ball game." She moved the shower curtain aside and stepped into the tub. "Maybe you should consider hiring me on as your coach."

What she started right there eventually moved out onto the bed. We let the sheets dry us off. Her smell and taste conjured memories of our carefree, blurry days in Austin—a whole life of unexpected turns, drop-offs, and rearrangements right around the corner.

Commitment had never really been in the cards. We'd never talked about it for any length of time that I could recall. Too much experience out there to be had, and neither one of us were going to impose such a thing on each other. We were both still fresh out of the forced, limited relationships of small towns, and the few connections we'd made in the city were still shaky. It seemed that everyone we'd met who had artistic ambitions were too self-absorbed and paranoid that their originality might be ripped off, leaving very little opportunity for pure, mutually productive connections. We were without mentors, and too naïve to really get a plan together. Had we gotten sage advice, would we have taken it?

And I wondered if I hadn't been such a single-minded, driven, ignorant asshole, might things have worked out between us? I remembered the constant feelings of self-doubt I had about her old-money background, worrying in my idle moments whether I'd ever realistically be able to live up to the sense of entitlement I assumed she had. All I could provide then was companionship, and even that began to fall off as I spent more time in the musty garage, under fluorescent tubes, drinking Pearl by the six-pack, trying to write my way out of an otherwise bleak future.

It saddened me to think about what she'd told me earlier that night, that she'd only wanted to go along for the ride, that she'd known she wasn't star material, and that, at the heart of it all, she only wanted to be in those moments we had together. Might things have been different if she'd told me that back then?

Did she ever tell me that she loved me? I couldn't remember.

I found myself on the verge of weeping as we settled on our backs, staring at the ceiling.

"Just like old times," she said.

"Better, I'd say."

She rolled onto her side, placed her leg over mine, and asked what I was thinking about. An illuminated wheel of birth control pills spun in my mind, but it was a fool's time to bring that up.

"Why did you wait?" I asked.

"Wait for what?"

"C'mon."

She sat up. "You weren't that easy to find."

"I don't buy it. It was the twentieth century. You knew where my folks were."

She swung her legs off the bed, stood and went for her purse, grabbing a cigarette. I reminded her that it was a non-smoking room, but it didn't faze her.

"I tried. I thought to call your parents, but I couldn't do it."

"Why not?"

"I made up my mind to do it alone, and that's that," she said, lighting the cigarette.

"You didn't think I was fit to be a father."

"I don't know," she began. "It's just what I decided to do. I could be a stubborn little bitch back then, if you remember. And a basket case."

"What did your parents have to say?"

"That it served me right."

"And they never tried to track me down?"

"I made it very clear to them not to do that."

I still couldn't reconcile why she'd chosen to raise Taylor on her own without at least telling me that was her intention. I reminded myself that she did have more than her share of self-righteous, bull-headed, superwoman inclinations.

"You had something to prove to the world."

"That had something to do with it," she said, looking at her cigarette with contempt. "It was strange. I hated you, I loved you, I wanted you to succeed. And yeah, I had something to prove." She walked into the bathroom and put the cigarette out under the faucet.

I stood and walked to the window, watching the traffic on the interstate. The sex should've knocked me out, but the Irish coffee had me awake, for a few more hours, I feared.

"Speaking of Loretta Lynn, are you on the pill?" I asked, as she emerged from the bathroom. "I don't want another kid that I won't be able to see for twenty years."

"Shush," she said, hopping onto the bed. She assured me I had nothing to worry about. "The last thing you needed was a child to slow you down."

"So you were doing me a favor? I don't believe that for a second."

"I told myself that after awhile."

"Ha."

"Would you have been able to do all you've done otherwise?"

"I think you're stalling."

"I'm telling you the truth."

"Did you ever consider how I might feel about all this? You had to know I'd find out eventually."

"How do you feel about it? I'm not even sure I know. Then again, sharing your feelings liberally isn't exactly your style."

"I've built my entire career on exploiting my limitations, if that's what you mean by style."

"Now you're the one who's stalling."

I sat at a small table in the corner of the room, irritated by her accusation of not being forthcoming with my feelings. "Feel free to stop me if I tell you something you already know, or should've already picked up." I ran down a detailed, exhaustive list of wrongs she'd committed over the previous few days, being explicit about the range of feelings each act had aroused in me. Anger, frustration, and the violated, self-disgust of having been manipulated was a common thread. "What else do you need?"

"I'm sorry, Carl. Interfering with your tour and making things difficult for you is not what I intended. And, to answer your earlier question—I've had time to consider pretty much everything, trust me. I just don't want you to feel like you have some moral obligation to make up for things that you never signed up for to begin with."

I stood and walked to the window again, struggling with Karen's assertion. I still didn't feel like I knew why she'd waited, or why this was the weekend to tell me. Sure, she might've been proud of her decisions, but what did Taylor think about them? On one hand, they were all he knew, so maybe they seemed natural and okay. On the other, I imagined his view of them had shifted somewhat now that his single-parent upbringing put him likely in the minority amongst the students at his college.

"All I'm trying to say here is that maybe your decisions were a bit selfish," I said.

"Oh, please. You try to make that choice under the same pressures I was under. You seem to be making no effort to imagine yourself in my position."

"I'm trying to imagine what our son has thought about all this."

She stood up and went for her purse again. "First off, he wouldn't be here if I'd not made a very key decision. Second, if he thinks he's been robbed of some perfect, traditional life then I guess it's his choice to be sullen about it. I've given him every opportunity and done everything I can for him. He never seemed the least bit troubled by his lot in life until the churchies got to him."

She lit another cigarette and joined me looking out at the interstate. "The potential in him is more than any parent could hope for. I don't want to see him waste it all pushing their agenda."

"What's so wrong with a Christian value or two? I don't really see the need for panic."

"He wasn't born a bad person, Carl. None of us are. He doesn't need to be told to repent or feel guilty. Why submit to thinking about yourself that way? What good does it do? If you have some insight, please share."

"I don't know. I pretty much left all my Catholic upbringing in a motel room in Gainesville in the early 80s."

She sat on the bed. "Seriously, I doubt you do your best work while you're feeling guilty about it."

"I suppose not."

"See, there you go. Feeling you're in the wrong before you even begin is no way to move ahead."

I watched the last hour of a John Wayne movie as Karen rested her head on my chest and twitched herself to sleep.

Though I'd learned not to take anything she said at face value, her concerns about Taylor were beginning to make some sense to me. It seemed as though she expected me to do something about it, but what could I do? He was an adult, after all, and free to choose to learn things the hard way just as all of his paternal male ancestors had done.

As I began to doze off, I had a vision of Rhonda standing atop Percy. I was spying on her again through the same opening in the fortress, except this time Satan caught me in the act.

14

Karen was dressed and ready to go at 8 AM, reprising the "Pina Colada Song" and making other superfluous racket to agitate me out of my slumber. I'd slept five hours, tops; my dreams infused with nonsensical infomercial dialogue. A small coffee maker popped and gurgled next to the television. I covered my head with a pillow.

"I wanna know more about this junkyard woman you've been seeing."

"What?" I tossed the pillow aside.

"Clay was talking about her at the show the other night. She sounds fascinating."

That asshole. I knew what he'd told her—everything I'd told him, multiplied by his interpretation, with some extra stretchers thrown in to make it all work to his advantage in some way.

"She's a mechanic and auto body specialist," I said, propping myself up against the headboard. "She did the plastic surgery on Percy."

"That's what Clay was saying. Sounds like you and her are pretty serious."

"I just met her last week."

She poured a cup of coffee. "That's not how Clay made it sound."

"Why would you believe him over me?"

"I haven't heard your side of the story, that's why I'm asking."

Something sinister was afoot. It was convenient that she'd waited until after she'd seduced me to bring it up. I tried to comfort myself with Clay's rule of thumb about foot rubs and fucks at our age.

"I can't wait to meet her," she said.

"You probably will," I said, using my pinkynail to backhoe sleep from my eyes. "Either tonight or tomorrow."

"Clay mentioned that she might be flying out. That sounds pretty serious." She handed me a mug of coffee. "She doesn't know anything about us, does she?"

"Us?"

"Yeah, us. This. The fact that we're traveling together."

"No. I thought you and I were just meeting up for a drink or two. That didn't seem to warrant a mention."

"Do you have a reason to tell her now?"

"Do I?"

"I would say you probably do."

"I don't think you want to be around for that." I stood from the bed. "She's a pretty tough broad. I wouldn't want to get in a scrap with her myself."

My breakfast at the hotel restaurant consisted of flimsy white toast, blueberry syrup-infused link sausage, and two fried eggs with the leathery ring cooked onto the edges. I looked at each item with disgust, listening to Karen's big plans for the day—the Art Institute, Sears Tower, and whatever else we could squeeze in. Fine. I didn't care where we went or what we did as long as we stayed out of the heat and my van would be safe from thieves. The radio jock warned that it'd be another "air-conditioning kind of day."

I got the phone call from Rhonda as we crossed into Chicago proper. She didn't sound especially happy or enthusiastic. I couldn't make out her words over the road noise, so I promised to call back once I got off the interstate. I hadn't called her since I left for the tour, and I assumed this had something to do with her somber tone. My mind raced, trying to come up with a suitable excuse. I had several, but none that I was prepared to share with her yet. I took the next exit, parked at a gas station, and called her back.

Bill was in the hospital. He'd had a stroke.

"About the biggest one you can have and still breathe on your own," she said. "I thought I should let you know."

She read me the dossier. The manager of Flo's had found him in his recliner just after seven that morning. He'd been watching television, and had a half-eaten bag of Corn Nuts in his lap. Bill's son, Alan, was flying in from Houston later that morning.

"I was planning to come to your Minneapolis show tomorrow night and surprise you, but I don't know what to do now."

"I probably oughta head back."

"Up to you. I don't know what your spiritual beliefs are relative to this sort of thing, but my guess is Bill isn't going to know either way."

It soon became clear that neither one of us were going to make a decision right then and there. She asked how the tour was going and why I hadn't called. I apologized.

"It's been a roller coaster," I said. "Lots of old faces coming out of the woodwork, keeping me out all hours of the night. I'm going to be glad to get home."

"Me too. Even Satan seems a little bummed that you're gone." She asked if I was still planning on visiting my friend in Cedar Rapids after the tour. "Because if you're not, then I was thinking maybe I could just get a one-way and then drive back with you—if I decide to fly out there, that is."

My ability to keep my truths and lies in order was nearing full capacity. I was so pissed off at Clay, and averse to any notion of visiting him, that I found it excruciating to tell a lie to the contrary, especially to someone as undeserving of deceit as Rhonda. One thing became clear to me as I chewed on what I should say next: everything about my not-so-distant future was uncertain, and seemingly out of my control. The only ass-saving maneuver I could think to do was buy some time.

"Are you still there?" she asked.

"Sorry," I said. "Just thinking about Bill."

"I hear ya. I'm sitting right beside him."

I told her that I might just cancel the rest of the tour. "It's only a couple of shows. No big deal. Gimme a few hours to think about it."

"Sooner the better, but no rush," she said. "I know someone at an airline who owes me big time. He can get me on pretty much any flight."

So, despite my attempt to buy some time, the pressure was back on.

I couldn't shake the news as Karen dragged me through the noise, panhandlers, and heat of downtown Chicago. I thought about what I had to return to in Forsyth, and it didn't amount to much with Bill gone. He'd become my rock. I figured I didn't have much time left in the guest house, and the prospect of finding another place and signing a lease didn't appeal to me. And, as much promise as my relationship with Rhonda seemed to hold, it was too early to be making any big decisions based on that. The more I put the pieces together the more it began to look like my days in Forsyth were numbered. Then there was the question of where I'd go after that.

Karen and I eventually made it into the Art Institute. I found myself struggling to feign interest in everything she pointed out to me. I'm not a complete ignoramus when it comes to the visual arts. I recognized many of the artist's names and a few of the paintings. Despite her generous attempts to enlighten me, the only images I could concentrate on were Bill lying in his hospital bed, a bag of Corn Nuts, safety goggles, and a brown sack containing fruit and Bill Clinton CDs.

I heard Karen talking: "Don't allow any of these pieces to force you into deciding whether they're good or bad . . ."

It really hadn't occurred to me just how close Bill and I had become. I guess he snuck up on me. He was the only reasonably close friend I'd made in Forsyth, despite my attempts to keep some psychic distance between us. Why had I needed that distance? Had he ever felt like I was being standoffish, or that I was trying to avoid him?

". . . Approach a piece and ask yourself how the work challenges convention, long-held belief, common sense—the typical automatic reactions one might have when experiencing it . . ."

Going back to Nashville was out of the question. But, where else would I go? What could I do in St. Louis?

". . . Impact—not necessarily quality . . ."

There was still that cabin in the mountains. But did I really need more solitude?

" . . . How and where does a piece break through mimicry . . ."

Somewhere in the contemporary art wing I got too close to some amorphous green blob setting in the middle of the floor and an alarm went off. That was it for me. I told Karen I had to find another way of spending the afternoon.

"This is too much for a washed-up old dog," I said.

"You're experiencing the aesthetic headache."

"I feel like my head is being used to plow a field."

"You get what you pay for."

A short taxi ride later, we found ourselves amongst the commotion of Navy Pier. This wasn't what I had in mind. Not ten paces into the crowd, a young girl dropped her snow cone as I moved past her. She pointed at me and began to cry.

"Just great," her mother said, scowling at me.

"Give her a dollar," Karen whispered, elbowing me in the side. I felt like slapping all three of them. I pulled a dollar from my wallet and held it out toward the woman. She waved it away, looking at me like I owed her more than I'd ever understand.

Stop the world and let me off, I'm tired of going round and round, I sang.

"I've got an idea," Karen said, grabbing my hand and leading me through the swarm of teenaged rollerbladers, Asian tourist groups, street performers, and security officers. I could sense where this was going, so I pulled back and stopped, looking up at the Ferris wheel.

"I don't think so."

"What, are you afraid of heights?" she asked, pulling at my arm.

"I'm afraid of lines."

And this is why: after no more than five minutes of waiting, I made fleeting eye contact with a man standing a dozen people behind us. His eyes lit up like we were long lost pals. I tried to avoid looking his way again, but after another ten minutes of baking on the walkway it became too much of a strain. Our eyes met again. He made his approach, and asked if I was who I was.

"Yep."

He introduced himself as Craig. "And that's my wife back there." He pointed. She smiled, waving her hand with humming-bird speed. "We're coming to see you tonight. Come all the way down from Green Bay. Why don't you ever play up in our country?"

"Just wasn't in the cards this time around."

"I don't have anything for you to sign or I'd bother you for an autograph."

"There's always tonight."

He slouched a bit, looking as though he'd expected me to be taller. "Between me and a good friend of mine, we have all your records."

I introduced Karen. Craig asked if she was my wife.

"No," I said. Karen shook her head in support.

He waited for one of us to expand, nodding slowly, but we left it at that. "What songs are you going to play tonight?"

"Not sure yet."

"I hope we hear some of the old stuff. When are you going to start writing like that again? I mean, the newer stuff is good, but those first few records are . . . *wow!*"

"You get older and the things you think about change," I said. "I'm sure you can understand."

"My buddy thinks you need to get out more."

I could tell Karen was holding back laughter.

"Is that so," I said. I felt like taking a swing at him.

"He calls himself a writer. He's got a knack for poetry."

"I'm sure he does."

"We have a bet going, him and me. I say the music comes first, he says it's the words. Which is it with you?"

"Neither. Where they end up is all that really matters."

"Say, would you like to join my wife and I for dinner before the show?" he asked. "My treat."

Did this guy really have no idea?

"Thank you, but I'm afraid we already have other plans," I said.

"We do?" Karen asked.

It wasn't the appropriate time or place to yell at her to shut up. Did she have no idea either? I told Craig that we had dinner arrangements with my publicist. Karen interrupted, saying that she hadn't been made aware of any dinner arrangements. I said that's the way it was. Karen said I should've told her. I told her she must not have been listening when I informed her of our dinner plans. She said she thought my publicist lived in Nashville. This continued for awhile longer before Craig got the hint that I was weaseling out of his invitation. He returned to his place next to his wife and said something to her that soured her expression.

I turned to face the front of the line. "What the fuck was that all about?" I asked Karen.

"Why do you have to let a fan down like that? You can't afford to lose one."

"*You* let him down. I was just lying to him."

"He was trying to be nice."

"You weren't listening very carefully."

"I was right here for all of it."

"*I need to get out more*—who says that kind of crap to someone they've never met?"

She turned away. "You need to calm down. We're amongst the public."

We didn't speak again until the carny had us shut in the gondola. It smelled barfy and sweet, just like every other carnival and amusement park ride on earth.

"Here's the thing with you, Carl. Are you ready to listen?"

"I'm kinda stuck here, aren't I?"

"You're becoming a fundamentalist in your old age."

"Not today, please. I've got enough on my mind."

"You've let your career and yourself slide on down with the rabble."

How dare she.

"The record company puts out the 'essential' Hog, and now you're choosing to believe it."

"Believe what?"

"That that's you, that there is an essential you. You've been going that direction for years now."

The Ferris wheel began to move.

"New-Agey bullshit," I said. "How would you know what direction I've been going in?"

"Let's have a look at the evidence: you don't tour with a band anymore, you leave your people in Nashville to live like a lone wolf, and your songs the last few years have been—well, pale imitations of your earlier stuff—to the point of being boring, more often than not. Solipsistic, at best."

"Good god, woman!"

"You've read the reviews. I'm not making this up myself."

"To hell with reviews," I said, looking south toward the Gary, Indiana, skyline as we began the slow climb.

"Even the hacks know when an artist is only running on one cylinder."

"They like to think that."

"Back when you started out, it was all new to you, the whole process. You didn't know what would succeed and what wouldn't, so you were working without a net."

"Big whoop."

"Then you achieve some success, and in an effort to maintain it, you get pressured toward sameness. You get bored with that, and it comes out in the music. The extended sophomore jinx."

"You talk about this like you've experienced it."

"Who says I haven't?"

"Are you trying to pick a fight?"

"My guess is you moved to Forsyth as a way of getting more in touch with the 'real' you. I'll bet it crossed your mind that the only way you thought you could continue writing good material would be to live like a hermit."

"Christ."

"We both know you're not happy with your work anymore," she said. "It's pretty obvious that's the case."

"Is that so."

"You've been living in your own shadow for awhile now. You've got to admit that."

"What is this? Are you my shrink all of a sudden?"

"No. This isn't psychoanalysis."

"What is it then?"

"You are unaware of the fact that you use your old success as a foundation for everything you've done since, and it bores the hell out of you. Am I right? I can't think of a more miserable, frustrating place to be in. I've been there myself. I'm probably there right now."

"Great. Shall we hold hands and cry it out?"

"We need to identify the problem before we can proceed."

"Enough already," I said, waving it away.

"Set your ego aside for a moment, Carl. I'm not attacking you."

At a loss for anything to say that might redirect the conversation, I began singing Tennessee Ernie Ford's "Sixteen Tons" as she continued her lecture.

"You don't want to make the same record over and over, though you continue to do so..."

Another day older and deeper in debt . . .

". . . It's all about surfaces anyway. Nothing has any built-in meaning, or good or bad quality. All of that comes from whoever is in the position to like or dislike it . . ."

Saint Peter don't you call me, 'cause I can't go . . .

". . . The inevitable result of fundamentalism is eternal crankiness and perpetual irritation. It's your choice whether or not you wish to take part in it . . . "

I owe my soul to the company store . . .

That night's gig was cursed from the start. No one from the new record label showed up as they'd promised. I broke a string halfway into the first song, and the better of my two amplifiers shorted out three songs later. A fight broke out during a love song. The merch table was knocked over and most of a pitcher of beer was spilled on Karen before the venue's one-man security force was able to move the fight out onto the street.

I was able to play through the fight and do another couple songs before thoughts of Bill started getting in the way of my words and I began forgetting the first lines of verses. A handful of people turned and exited the venue. I'd only played forty minutes when I set my guitar down, apologized for the short set, and thanked everyone for coming. In an effort to save face, I told everyone to grab a free CD on their way out, and then I left the stage. My cheeks were full with vomit before I got the alleyway door open.

We got a room an hour northwest of Chicago. Karen and I hadn't said much to one another since the Ferris wheel ride. We took showers, brushed teeth, and then sat on our respective queens staring at the television as I cycled through the channels. She commented on my not having any drinks that day, and asked if I wanted to share a joint.

"No," I said. "I've got enough to think about without thinking about thinking about it."

She apologized again for her verbal attack that afternoon. "I'm really just trying to help."

I tossed the remote onto her bed and rolled onto my side preparing for sleep. A lyric had been bouncing around my head since leaving Chicago. It seemed like an appropriate time to try it out on another set of ears. I let out an aggressive, iambic fart. "You're free to think whatever you want about me," I said. "But in the interest of full disclosure, why don't you keep it to yourself."

15

Any farmer will tell you that waking early and getting outside while the atmosphere's still cool is the only way to face a day of impending, oppressive heat. I left the motel, walked across the overpass, and kept along the roadside. Patches of fog hovered low over the corn and bean fields. Wafts of diesel exhaust mixed with the dew-drenched crops to pass for fresh air. Grain silos and a water tower lay a mile or so ahead, which meant that breakfast at a mom-and-pop diner was to be had, so I made the commitment.

It was too early to call Rhonda and find out what she'd decided to do. If she were to make the flight that day, then I'd have to figure out a way of getting Karen out of the picture. She couldn't be trusted to mind her own business, and it seemed almost counterintuitive to imagine her not getting catty and making some kind of scene. How I was going to achieve this was the big question.

I found the town diner, and took a seat at the counter a few stools down from a trio of grumbling, retired farmer types. They looked at me as though I were a dangerous new strain of corn fungus. I ordered biscuits and gravy, coffee, a pen, and a sheet of paper. A potentially difficult challenge lay ahead, and I wasn't about to blow it on account of my own laziness or lack of preparation, so I began drawing up a flow chart.

By the time my breakfast arrived I had both sides of a page filled with possible scenarios. If Rhonda didn't make the trip, then I had nothing to worry about. If she did, and I couldn't convince Karen to catch a bus back to Cedar Rapids that morning, then I had serious problems. I hadn't even filled half of the first side of the page before I wrote: *Ditch Karen at a truck stop somehow?*

It was 6 AM Colorado time as I began the long walk back to the motel. I called Rhonda. She didn't sound enthused. I asked what she'd decided.

"Your friend Clay called last night," she said.

Uh oh. I could already sense that their conversation had strayed from subjects automotive, but it was too early to admit to anything specific, so I stalled.

"That bum. Did he try to make an offer on your place?"

"I almost spent three hundred dollars on a ticket to come see you, not you and some other woman. This explains why you haven't been calling."

Clay was going to suffer for this. "I've got some explaining to do," I said.

"I doubt that you do, actually."

"Are you gonna listen to me?"

"No. I've got too much to do right now."

"Just give me a minute—please?"

"Listen, Carl, I'm not young and naïve enough to sit here and suffer through a bunch of bullshit excuses and lies. Frankly, I'm insulted that you're offering."

I attempted to launch into an explanation.

"No, Carl. Not having it. We'll talk when you get back. I'll need to get paid for the van." She told me in the fewest words possible how Bill was doing. His condition hadn't improved. Alan had flown in and was trying to make arrangements to move Bill to a hospital in Houston. "Why don't you talk to Alan from here on out," she said. "He's been asking about you."

She gave me his number before hanging up, but I didn't have any way of writing it down, and she didn't stay on long enough to repeat it.

I suspected Clay knew why I was trying to reach him, and that's why he neglected to answer his phone most of the day. Karen and I were three hours deep into Wisconsin before he picked up. It wasn't a conversation Karen needed to hear, so I pulled the van over and tore into him as I walked down the highway embankment.

"Sorry, buddy," he said. "I didn't realize you hadn't told her. You should've said something."

"What business do you have calling her anyway?"

"To see if she wanted to sell."

"You're bullshitting me, Clay. There's that stink to your voice."

"You gave me her number, remember?"

"Not for you to actually use. What sort of idiot would even think to make that call?"

No response.

I demanded he tell me exactly what they'd talked about and what he'd told her, since Rhonda hadn't given many specifics, and could've been speculating about many things. He claimed they talked cars for a few minutes before she started asking about the Cedar Rapids show, and about me.

"I told her that Marnie and I were a little disappointed that you left so early," he said.

"Then how did Karen get brought up?"

"I don't know."

"C'mon."

"I don't remember. I might've said 'they' instead of 'you'."

"Well?"

"Shit, Carl. How do you expect me to remember a detail like that? It sounded to me like she already knew. All I told her is that you had some professor riding around with you working on a paper or some shit."

"Then how did she find out the professor is also a woman?"

"She asked me."

I began the slow climb back toward the van. Clay assured me that he hadn't told Rhonda anything else about Karen, or our history, or about Taylor. So, all Rhonda knew was that I had another woman riding along with me that I hadn't told her about. I asked Clay to verify this.

"That pretty much sums it up," he said. "But look at the positive side—there's no way she could get more pissed off than she is now once she learns all the facts."

"That's very comforting."

"I thought you weren't gonna pursue that chick."

"I never said that."

"Ah, well. Doesn't matter. Save yourself the trouble. She sounds like too much woman for you anyway. How were the last two shows? How are those pills treating you? How's that rash?"

Click.

Karen was so aggravated and stressed by the heat and traffic congestion of downtown Minneapolis that she stopped the van in the middle of a lane, turned the hazards on, and had me drive the last few blocks.

I parked the van in the alley behind the venue. She told me she was going to take a walk alone. I made no protest, as I was plenty annoyed with her after seven hours of listening to her sighs and complaints about our traveling conditions.

My mood improved as I entered the air-conditioned club. I asked the bartender to point out the person in charge. He said the owner was out, as was the soundman.

"We might have a problem," he said. "I don't really know. I just pour drinks."

"What sort of problem?"

"Sounds like the night got double-booked. We've got you and some metal bands from Milwaukee."

"Well, we can't have that."

I asked him for the owner's number, and he gave it to me.

"He was just in here about an hour ago," he said. "I'll just say that it's his birthday and he got started early."

I called and got the owner's voicemail. I left a short message, repeating what the bartender had said about the double-booking, and expressing my strong desire that it wasn't true.

All I could do was wait. Their green room had all the charm and comfort of an Alcatraz cell, so I took a seat at the bar. A half hour passed. I'd spent three dollars on the touch-screen trivia machine and was on my second beer when the first wave of metal dudes stumbled through the front door. Their guitar cases were coffin-shaped and their amps covered in diamond plate steel. They'd stenciled each piece of equipment with the name of their band—Mung of Mary.

The whole pack was visibly drunk and high, wearing the uniform of their genre: black shoes, black jeans, and black T-shirts emblazoned with the logos of other metal bands. Someone who looked like a member of their entourage broke away from the rest and got the bartender's attention. The bartender pointed at me and then the man approached.

"Mr. Mahogany, glad you made it," he said, extending his hand. "I'm a big fan."

"Who are you?"

"Steve, the owner. Call me 'Snake.'"

"We have a bit of a conflict here, it seems, Steve."

"Yeah, things got a little screwed up," he said. "We have three other bands booked tonight."

"Three?"

"I was thinking you could do the agreed-upon ten o'clock slot and we'll work around that."

"You want me to play in the middle of three metal bands? You didn't read the contract you signed."

"I think it'll work out fine. These people will dig your stuff. Can I buy you a beer?"

I thought a moment, looking around the barroom that was beginning to fill with people who were obviously not fans of mine. I told the bartender that I'd take a pitcher of stout, and he began pouring.

"A stout drinker," Steve said, giving me a pat on the shoulder. "Good man." He asked how my drive went, as though the matter were settled. His eyes darted around the bar, his attention drawn elsewhere, so I didn't bother to answer the question.

"Did you read the contract?" I asked.

He looked back at me. "I'm sorry. Come again?"

That did it. I stood up from the barstool, grabbed the pitcher, and told him to follow me. He did. I walked toward the back of the room, stopped at the sound booth, and acted like I had a secret to tell him. He leaned in toward me.

"Watch this," I whispered.

I poured the contents of the pitcher across the faders and knobs of the mixing console. The pitcher was completely upturned and dripping foam before he seemed aware of what he'd just seen. I shoved the empty pitcher against his chest and went for the side exit.

He and a few of the metal dudes got some kicks and punches in on the van as I sped down the alley. It didn't worry me. There wasn't anything they could do to Percy that nature hadn't already tried. I could see in the sideview that one of them had fallen face-first on the asphalt during their pursuit. I watched as the gang helped their fallen comrade to his feet. The diversion of attention caused me to sideswipe a parked car. All I knew for sure was that I'd clipped its side mirror. The alley was poorly lit, and there was no foot traffic, so I kept driving. I doubted any of my pursuers had seen it, but I couldn't be sure that someone else hadn't, so I made my careful way to the interstate.

I called Karen from a small tavern fifteen minutes south of downtown. She answered, telling me to hang on so she could escape the noise of wherever it was she was at. I couldn't make out the specific song that was playing there, but it was from the disco era. The noise died down and she told me she was at a club called The Gay Nineties.

"Sounds pretty gay," I said.

"I got a call from Taylor," she said, sounding surprised and thrilled. "He's in St. Louis. At the house."

"Oh yeah?"

"Yeah."

"You need to get a cab," I said.

"What?"

"You need to call a cab."

"Why?"

I told her my location and laid out her options for getting home—either she could get a taxi to where I was, or else she could take any combination of bus, train, or plane to her car in Cedar Rapids.

"Aren't you supposed to be playing soon? What happened with the show?"

I told her just enough about the contract dispute and the hit-and-run to justify my not driving back into downtown to get her. Despite this, she seemed hesitant to submit to calling a taxi.

"I'll give you an hour," I said. "Let's see some hustle out there."

And so, a little over an hour later, the lights of Minneapolis were behind us. The tour was over, and the fact of it was a welcome relief, as though I'd just shed some chronic, soul-crushing burden. The thrill of knowing my contract with the old label had finally run its course trumped any ill feelings I had about the downward trajectory of the tour. A few failed shows weren't that big of a deal in the grand scheme of things. At least I could take pride in the fact that the last gig would be a memorable one, even though it never happened.

But none of this seemed all that significant now that I knew I'd be meeting my son the next day. I was excited and a little frightened at the idea. What do you say to a son you never knew you had?

After a couple cycles through the FM spectrum, Karen settled on a classical station. I don't know much about classical music, but the piece was dark and heavy—a palate of sounds one might use to evoke an epic wintertime battle between the Nazis and the Russkies; hundreds of thousands of corpses, stretching as far as it takes to notice the curvature of the earth.

"Well, there you have it," I said. "The final Carl Mahogany tour. Was it all you hoped it would be?"

"Final tour? Right. You people are always retiring."

"It feels great to say."

"You can add me to your list of people who aren't too anxious to do it again."

I laughed. "Oh, come on. That was nothing. You should've been on the '87-88 tour. Eleven months, two overdoses, three divorces, two missing persons reports—*that* was a tour."

16

I parked the van in Karen's driveway, hopped out onto the lawn, and stretched my back. She and Taylor were sitting on the porch swing. Karen hadn't been there long, as her Subaru was still clicking and hissing. They stood and met me at the top of the stairs.

"Here he is," Karen said, an arm around Taylor's waist. I stood square with him and put forth the glad hand.

"A pleasure to meet you finally," he said. His eye contact was solid and confident. He had about an inch on me, with wavy brown locks like my own, but had most of his mother's features. He'd definitely inherited a pretty-boyishness that I never had to suffer through.

"Your father announced his retirement last night," Karen said. "He's still under an impression."

"You don't look old enough," Taylor said.

"It's feeling it that counts, but thank you."

Karen walked in the house while Taylor returned to the swing. He rabbit-eared his spot in the book he'd been reading and tossed it onto the table between us—a book called *Steppenwolf*. He asked if I'd read it.

"I don't read band biographies. Too depressing."

He let me know that the band got their name from the book, and not the other way around. I knew this, but instead of acknowledging it, I mentioned listening to *My Life* on the drive out. He laughed.

"Of all the titles out there, it's funny what people choose."

This was his mother talking, so I tried to save face by claiming it was research for the country-rock opera I was planning to write.

"It's too bad you decided to retire," he said. "That could've been a hit."

"That's true. I may have to reconsider."

Karen nudged her way through the screen door with the necks of three Miller High Life bottles nestled between her fingers. "One for you, one for you, and one for me," she said, setting them on the table. She offered me a chair, but I declined for the moment, still achy from the drive.

"I like your van, by the way," Taylor said.

At least he knew how to get on my good side. He asked if it'd ever been tagged.

"Tagged?"

"Yeah," he said. "Tagged. Grafitti'd"

"No. I guess it hasn't," I said. "Who'd think to improve on a machine like that?"

Taylor laughed. Karen sighed.

I continued: "Your mother seems to think it's some manifestation of a personality flaw, but that truly is the Rocky Balboa of vans. The first movie, anyway."

Karen groaned. "I hope I never spend one more second in that thing. No air conditioning, the constant smell of exhaust—and you don't dare touch anything inviting, like a door handle, or a sun visor, in fear of it breaking off."

"Percival has circled the globe almost eighteen times. What have you done?"

Our little spat about the van amused Taylor, but it'd run its course, and I was at a loss for anything else to say about it. Karen was already worked up, so I took advantage of it by asking Taylor about his Mexico trip. He told us of the places he'd visited, and went on at length about the large sums of money the legislator had tossed around. I was impressed with Taylor's eloquence. It was almost formal, but not stuffy like his mom's. He didn't abuse the word "like" while describing things that he'd seen, or interactions that he'd had. I assumed Karen's tutelage had much to do with this, and I thought to mention it in a complimentary way, but it wasn't in the natural flow of conversation.

"You'll be pleased to know that I've decided not to return to college in the fall," Taylor told his mother. "I'm going to take a year off."

"What are you going to do with a year off?" Karen asked.

"I thought I'd come back here, work a little, get my act together."

Karen leaned toward him. "I would recommend finishing your degree before tackling something as vague as getting your act together. You only have two semesters left."

Taylor looked up at the hanging flowerpots lining the porch. "Ah, well. You never liked that school anyway."

"Now you're making it sound like you don't plan on going back there at all."

"That wouldn't break my heart."

After all of Karen's badmouthing of the school, I was a little surprised that she was acting so upset by the news. They bickered over the finer points, about him giving up his scholarship and the inevitability of credits not transferring to his next college of choice. I felt compelled to throw in my two cents, but it seemed pretty clear that my opinion would have no real bearing on the matter.

"I have outgrown their mission statement," Taylor added.

"Simple as that."

"Nothing is ever 'as simple as that'," Karen said, making finger quotes.

Taylor mocked her finger gestures. "Oh, 'you'd be surprised.'"

Visibly frustrated with the direction their conversation was taking, Karen began reviewing some of the more positive experiences she and I'd shared over the previous week—the art museum, karaoke with Darrel San. Somehow, her recollections of the bio-hazardous hot tub segued into her asking Taylor why he hadn't mentioned anything about his girlfriend.

"Out of the picture entirely," he said, his glance wandering toward the street. "I no longer fit her requirements. Quite a relief, actually."

Karen picked a cigarette from the breast pocket of her flannel shirt, looking a bit smug. She lit the cigarette with the mosquito candle. "Well, that's a shame. She was a very sweet young lady."

"Gimme a break, ma. You couldn't stand her."

"I wouldn't say that, exactly." Karen sat back and crossed her legs. "At least I got used to the idea."

Taylor turned to me and mentioned the ex-girlfriend's visit to St. Louis the previous Christmas. "This place was a madhouse of negative alpha female traits. Be glad you missed it."

Karen attempted to redirect the conversation by asking what I'd done the previous Christmas.

I had to think about it for a moment.

"Bill and I went rabbit hunting," I said. "I think we got fourteen total. Cooked them up on the grill, drank scotch, and watched *Spartacus*."

Karen and Taylor looked at each other as though they were embarrassed by what I'd just said.

"Huh," Taylor said, before taking a sip of his beer.

Karen stood from her chair. "Sounds festive." She excused herself and went inside the house. The music stopped, and I could hear her sorting through a stack of CDs.

"No more World Music, thank you," Taylor shouted. I seconded his motion, but to no avail. We were soon listening to a hand drum and the drone of a didgeridoo, awash in reverb worthy of a Phil Spector production.

I asked Taylor if he had a job lined up.

"Not really, but I can always go back to delivering pizzas."

Karen returned to the porch carrying another round of beers. "You'll be wishing you kept on with school after a few weeks of that."

"Don't knock it 'til you've tried it," Taylor said.

They went on talking about job possibilities and people I didn't know. It grew tiresome. I began mimicking the sound of the didgeridoo, and a thought crossed my mind—why not ask Taylor to ride back to Colorado with me? He didn't have anything better to do. I could use an extra hand preparing to move, and I suspected there'd probably be other work to be done around Bill's place. I had nothing to lose by asking, so I did.

"That sounds like a great idea," Karen said. "What do you think, Taylor?"

He looked interested. "I've never seen the Rocky Mountains."

There were no mountains to see from Forsyth, but it was no time to bring up that detail. I couldn't muster any other selling points to convince him, so I let him consider it a moment.

"We'll need to leave first thing tomorrow."

"Sure. Why not?" he said. And so it was decided.

We were on our third round of beers when a carload of Taylor's friends dropped by and stole him from us. Karen and I sat silent, watching the car drive away.

"Well, what do you think?" she asked. "Is he what you expected?"

"Not at all. I find your earlier descriptions to be severely lacking."

She began gathering the empty bottles. "I'm as surprised as you are—believe me. I didn't see any of this coming."

Karen brought the bottles inside and suggested we go for a walk. A storm system had passed, revealing the early stages of a brilliant Midwestern sunset. I followed her out to the sidewalk.

"I'm impressed," I said. "He seems like an all-around good kid."

"I got very lucky. There's only so much control you have as a parent, really. It's a hot commodity." We turned a corner and an old two-story school building came into view—the elementary school Taylor had attended. She continued. "I must say that I'm thrilled he's no longer looking at the world through stained glass windows. Though, it's probably too early to get my hopes up."

"You didn't sound so supportive an hour ago."

"You can't flat out approve of every decision a child makes without some qualifications and a bit of resistance."

I thought about my mother, imagining how she might've reacted to similar news. "I certainly don't know any different," I said.

We squeezed through an opening in the chain link fence surrounding the school's ball field.

"I would like to know what changed his mind," she said. "That's a huge leap to make."

"It could just be native intelligence."

"Ha. Wouldn't that be nice. There has to be something else, though. I hope he's not in trouble."

We walked across the ball diamond. She mentioned Taylor's T-ball and Little League years and how he was always more of a team clown and screw-off than a serious competitor. "I was glad that he chose to retire from baseball," she said. "Being the only single mom at his games came with certain annoyances."

We made it across the field and onto the playground. Karen jogged ahead toward the swing set. The playground was covered with interlocking panels of black cushioning instead of sand. I mentioned this as I sat in the swing next to hers. "It seems they're just making it more and more difficult for kids to learn the hard way," I said.

She asked how long it'd been since I'd stepped foot on a playground. "Because, you know, a lot has changed since the Ford administration."

"I guess I had no good reason to visit a playground since then, did I?"

"Don't go there."

We talked about the drive Taylor and I would make the next day, and speculated as to how the upcoming week might unfold. All I knew for sure was that I'd have to move out of the guest house, and that everything else depended on Bill's condition. Any mention of Rhonda seemed superfluous.

Karen asked if I'd decided where to move next. I had no idea, nor did I have any desire to discuss it right then, so I threw her a knuckle ball.

"I thought I'd move here and make an honest woman out of you."

"What? You can't be serious."

"Why can't I?"

"What makes you think I would marry the likes of you?"

"Body english."

"You are truly beyond help."

We continued swinging up and back, up and back, listening to distant sirens and the thumping subwoofers of lurking automobiles. Why it came to me, I don't know, but I broke out in song:

Boy, the way Glenn Miller played
Songs that made the hit parade
Guys like us, we had it made

Karen joined in:

Those were the days.

17

The weather inside the van was in the low 90s by mid-morning. Taylor slept the first three hours of the drive, as he'd failed to return home at a reasonable hour the previous night. Getting him out of his bed and motivated had been a challenge, and the effort led to a rather unceremonious parting between his mother and me. We hadn't even managed to hug one another, which felt strange considering she'd re-seduced me mere hours before.

I completed the *My Life* marathon about the time we passed Columbia. I looked back to check on Taylor. He was lying on the mattress, staring at the roof. I wasn't sure he'd heard me when I asked how he was doing, but a minute later he was sitting in the passenger's seat removing his shirt.

"How can you travel in this thing?" he asked. "Is it always this miserable?"

"God willing."

He tossed his shirt onto the dashboard. I asked how long he'd been awake.

"A half hour maybe. Just thinking about some stuff." He asked for one of my cigarettes.

"You smoke?" I asked.

"Not much. Never around mom."

"You should quit while you're not too far behind." I tossed him my pack. "What's on your mind?"

"I'll tell you. But you can't tell Karen before I do."

"Nothing would give me more pleasure than keeping a secret from your mother."

He lifted his feet onto the dashboard and blew smoke out the window. "I was expelled. That's why I'm not going back."

Okay—not the end of the world. I assumed his former school had a more restrictive code of conduct than other schools.

"For a little bit of pot," he continued. "My roommate ratted me out, the little prick."

"How much is a little?"

"Two ounces of glorified ditchweed."

I looked over at him with one brow raised high enough to lose focus in my other eye. "What were you doing with all that?"

He launched into the story—he'd been running late for a final exam and left the pot in a backpack in his dorm room. Campus security was waiting for him outside the lecture hall after he finished his test.

"So I get escorted to the Dean's office, and an hour later, half the dorm residents are watching me clear out my room, many of them on their knees praying—it was a sight to behold."

"Were the cops involved?"

"Good god, no. That place won't handle that sort of publicity."

It seemed strange to me that the school hadn't notified Karen somehow, so I asked why they hadn't.

"They thought it would be more effective if I told her myself."

"How do you think she's going to take it?"

"She'll be pissed—if I tell her, that is. Not sure it's necessary. I don't think she'd find out any other way. All my grades and other stuff will stand, I just can't go back there."

"That's a pretty good deal, I'd say."

He shrugged. "I probably shouldn't have told you. I know how parents interact."

"Your secret is safe with me," I said. "For twenty years, at least. Scout's honor."

A couple miles passed as I chewed on what he'd told me. I doubted that it was the whole truth. I could understand his not wanting to disappoint his mother, but the marijuana aspect seemed a bit askew, considering Karen made no secret about her own pot intake. It wouldn't surprise me to discover that she'd founded her college's pot legalization club. It occurred to me that he hadn't answered my earlier question regarding why he had two ounces, so I asked again.

"Selling weed to theology students is a lucrative business. You get into the upper level courses and there's no other way to come up with the kind of outlandish shit necessary to impress some of those professors," he said. "Do you smoke?"

I looked at the passenger's sideview and changed lanes. "Very rarely anymore. It seems to rectify my dyslexia, which freaks me out." I wasn't going for humor, but it struck enough of a chord in Taylor to cause him to get convulsive with laughter. I waited for it to pass. "You didn't get that nasty gene from me did you?"

"Dyslexia? No. I don't mean to laugh about it. That just sounded funny to me. Sorry."

"No worries."

"I'm just glad to get that shit off my back. I haven't been able to tell anyone worthy of hearing it until those friends of mine showed up last night. Sorry for dragging ass this morning. I know you wanted to leave earlier."

"No big whoop. I just wanted to beat the heat. It's an old farmer thing."

We veered off course a bit in order to patronize a Flying J truck stop on the northeast edge of Kansas City. Any seasoned road dog knows that the major truck stop chains are the only safe bet for certain necessities. While they do not always exceed customer expectations, they can be counted on for having fully-enclosed stalls and sturdy locks, providing world-class privacy for the discerning traveler.

I exited the TRUCKERS ONLY restroom and spotted Taylor at the soda machine. He remained shirtless—in flagrant violation of convenience store dress code. I walked behind him and asked where his shirt was.

"Don't be messing around with the holy trinity," I said.

"To hell with it," he said, filling up a 64-oz. cup with ice. "The world's full of general guidelines."

I paid for the fuel and waited in the van. My dashboard thermometer read 115° F. Just as I was beginning to grow impatient, Taylor emerged from the store wearing a black T-shirt depicting an Olan Mills-inspired composition of a wolf-in-profile alongside a much smaller Native American warrior-in-profile, each looking in opposite directions. Maybe it was artist incompetence, but both creatures looked frustrated with one another and their lot in life, as though they were tired of being crammed onto the same T-shirts. Taylor hopped up into the van and immediately removed the shirt.

"Did they make you buy that?"

"No, I just slipped it on. I didn't feel like fuckin' around in there."

Talking over the wind and engine noise proved to be too much. We drove for long stretches without any meaningful conversation. I eventually put earplugs in and Taylor his headphones.

It did seem odd that in our few hours together I'd seen no evidence of what Karen thought she should "prepare" me for. The circumstances of his expulsion and his petty theft from the truck stop suggested the behavior of a touring musician or roadie, not an uptight, straight-A college student with a Christianity problem. Maybe she'd been exaggerating. But what for?

We switched seats in Hays, and I made several attempts at a nap before the exhaustion of trying finally overcame me. When I woke, I noticed we were no longer on I-70, but on a two-lane heading north. There was a storm front ahead. The temperature had dropped enough to allow us to drive with the windows up. It seemed that Taylor had been taking liberties with the accelerator. I checked the time and did some calculations. We were an hour-and-a-half ahead of schedule.

"You might consider slowing down a bit," I said. "There are some ambitious cops along here."

He looked over at me, seeing that I was trying to tell him something, and removed one of his headphones. "Your speedometer doesn't work," he said, delighted, as though it justified his speeding.

I didn't believe him, so I leaned over to see for myself. Sure enough, the needle was dead at the seven o'clock position. Sheets of rain started to fall after a few more miles, slowing Taylor's driving a bit, but not enough for my tastes. I stated my opinion, and he let off the gas a little, or so I thought.

"Is your gas gauge broken too?" he asked, as Percy began to surge and then hesitate. "It says we have half a tank but it feels like we're running out. I've got it floored."

"Could be the distributor is wet," I said.

"Been acting funny the last few—"

Then POW. Smoke filled the cab. The engine sounded like a couple of bricks in a clothes dryer. Taylor stepped on the brakes, navigating blind through the smoke and rain, trying to pull us over safely.

We came to rest in the bar ditch, almost perpendicular to the highway. I opened my door and noticed a rapid stream of water passing beneath the van. The smoke was thickening, so I got out, lifted the hood, and doused the flames using Taylor's 64-oz cup. The engine had blown a rod and there was nothing else we could do until the rain stopped, so we hurried back into the van.

Within a couple of minutes the rain turned to hail.

It was at this point that we decided to turn to whiskey.

Twenty minutes passed before the hail and rain let up. The stream in the ditch had risen several more inches. I jumped from the van to the ditch bank and walked to the blacktop looking for the nearest mile marker. I could see the outline of one a hundred yards or so to the north, so I began a slow jog toward it, weighing our options. Should I hassle with finding a tow truck driver between there and Forsyth and pay him a couple hundred bucks to tow us back to town, or should I swallow a little pride and chance it with Rhonda?

The mile marker placed us about forty miles east and south of Forsyth. We sat in the cold van for ninety minutes before Rhonda arrived.

She was all business. Taylor and I offered to help, but she wouldn't have any of it. She ordered us to sit in the cab and warm up.

Taylor and Rhonda didn't get a formal introduction until the tow truck was at cruising speed and Rhonda's hand lifted from the gearshift.

"You never told me you had a son," she said.

"I just found out myself."

She nodded once and left it at that. Despite my showering her with praises and thank yous, she seemed in no mood to perpetuate conversation of any kind. I could sense that she had plenty to say to me, but was hesitant to do so with Taylor in the cab. The fact that I'd chosen to sit between her and Taylor, and that our bodies were in contact made it all the more awkward. Eventually, she did have something to contribute.

"You two reek of whiskey and B.O."

I told her we'd taken a few swigs to stay warm.

"Well, don't be selfish," she said.

I told her I'd left the bottle in the van. She immediately turned her hazard lights on, took her foot off the gas, downshifted, and made an abrupt stop in the middle of the lane. As soon as our backs hit the seat, she turned to me and said, "It's not doing any good back there now is it?"

A few pulls off the whiskey made her more talkative, but it didn't seem to lighten her mood any.

"Been one hell of a week," she said. "It's always a treat to have Alan in town. You'll have the pleasure of meeting him tomorrow. He's pretty bent out of shape. Something to do with you, apparently."

In my dozens of hours of conversation with Bill, he'd only mentioned Alan a couple of times, and always in passing. I'd gotten the sense that Bill was ashamed of him for some reason, but whether it was because of one abominable act or a lifetime of persistent assholery, I had no idea. Either way, I'd given Alan no reason to dislike me. I'd never even talked to the guy.

"All I've ever done is keep his father company," I said. "He should be grateful."

Rhonda grabbed the bottle from my lap. "That'll have to be between you, him, and the lawyer."

Mention of a lawyer made me wonder if Alan had been

screwed out of something in his father's will, and thought I was to blame. I couldn't think of anything else it might be.

Rhonda drank the last few swigs, and then rolled her window down as if preparing to throw the bottle toward the ditch. She then reached behind me and opened the sliding rear window. The breeze smelled of wet pasture and distant feedlots.

"Like a couple of transients," she said. "I should have the both of you riding in the back." She set the empty bottle in my lap.

I was able to borrow Helga with minimal ado, and Taylor and I started for the back roads. I thought Taylor should experience the full extent of Helga's unlikely awesomeness. I'd just turned out of the junkyard when he asked how long I'd been seeing Rhonda. I pushed myself back from the steering wheel, sure that neither Rhonda nor I had said anything during the previous hour that was remotely suggestive, or even tender. "Where'd you get that idea?"

"I may be a savant, but I'm not an idiot."

Had Karen already told him about Rhonda? "We met long before your mother decided to get back in touch with me."

"I can't blame you," he said. "She's an attractive woman. Low population densities like these—hell, I can imagine people your age feeling the need to scramble for a piece."

The audacity.

I turned onto the straightaway and floored the accelerator. Taylor's feet lifted off the floor and his head snapped back. I shouted: "Your mom sure taught you how to spout off at the mouth."

He took a shower when we got back to the house. I put a record on the hi-fi, tossed some beers in a cooler, grabbed my pellet rifle and a box of pellets from atop the fridge, and went out to the porch.

I was overcome with sadness and nostalgia as I began shooting toward Bill's junk pile. It was the end of an era. Never again would I see Bill saunter across his lawn to join me for beers and meandering, off-color conversation. And, while the future of my career was still uncertain, it pained me to think I'd be leaving behind the best songwriting porch I'd ever known.

Taylor walked outside wearing only his boxer shorts. I pulled the trigger on the rifle, and the pellet hit what was most likely a paint can or other metal container. Sounds were all I had to gauge any feats of marksmanship. He had a brief look at me and what I was doing.

"Lifestyles of the rich and famous," he said.

He was a mouthy little shit—I'd give him that—but at least he talked. I suggested he go get my other pellet rifle and pull up a chair. "Get in on some of this reflected glory while it lasts."

I was surprised that he knew how to handle the gun, until it occurred to me that he might've learned a thing or two from Karen's father, who had a caliber of firearm for every mood, according to Karen.

"What are we aiming at here?" he asked.

The question struck me as one ripe with existential possibilities. "Just aim at the Zen of the thing and blast the shit out of it."

He lifted the barrel in the general direction that I'd been shooting in and pulled the trigger. We waited for the report, for many seconds after the pellet had probably come to rest in the brush thirty yards away.

"Did you hear that?" I whispered.

"Hear what?"

"That's what I thought."

We shot round after round into the darkness until our arms grew weak from pumping the rifles. The gun Taylor was using had been a gift to me from my grandfather. At some point in my early teens, I'd etched JIMI HENDRIX into the stock with a pocket knife. Taylor commented on this.

"You've come a long way from Hendrix to whatever crap you've got us listening to now," he said. "What is this?"

"Early post-pompadour era Conway Twitty."

"Now I know what you meant when you said you wouldn't wish your musical tastes on anyone," he said.

This was something I'd never said to him in person, so I asked where he'd heard it.

"I read it in one of your old interviews."

I couldn't remember which interview it came from, but it sounded more like late- rather than early-period Mahogany banter. It was unsettling to think that everything Taylor knew about his dear father, other than whatever his mother had told him, he'd learned from the media.

"You must've done some serious archeology," I said.

"Mom's got the magazine back home. *Professional Songwriter,* June 1999. I just happened to pick it up the other day."

I tried to recall what else I might've said in that particular interview, but I couldn't. "What's your mom doing with a copy of that laying around?"

"She's got a whole stack. Probably 30 or 40 different magazines."

That had to cover just about every magazine interview I'd ever done. "Has she been collecting them all these years?"

"Not that I'm aware of. I think she's been buying them off the internet."

I'd forgotten about Karen's so-called project. She'd made no mention of it since the night she told me about Taylor, which seemed to cement the fact that she'd just been using it as a screen to ease her way onto the tour. I mentioned what little Karen had said about the project, hoping Taylor might be able to shed some light on it.

"She's working on something," he said. "I don't know what, exactly, but, she's got all those articles highlighted and marked up like a used textbook."

"She's never said anything to you about it?"

"No." He loaded another pellet and began pumping. "And I've learned not to ask her about her projects unless I've got exactly nothing better to do for the next hour or three."

This led into a prolific stretch of Karen-centric anecdotes. I told him in great detail about the night she hit me with the lawn chair, along with several other more minor incidents that occurred during our brief relationship in Austin. I had no reason to withhold anything, so I laid it all out there, and once he sensed this, there was no stopping him. We traded story after story. He had far more material than I did, and tossed it at me until my face hurt. By the time he let up I felt as though I'd been beaten with laughter.

I still didn't know why he'd waited until this particular time in his life to find me. It'd been one of the few things Karen didn't seem to know either. I asked him, and he looked as though the question caught him off guard.

"Is it something to do with you getting expelled?" I asked.

"No. What did my mom tell you?"

"Not much, just that you'd decided it was time. She didn't give any reasons."

"That's funny. I thought you were coming to find me," he said.

"I knew nothing about you until last Saturday."

"I thought she told you a couple weeks ago."

"Could it be your mother has been jerking both of us around?"

I recounted my version of things, and he told me his. Karen had orchestrated our meeting, and it had all gone according to her plan. Taylor had known about it for months. He'd already been in St. Louis for two days when Karen feigned surprise during our phone conversation after the Minneapolis debacle. I was just happy to finally meet my son, but why all the bullshit? There were countless ways Karen could've handled breaking the news to me and bringing Taylor and I together. Why had she chosen to complicate it with so many unnecessary lies and deceptions?

After having tolerated these for a solid week, I was ready to be done with them. Taylor and I continued drinking beer, shooting pellets into the darkness, and listening to Twitty. I took comfort in the favorable odds that the worst of Karen's scheming had passed. What else could she possibly have to hide from me? I couldn't think of anything, but I knew better than to rely on my own imagination.

18

Bill had another stroke just after midnight. Rhonda called me at sunrise with the news. There was to be an informal memorial brunch at Flo's starting at 9 AM.

I tried to fall back asleep, but was kept awake by regret that I hadn't made it back in time to visit him before he passed. He may not have known either way—as Rhonda had said—but I still felt like I owed it to him. I got dressed and tried to walk it off.

His pastures were busy with killdeer and prairie dogs. A hawk rested on a power line to the east, looking down on it all as though it were a breakfast menu. I came across a bull snake stretched out across my usual walking path. I picked it up and carried it with me for a while, entertaining the idea of placing it on the bed next to Taylor as payback for his ass-dragging the previous morning. I was halfway back to the house when it shat on my arm. I took it personally, and so let it go.

It seemed strange that Alan hadn't been staying at his father's house. There was no evidence that he'd even stopped by. I tried the front door. It was locked, which was unusual. Bill took pride in the fact that he never locked his doors. "There's no reason to," he'd say. "I got nothin' to steal. And who'd think to leave something?"

I walked around to the west patio and tried the sliding glass door. It opened easy as spinning a roulette wheel.

I'd only been in Bill's house a handful of times, and had only gone as far as the front room. There was worn shag carpet by the quarter-acre, mossrock, gold leaf-infused wallpaper, and the entire spectrum of yellows, greens, and browns spread about. Any dedication Bill's wife may have had to staying hip to current trends in interior decorating seemed to have been derailed by the question *who shot J. R. Ewing?*

I wandered the house convinced that I'd find a stash of rare firearms, baseball cards, or other precious artifacts. No one of his generation worth millions of dollars could go without having a collection of something. I scoured the main floor and found nothing remarkable, then headed for the basement.

Nothing to speak of there either. Just a lot of big rooms, each one cold, dusty, dark, and lonesome as the next.

I made another pass through the house looking for portals into Bill's past. There were many old photos of him and his wife, but only a couple of Alan as a child. Rhonda's 8 x 10 junior and senior year portraits were framed and sitting atop an upright piano near the dining room. I knew that Bill and Alan were more-or-less estranged, but it seemed odd that Rhonda's photos were so prominently displayed. Was she aware of this?

A dozen or more of Forsyth's elders stood outside Flo's waiting to get in. Taylor and I listened in on their conversations as they reached consensus that it was a lovely morning, an impressive turnout, and that Bill would've been pleased. The host wrote my name on the waiting list before I spotted Rhonda sitting with a few others in a far corner. I noticed they had an empty seat, and I hoped we might be able to join them and avoid the 20-minute wait, so we walked over to their table.

"I should've known you wouldn't pass up a free breakfast," she said, before gesturing toward the man sitting across from her. "This is Alan."

He gave me a brief glance before taking an immodest bite of chicken fried steak, holding his fork like a shiv. Rhonda introduced Alan's son, who, like his father, seemed inconvenienced by our presence. I don't remember his name.

Taylor took the empty seat next to Rhonda as I negotiated with the people at an adjacent table for their unused chair. There was no clear place for me to sit that wouldn't put me in the way of waitresses and bussers. Alan was visibly irritated by my effort. I asked him where he was staying. "I'd figure you'd be out at your dad's place."

"You'd figure," Alan said.

Rhonda set down her coffee mug. "They're out at the new hotel by the interstate."

I expressed my condolences to Alan, mentioning how I'd gotten to know Bill pretty well over the last year.

"That's what I gather," he said.

I considered the possibility that he was tired of talking about his father. However, it was clear that he was upset with me specifically, for some reason. He wiped the corners of his mouth and began folding the napkin.

"I'm going to need you out of the guest house by Monday night at the latest," he said.

"This Monday?"

"You heard me." He waved his hand to get the server's attention.

I knew I had to move out sooner or later, and was prepared to do so, but three days didn't give me much time.

"What's the big hurry?" Rhonda asked.

Alan reached into his pants pocket. "That's just how it's gonna be. We need to get that place cleaned up."

In my defense, Rhonda mentioned how the estate sale they'd been discussing was still several weeks, if not months away.

Alan pulled a crisp fifty from his wallet, folded it width-wise, and set it on edge at the center of the table. "It's not up for debate." He stood and brushed crumbs from the front of his khakis, and his son followed suit. Neither one had finished half of the food they'd been served. "No one at this table has any say in the matter. And the sooner you all accept that, the better off we'll all be." They started for the door.

"You're a real gem, Alan," Rhonda shouted.

I waited for them to exit the diner before taking Alan's chair. "Has he been like this the whole time?"

"He's been that way since 1976," Rhonda said, looking exhausted. "I cannot wait until this is all over and I never have to see that asshole again."

Just about everyone passing through the diner stopped by our table to talk with Rhonda. They spoke to her as though she'd just lost her own father. I thought about her high school portraits, wondering if I'd missed some key information about the true nature of their relationship.

A man who looked about Bill's age stopped by as we prepared to leave. He and Bill had obviously shopped at the same haberdashery. Rhonda stood and put her arm around him before introducing us.

"This is Bill's attorney."

We shook hands. "Call me Jed."

Rhonda began explaining who I was. Jed wasted no time interrupting.

"So, you're the famous Carl Mahogany. Billy told me a lot about you."

I struggled to come up with a suitable reply, hoping to make a good impression on him. Bill had never mentioned anything about Jed that I could recall, so I lied. "Great to meet you finally. Bill spoke very highly of you."

He looked amused. "That comes as a great surprise to me. He must've been up to his neck in scotch."

The four of us began walking toward the exit. Jed suggested that I meet with him at his office sometime that afternoon. "No reason to put it off. Won't take but twenty minutes."

"I'm not in trouble, am I?" I asked, hoping he might hint at what our meeting was to be about.

"That'll depend on your definition of the word."

I couldn't wait, so I arrived at Jed's at twelve o'clock sharp. I parked at the end of the walkway leading up to his law office—a three-story stone mansion that stood directly across the street from the main entrance of the county courthouse. I stepped out of the car and noticed Jed sitting alone on his porch swing holding a tall glass of something.

"Mr. Mahogany," he shouted. "It is one hot sonofabitch. Get on up here in the shade."

It put a smile on my face to hear such a pronouncement from the old man. I walked up the half dozen stone steps onto the porch. "I'm getting too old for this kind of heat," I said, in an attempt at polite conversation. "I don't know how you do it."

He lifted his glass toward me and pointed at it with his available index finger. "I fill a cool glass halfway with a reputable bourbon, and let fate take its course."

He stood up from the swing, set his drink down on the window ledge, and extended his hand. We shook and he offered to get me a drink, but I declined under the pretense that I had a busy day ahead. I sat on an oversized antique rocking chair. He asked how long I'd known Bill, and I told him. Then he asked how much I knew about Bill's personal affairs.

"Very little," I said. "He didn't talk much about his past."

"That sounds just like Billy," he said. "The only reason I know anything is because I'm his attorney."

I mentioned what little I knew about Alan, focused mainly on the fact that he and Bill had been estranged to whatever extent, and for reasons unknown to me. I hoped Jed might illuminate some of those reasons, but he didn't. Instead, he launched into a general explanation of the importance of maintaining a long-haul relationship with a competent lawyer, and one with the ability to see the larger picture.

"Not that it did Bill much good," he said. "Someone as contrary and impulsive as he was has no use for cautionary, pre-emptive legal services. That being said, there are certain provisions in his will that are sure to cause controversy, particularly with Alan."

"That's the feeling I've been getting."

"You stand to receive a substantial sum from Bill's estate. A small fraction of the total, but a good deal of cash nonetheless."

"How substantial of a sum?"

"Once everyone takes their bite, you'll be looking at around one hundred thousand."

I didn't know what to say. Blood rushed to my face.

"Now, are you ready for that cold beer?" he asked, laughing.

This was more money than I'd ever seen on any balance sheet with my name at the top. I asked when Bill had added this provision to his will. Late June sometime—several weeks before the storm rolled through, and a date with no other apparent significance. I asked Jed if he knew anything that I didn't as to why Bill had chosen to do what he did.

"I was hoping you might be able to tell me," he said.

I thought a moment. "Well, we shot a lot of rabbits and drank some scotch together. Is that worth a hundred grand?"

"Sounds like good work if you can get it."

He stood from the swing and told me we'd work out the details after the reading of the will, which was scheduled for Monday morning. "Your attendance is optional," he added. "I will say that Alan is somewhat aware of what you and I've discussed. I imagine he's not going to be very pleased with the overall content."

I asked if anyone else knew any details about the will. He said no, and recommended I say nothing about it to anyone until after the official reading.

"I know Alan wants you out of that house by Monday, but I'd suggest you be out of there before then. He can be a loose cannon, and he can afford to change how his actions are interpreted in the eyes of the law."

Rhonda called soon after I returned from Jed's. She invited Taylor and me over for beers and burgers and to meet her daughter who'd just arrived from Greeley. She sounded happy to talk to me, which was a welcome surprise, so I accepted her invitation. It seemed as though she'd either forgotten, forgiven, or had chosen to ignore the entire Karen ordeal.

I didn't mention anything to her about Bill's gift right then, but I found it impossible to keep the news from Taylor. We spent the rest of the afternoon cleaning and packing, discussing what might be done with the money. Nothing either of us came up with seemed to stick, other than my conviction to get Percy running again.

Taylor gave me an earful about it on our way to Rhonda's, appealing to logic and emotion in equal measure, enumerating several valid reasons why I should junk Percy. What his limited years didn't allow him to understand was the sense of history and loyalty that the van had come to represent, and how impossible it would be at this point in my game to develop another relationship comparable in complexity, depth, and nuance.

"Whatever, dude," he said as we stepped out of the car. Rhonda's parking lot was still damp from a brief late afternoon shower. Shannon closed the junkyard gate behind us, and was still many yards away when she introduced herself. She expressed her pleasure that Taylor and I had agreed to come over and share the evening with her and her mother. Her kindness and enthusiasm seemed a bit rehearsed. Regardless, she did have an effervescence one might expect of an attractive, confident, young woman who hasn't yet been subjected to life's erosions—the kind that often result in people like me making hasty, unwarranted, and usually negative-leaning judgments about their character.

Rhonda emerged from the house wearing sunglasses and carrying a tray of ground beef patties. Taylor had already begun asking Shannon college-related questions. They seemed capable of entertaining themselves, so I left them alone and walked over to Rhonda. I offered to help cook the burgers, but she refused.

"I'm sorry that I've been such a bitch," she said, lifting the lid of the gas grill and leaning away from the heat. She seemed upset, as though she'd just stepped away from a difficult phone conversation.

"No need to apologize," I said.

"Bill never really told you much, did he?"

"About what?"

"Ah, forget it," she said, placing the patties on the grill. "I'm done thinking about it for today."

I didn't want to let the subject go, but thought it might be best to honor her wishes. We would soon be a few beers toward a more appropriate frame of mind for such discussion.

"I've decided to put a new motor in the van," I said.

She closed the lid of the grill, turned to face me, and placed a fist on her hip. "You can't be serious."

"I can't talk myself out of it."

"Maybe you should try harder. Don't give up on yourself so easily."

I mentioned Jed's recommendation that I clear out of the house before Monday. "I think Taylor and I could have the van loaded and the house cleaned out by tomorrow night."

"How are you going to get the van over there?"

It was already Friday night, and the funeral was set for Sunday. I had no idea how long it would take her to swap out an engine, but I guessed she had better things to do the next day, and I didn't want to rush her.

"Could we tow it?"

She looked at me as though she were about to knock on my forehead to see if I was still home. "What's the big hurry, anyway?"

"Jed seems to think Alan isn't going to be very happy about the will."

"So what?"

"I'm just trying to stay out of the way. It's what Jed suggested."

"What's Alan going to do, seriously."

"How would I know? I just met the bastard."

She began walking toward the house. "It's not like he's going to do something stupid."

I reminded her of the arrow protruding from the rear of my van. "I question your ability to predict the behavior of desperate men."

I followed her inside the house and she put me to work slicing tomatoes and onions. She mentioned getting started on the van the next morning. I insisted that she put it off until after the funeral.

"No," she said. "I could use the distraction, believe me." She began filling a small box with condiments, napkins, and such. "So, once the van's fixed, are you just gonna up and leave? Is that it?"

I reminded her that I no longer had a place to live, or a job, and that Forsyth had nowhere for me to put my limited talents and abilities to good use.

"Sounds to me like you need a little time to figure out your next move," she said. "Why don't you stay here for a couple weeks? God knows I've got the space."

I thanked her for the offer and said that I'd think about it.

"I'll put you to work," she added. "I can think of a million things that need doing around here."

"If my last three gigs are any indication, I should probably start looking for a new career."

"There you go. Country music star to junkyard associate—almost overnight."

The four of us sat outside the garage as we ate. Despite my best efforts to deflect and redirect certain topics, the conversation kept returning to the exploits of my recent tour. I don't mind talking about such things, but I had to be considerate of Rhonda's feelings; the fact being that Karen's presence was inseparable from nearly every story worth telling.

I hadn't anticipated Shannon's persistent questions. They were easy to field at first, but it soon became impossible for me not to mention Karen, and I could tell it was making Rhonda uncomfortable. I'd been skirting the issue long enough that it became an embarrassment to the virtue of honest, open conversation amongst adults. My not having mentioned Karen at the outset had Shannon confused, and so she began revisiting my earlier answers, attempting to place Karen within them.

It became too much for Rhonda. She pointed toward the cemetery of automobiles. "Shannon, why don't you go give Taylor a tour."

They were quick to flee. We heard the two of them burst into laughter after they disappeared around the far side of the garage.

"Well, that was embarrassing," I said.

She finished her can of Coors Light, then twisted and crushed it between her hands. "Yes it was."

"I feel like I should tell you the truth about it all," I said. "But do you want to know?"

"Did you set out to hurt my feelings?"

"No. Of course not. I had no idea what I was getting myself into."

"Did you sleep with her?"

I lied.

She pitched the can like a horseshoe toward a large barrel deep within the garage. "Well then, do I really need to know anything else?"

"I guess not."

"You've already made up your mind to leave."

This was only mostly true. "I really have no idea what I'm going to do. I'm still playing catch-up with things that happened twenty years ago."

We cleaned up, put the leftovers away, and returned to our chairs outside the garage. Taylor and Shannon had been gone well over a half-hour. After a very brief discussion as to what they might be up to, we decided not to organize a search party. There was fear about what we might discover. I mentioned Taylor's marijuana bust and expulsion, before it occurred to me that it might not have been time-appropriate. The implications of this seemed to comfort Rhonda, however. She suggested that the two were probably just sitting on a tailgate burning a J, and this was acceptable. She mentioned that the southwestern corner of the junkyard had been a pot smoking destination for two or three generations of spirited youths.

In short time we'd moved our chairs onto the lawn, between a pair of tiki torches burning citronella. Judas Priest's *British Steel* album played on the stereo in the garage, quiet enough that both of us noticed the sound of a vehicle driving unusually slow past the junkyard. Rhonda mentioned that she thought she'd heard it earlier.

"No doubt a Chevy 350," she said. "With a loose valve lifter. Which only eliminates about half the vehicles in town, unfortunately."

We had no way of identifying the vehicle without peeking through an opening in the fortress walls, though we could tell its headlights were off. This fact alone made the driver guilty of something. It sounded a little like Bill's truck.

"I wonder what Lloyd's up to tonight," Rhonda said.

We heard the crunching of gravel before Taylor and Shannon appeared.

"Just grabbing a couple more beers," Taylor said. Shannon followed him into the garage. Her posture had sagged a bit and she avoided eye contact. Rhonda's eyes rolled. The kids emerged from the garage looking hell-bent on returning to wherever they'd been hanging out.

"Come here a second, sweetheart," Rhonda said.

Shannon stopped and turned to face us, looking like she'd just been accused of something. "What?"

Rhonda laughed. "Holy Christ. What kind of trouble could you two possibly be getting into back there?"

Neither of them had a quick response. Perhaps it was too open-ended a question to ask people in their state of mind.

"Do all of us a favor," Rhonda said, before mentioning the lurking Chevy. She asked if they'd sit out by the road, somewhere inconspicuous, and keep a lookout in case it passed by again. The kids looked at each other, and exchanged subtle nods and shrugs before agreeing to do it and walking away.

After some discussion about whether it was Alan or Lloyd creeping outside the fortress, Rhonda asked if Bill had ever told me about the accident.

"He never mentioned any accident," I said, assuming this is what she'd been referring to earlier when she asked about Bill not telling me much.

She paused a moment and sipped her beer. "Alan caused the wreck that killed my father."

She told the story. It happened when she was sixteen. Her dad had left in the tow truck around 1:30 AM on a Sunday to pick up a stranded vehicle fifteen miles southeast of town. A motorcyclist noticed the tow truck upturned and tangled in a barbed wire fence about fifteen minutes later.

Her father had hit the brakes and swerved to avoid something and lost control. The truck rolled and then slid until it was slowed by the tension of the wire. There'd been no evidence of a collision, or any weather to speak of. Rhonda was certain her father would never have gone that far out of his way to avoid a deer or other creature.

It happened a couple miles north of a creek bottom where Alan and his friends used to get drunk. They'd been there that night, and Alan had left the spot in his pickup around that same time.

Several days passed before anyone began to suspect him. He denied having anything to do with it.

"We all knew," Rhonda said. "You can just tell when it's someone you've known for years. He quit talking to anyone. That was as good as an admission of guilt. He skipped town right after graduation. Hasn't been back more than a couple times since."

She explained how Bill stepped in to help her family afterwards. No one resented Bill or his wife for any of it. "No one much cared for Alan anyway—before or after."

"Bill didn't seem to care much for him either," I said.

"He was a pretty good judge of character."

We sat on that for awhile. Why had no one mentioned anything about the accident before? I could understand Bill and Rhonda not wanting to bring it up, but it was the type of story Lloyd would've told me.

Satan had been lazing on the grass for the better part of the evening. She caught a scent or heard something that sent her running and barking toward the northeast corner of the junkyard. I asked if it might be a coyote or raccoon.

Rhonda stood and began following Satan's trail. "I doubt it. She knows better."

I followed, and Taylor and Shannon were soon jogging toward us. Satan had given up trying to scale the chain link fence that lined the interior of the fortress, and was beginning to tunnel. Rhonda kneed her in the side and peered through the gap.

"Can you see him?" Taylor asked.

"See who? What did you see?"

"We just saw an outline," Taylor said. "Looked like maybe he'd sprained his ankle."

Taylor wanted to chase the man down, but I already knew where to find him—in the remarkably least-maintained half of a dumpy beige brick duplex.

19

I couldn't allow my son to come all the way to Colorado without seeing the Rocky Mountains, so that's where we headed Saturday morning. We took the most direct path, yet he whined about it taking so long before they came into view. It became tedious, so I quipped about him inheriting an entitlement complex from his mother, and that put an end to it.

We cut north of Fort Collins and started up Poudre Canyon. Our plan was to make it to the Continental Divide, but this was not to be. The elevation and Helga's inability to go below the speed limit around the tight corners got the best of him. We weren't ten miles into the foothills when he demanded I pull over immediately, and he vomited behind a just-emptied school bus of pre-adolescent river rafters. Most of the kids cringed and turned away, some laughed, and a couple decided it was also a good time to barf.

He was visibly traumatized by the spectacle, but insisted we keep going.

"If it'll make you feel any better, I puked on stage in front of three thousand people in Tulsa," I said, before going into unsolicited detail. We made it around a few more bends before he leaned out the window and barfed again.

So, we turned back.

There's a lot to see along the stretch of highway that connects the Rockies and Forsyth. Fences, tumbleweeds, cottonwood trees, abandoned homes, and a couple of soon-to-be ghost towns. I pointed out a cloud that resembled a beaver skull. There weren't many clouds to work with, but we made the most of them. Taylor saw a seahorse playing a theremin, and I managed to pick Mary Lou Retton's 1984 Olympic vault landing out of the same formation minutes later.

He became fascinated with the idea that we were in the midst of a national park. "It's unbelievable. There isn't shit to see out here."

"That's why it is what it is."

We began passing signs for the Pawnee Buttes. Many locals had recommended I visit the site, including Lloyd, who'd claimed it was "where hippies go to get in touch with their two-percent Cherokee heritage and hope it'll turn into a scholarship."

It was early afternoon, and we had nothing else to do, so we turned north and followed the gravel roads.

We hiked the footpath, and it led us to the edge of a cliff so steep that I got paranoid that I'd already made the plunge in some not-so-distant-future. A legion of wind turbines loomed on the distant edge of the valley. Taylor pulled his wallet from his shorts pocket and sat on a chunk of sandstone.

"They kinda ruin the view, don't you think?"

He'd been looking at them since we arrived. "You were the one complaining about nothing to see around here. Now you can't keep your eyes off of 'em."

He responded by pulling a joint from his wallet. "Feel like rectifying some of that dyslexia?"

"Why not."

I mentioned the last time I smoked pot, and Blaine. Taylor knew about him.

"He's got a crush on mom," he said. "Pretty much all of her students do. He purposely won't graduate so he can continue taking her classes."

I assume Karen's never had any problem getting any man she's wanted, though I wondered how many boyfriends she'd run through Taylor's life. She hadn't mentioned any during our travels. I asked Taylor about this.

"She dated, but nothing too serious, as far as I know. No one ever moved in with us or anything." He lit the joint and took a drag. "Most of the dudes that hung around the house were gay, or are gay, rather—in various stages of denial. Mom likes to call them her 'inflammables.'"

I asked about Don Johnnie.

"You mean the Sleestak?"

I'd forgotten these creatures from the old *Land of the Lost* TV show. "Yes. That god-awful abomination."

Taylor passed the joint to me. "He's another of mom's charity cases. You didn't shake his hand did you?"

I admitted to it and we had a good laugh.

"Talk about a thunderstealer," he said.

I took a puff and asked why he supposed his mother never married.

"I have no idea," he said. "Grandma bugs her about it all the time, though. Mom always says she's too busy."

This was also my general excuse. "Some people just aren't cut out for it," I said. "I can't say I ever really had that ambition. What about you?"

"It'll happen someday, but I'm in no hurry."

We watched a bird of prey circle overhead as we burned our way through the rest of the joint. I thought about my extensive list of failed relationships. Some aspect of my career could be blamed for most of them, but it was more often just an easy excuse. A pattern had begun to develop by the time I was in my mid-twenties, and so I began telling any prospects that if they were looking for a conventional life with regular hours, then I wasn't their man. Of course, this turned out to be a worthless deterrent, but at least I could say I told them so.

He asked if I'd decided where I was going to move. I still wasn't sure, but I mentioned St. Louis.

"I'd like it if you and I could hang out once in awhile," I said. "We've got some catching up to do."

"I'll say."

St. Louis was beginning to sound like a real possibility, though a lot depended on whether Taylor planned to stick around there. I asked him what he thought he might do, and he said he'd probably finish his degree at Karen's school.

"After that, who knows," he said. "Aren't you supposed to have some advice for me, being my father and all?"

I tossed a rock off the cliff. "It's been the destiny of all successful Mahogany males to ignore all advice and opinions. So you might want to consider that as an option."

20

Bill's visitation began at noon, but we didn't arrive until a half-hour before the memorial service was to begin. I didn't know anyone there aside from Rhonda and Jed, and they were both busy skipping from small crowd to small crowd. I approached the casket to pay my respects, and got halfway through a recitation of the Lord's Prayer in my head before being distracted by the aesthetic work the preparer had done on Bill's face. It reminded me of Ted Turner's ill-conceived attempts at colorizing classic black and white films. Bill's once-stately appearance had become a vehicle for an ambitious novice's portfolio enhancement. I imagined Bill asking St. Peter: "Is there somewhere in there I can wash this crap off?"

We sat along the back wall on stackable chairs, drinking coffee out of styrofoam cups. People of all ages walked past us, clueless as to whom we were, but they all smiled and said hello. I felt sorry for the kids in attendance—church all morning and then a funeral in the afternoon. Some Sunday. Despite this, I wanted to grab each one by the back of the neck, shake them, and say *it's later than you think!*

The pastor asked that everyone be seated, then thanked everyone for coming, and began the service proper with a prayer and a couple passages from the *Bible*. One of these was Ecclesiastes 3:1, also known as the song "Turn! Turn! Turn!" made popular by the Byrds.

Bill had never been a regular church-goer to my knowledge.

The baby-faced pastor confirmed this as he began his short sermon: "After walking around this room and having a chance to speak with many of you, I have learned many things about Bill," he said. "Not only was he a beloved father and husband, he was a well-respected businessman, civic leader, philanthropist, gardener, and rabbit hunter."

Gardener? I never heard such a thing. Did noxious weeds count?

Alan emerged out of nowhere and gave the shortest eulogy on record, appearing annoyed by his own attendance. He expressed regret that he and his father didn't have a closer relationship. This seemed to create a collective anxiety in the room; an anticipation that he might snap and unleash years of pent-up anger and frustration. I sure felt it, enough that it distracted me from listening to the rest of what he had to say.

One of Bill's ex-girlfriends took the podium immediately after Alan. She introduced herself, saying she was from Fond du Lac, Wisconsin, and told of how she'd met Bill while working at an ice cream shop in high school. He'd been working on his uncle's farm that summer.

"We'd only been dating a couple of weeks," she said. "He talked me into hopping a train. We rode on top of a boxcar all the way to Oshkosh. It was the scariest hour of my life…and I lost all dating privileges until I left for nursing college."

At least a dozen of Bill's friends got up and spoke, and there was no shortage of laughs and surprises. One of his former classmates told the story of how Bill had been hired to construct a bomb shelter in the back yard of a notorious local crone named Florence—the woman who'd become his diner's namesake thirty years after her death. All but the roof had been completed when

Flo realized the space wouldn't be sufficient to accommodate her and her fifteen cats.

The man looked up, and began folding the sheet of yellow legal paper that he'd been reading from. "And after several minutes of heated argument about the role of housecats in post-nuclear holocaust Forsyth, Billy found himself searching, once again, for gainful employment."

Rhonda was the last to speak, reading aloud from the pages of a notebook. She talked about her father's death and how Bill's kindness and generosity kept her family and the family business afloat.

"He once told me that there's nothing easier to do than taking what God has given you for granted, and neglecting those who've made you who you are."

Guilty.

She continued: "And it's the people who really know how to live that aren't afraid to wake up each and every morning and put in the effort."

I chose not to speak, having nothing to say that could top that.

Taylor and I followed the procession of cars to the cemetery. I asked him to repeat what Alan had said during the last part of his speech. He said it was a story about a fishing trip, but it had no point or moral, no vivid details or narrative arc, and shed no light whatsoever on the dynamics of their relationship.

We drove up the cemetery's narrow gravel road marveling at the insurmountable odds Alan had to overcome in order to create and share such an anti-story.

Bill was buried next to his wife, with whom he shared a modestly-sized, unadorned red granite monument.

21

"Pull!"

Taylor frisbeed a copy of the *Essential Carl Mahogany* CD over the burn pile, and I blasted it with one of Bill's shotguns. A box of 300 authentic, label-released discs had finally arrived that morning. Compact disc cases aren't designed to soar gracefully, so it took a few tries before we figured out the best way to achieve maximum distance and loft. We'd gone through two dozen shells before Taylor noticed Rhonda watching us. She was leaning against the house, arms folded, shaking her head.

"If this isn't straight out of the redneck handbook," she said.

"Wanna take a crack at it?" I asked.

"Sure."

I loaded two shells and handed the gun to her. She knew what to do. Taylor sent a disc flying toward the wall of Russian olives and Rhonda vaporized it.

I screamed like Howard Dean. I guess I knew exactly how much fun I was having at the time I was having it.

Rhonda looked pleased with herself as she handed the gun back to me.

"Aren't you gonna take a few more shots?" I asked.

"I didn't come here to dominate."

I held the gun out toward her. "Here. I insist."

"Okay."

Taylor tossed disc after disc and Rhonda killed every one. She'd blasted ten or eleven in a row before she'd had enough.

"Don't stop! We've still got a couple hundred discs to obliterate."

She handed the gun back to me. "I guess you can afford the ammo," she said, giving me a gentle punch on the shoulder. "Aren't you a lucky sonofabitch."

I assumed she was referring to what she'd learned at the reading of the will that morning, and I was correct.

"Alan didn't even sit through the whole thing," she said.

"Well, I didn't earn it buying lottery tickets."

We walked around the front of the house to have a look at Percy.

"It's a goddamn miracle," Rhonda said. "If that odometer makes it past 500,000 miles, I'm calling the Guinness Book people."

She walked toward Helga and suggested I treat everyone to dinner and a round of miniature golf at the new funplex. "Pick us up around five?"

"Sure."

Taylor and I had the house emptied within an hour. Everything fit in the van but two large boxes that we tied to the mangled roof rack with baling twine. The remaining *Essential Carl Mahogany* CDs came to rest at the bottom of Bill's dumpster.

I locked the doors of the house, slid the key through Bill's mail slot, and then took off down the long driveway. Tears began to well up as I saw his mansion shrinking in the sideview.

We left the van at Rhonda's and took her Bronco downtown to Jim's Steakhouse. I ordered Beef Charlemagne, and this confused the young waitress.

"Your chef will know what to do," I said.

Rhonda let everyone know that Bill had willed her the junkyard, all bought and paid for, plus an amount of money that she didn't disclose.

"So, it looks like I'll be sticking around awhile longer," she said.

I brought up the possibility of her selling it and starting a new life somewhere else.

She laughed, and her eyes rolled. "Please. I'm too old for that nonsense. Though feel free to start over yourself. Don't forget to write. I'll want to hear all about it."

I'd made brief eye contact with the chef, and he clearly wasn't thrilled about it, but the Beef Charlemagne arrived with no fuss. It tasted much better than my attempt, and so I left him a more-than-generous tip.

Don Q's Fun Park had opened for business sometime during the week I'd been away. Only the miniature golf courses, concession stand, and batting cages were up and running. The eastern half of the two-acre park consisted of a rectangular pond, on which fun-seekers willing to wait until the next spring would be able to wage battles in state-of-the-art bumper boats. Two nine-hole courses, six batting cages, and a parking lot made up the western half.

The design of the mini-golf course was impressive—by far the most artistically ambitious thing of any permanence that Forsyth had ever seen. It was quickly established that Taylor was the only one among us who had actually read Don Quixote. Shannon mentioned that she may have seen the movie version at some point, but Taylor was quick to cast doubt, informing us that the story was cursed, and had proven nearly impossible to make into a worthy film. "So, we have to settle for the mini-golf version," he said.

Each hole of the course represented a key scene in the novel, consistent with the order in which they occur in the story. Hole number four was a par five: a windmill challenge. I set my ball on the tee.

"We're at the most famous scene in all of Western literature," Taylor said. "So, don't fuck it up, Dad."

I proceeded to hit the ball into one of the motor-driven rotating blades. The ball meandered a few feet back toward me and stopped, as though it'd just been knocked unconscious. Taylor put his hand on my shoulder and assured me that it would be okay—or at least in keeping with the novel—to attack the windmill with my club.

The quality of my putting never recovered. Rhonda beat Shannon and Taylor by two. I placed a distant third.

The victor bought a soft-serve ice cream cone for each of her underlings. We walked out to the edge of the pond and sat at one of the dozen picnic tables dividing the pond area from the mini-golf area. The sun was just beginning to set, giving the sparse westernmost clouds the appearance of melted orange creamsicles. Don Q's public address horns played AC/DC's "Hells Bells."

We talked about what the next few weeks and months had in store for each of us. Taylor expressed the notion that life is what happens while other plans are being made. He said he was going to focus attention away from plan-making and goal-achievement for awhile.

"Don't forget to write," I said.

Shannon had been the most reticent about the subject. Rhonda asked her to contribute something to the conversation, but something grabbed her attention before she had a chance to speak. She looked over my shoulder toward Main Street, horrified.

"Isn't that your van?" she asked, pointing behind me.

"What in the hell," Rhonda said, the first to stand up from the table.

I was hesitant to take the bait, figuring they were just playing a practical joke. Not until Shannon stood up did I turn to face the action.

Indeed, there was Percy, held aloft by Rhonda's giant forklift, the whole package turning off of Main Street and heading directly for the pond. All that stood between the street and the water was twenty feet of dirt, a fence consisting of a single steel cable, and then three or four more feet of dirt.

Rhonda was already several paces ahead of me, running around the northwest corner of the pond, shouting at Lloyd. The forklift had come to a stop at the fence. The forks rose several feet before Lloyd tipped them forward. The screech of metal on metal came to a crescendo, and then my van plunged headlong into the water.

Lloyd sat behind the wheel, smiling, never once taking his eyes off the sinking van until I jumped up the side steps of the forklift and punched him in the temple. Gravity brought him to the hard dirt shoulder-first. He writhed like a beheaded snake. I kicked dust and gravel in his face, but he showed no sign of standing up and defending himself.

Rhonda shut the forklift down. Strangers began to gather and whisper to one another, watching bubbles surface around the van. Within seconds, it'd sunk as far as it was going to. All but half of each wheel and a section of muffler were submerged.

Fire, police, and ambulance soon made their appearance. I filled out some reports and answered questions. They hauled a barely conscious Lloyd away on a stretcher.

Redneck ingenuity tried to intervene and assist in the rescue effort. Countless feet of rope, chain, and winch cable were offered up, along with several conflicting strategies as to the best way to remove the van from the water. Rhonda eventually had to shout at everyone—mostly high school-aged boys in ball caps, sleeveless shirts, and Wrangler jeans—to get lost.

She had everything under control.

We had the van out of the water, turned upright, and set down in front of her garage before midnight.

22

The van rescue effort had left Taylor and me without a dry article of clothing between us. I walked downstairs to the kitchen the next morning wearing Rhonda's only pair of boxer shorts—a cheery little set, peppered with the logos of college football teams, and the phrase BRING ON THE BIG TEN! printed in an arch across the butt. Shannon and Rhonda failed to contain their laughter as I turned my back to them and poured a mug of coffee. Taylor was quick to join them as he entered the kitchen wearing respectable shorts and a shirt. They had the choice whether to look at my exposed ass or turn away as I left the kitchen for the laundry room.

I pulled my clothes from the dryer, noticing their new blue-green hue. The chemical that the Don Q people used to treat their pond water had not washed out, which meant that everything I owned that was permeable and salvageable would probably be blue-green forevermore.

I sat square with the kitchen table, staring out the window toward the road as I ate the bacon, eggs, and toast that Rhonda had prepared. I'd been avoiding the south window, not ready to face the van in all the glory of daylight.

"Are you ready for this?" I asked Taylor.

"Ready when you are."

"We won't be able to wait that long."

I lifted Rhonda's pack of Marlboros from the table and looked at her.

"All yours," she said.

Shannon refilled our coffee mugs, and Taylor followed me out the screen door, down the steps, and onto the driveway.

There it stood, surrounded by a ring of wet ground, roof caved in slightly, windshield shattered, large sections of the exterior coated in mud and god-knows-what else. Lloyd's arrow had bent, but was still lodged in the rear door.

I pried it open with a crowbar and took my first long look. I could see that the milk crate full of my earliest spiral notebooks was ruined, as was my box of yellowed newspaper clippings, hand-printed showbills, exotic fan letters, and other irreproducible artifacts.

I swallowed hard.

Taylor stood a few feet behind me. I told him to go put something worthwhile on the garage stereo and bring me any tarps and towels he could find. Within a couple minutes he had a large blue tarp spread out beside the van. Black Sabbath's "Hole in the Sky" roared from the garage speakers. I thanked him. He asked what else he could do.

"How about you go hang with the ladies for awhile," I said. "Let me peel this onion by myself."

Everything was spread out on the tarp and drying within an hour. I hadn't sorted through all of the boxes yet, but I knew most of it would end up in the dumpster, along with the computer, stereo, and just about everything else.

The Martin (which had miraculously survived the tumble from the wall weeks earlier) was ruined, as was a '55 and a '62 Fender Telecaster, '64 Fender Vibroverb, and a '59 Fender Bassman. This amounted to $200–300,000 worth of vintage gear. Another five grand worth of classic microphones and effect boxes were destroyed.

I'd managed to hold back the waterworks until I pulled a milk crate of old friends' recordings from the muck.

Producing a vinyl record used to be a monumental achievement, especially if you were an artist or band with no record label support. You worked your ass off, and saved enough money to do the recording and have a few hundred copies of your album pressed, and if your band imploded before you ever got noticed, this was the only solid proof that you'd ever accomplished anything.

I peeled each of the wet record sleeves apart, each autograph and personal message distorted and diffused by the ubiquitous blue-green juice. I looked at their posed band photos, putting faces to names, remembering all the after-parties, petty crimes, and horrible stagewear, wondering what became of everybody. Most of them got out before the getting got worse. Some of them had found modest success on the fringes of the music business as session players, recording engineers, and music instructors. A few ended up doing the Branson thing. One guy eventually got into writing and publishing songs for kids, which affords him modest homes in Aspen, Cabo San Lucas, and a ranch near Missoula, last I heard.

Taylor walked up carrying a couple bottles of beer while I was still separating the albums. "Looks like you could use a beer right now," he said.

"I could use about eighty-seven beers right now."

We worked into the early afternoon, sorting and cleaning. Taylor helped keep me calm, and talked me out of throwing several things in the dumpster out of frustration.

"You're mistaking 'damaged' for 'destroyed'," he said. "A lot of this stuff would probably serve its original purpose if you just let it dry out."

He suggested I let these things be a reminder, someday, of my "blue-green phase."

"That sounds like some bullshit your mom would conjure up."

Karen called him as I searched for the library's cookbooks that I'd left on the dash, intending to return on the way out of town. They were nowhere to be found.

So, the cookbooks, the karaoke cowboy's demo CD, a half pack of Gunsmokes, and a few other treasures are resting on the bottom of Don Q's pond to this day.

I couldn't help listening in on Taylor's conversation. There were many choppy sentences involved. His mother had obviously found out about his expulsion somehow.

Pizzas were delivered. Rhonda, Shannon, and I sat in the air conditioned kitchen and dug in while Taylor had it out with his mom. I told them what was going on. Rhonda looked at her daughter. "I hope we never have to have that conversation."

The two of them snapped back and forth, long enough that Rhonda was able to extort from her daughter a denial of any past wrongdoings and an oath of virginal behavior henceforth.

I'd been thinking about Helga, and asked if Rhonda would sell her to me.

She hemmed and hawed.

"What's your offer?" she asked.

"Save me the guessing."

"For you, fifteen hundred."

I thought a minute, considering the recent reduction in the total cubic footage of my belongings. There was a good chance that what remained could be packed into and atop Helga. I could rent a small trailer if necessary.

"It's a deal."

Taylor entered the kitchen minutes later looking exasperated. Rhonda told him to grab a slice of pizza. I played dumb and asked him how his mother was doing.

He sat down and stared at the center of the table. "I swear. You can't tell if she's just having a bad day or if she's passing a kidney stone. At least you haven't had to deal with that for the last twenty years."

"I've been counting my blessings all morning."

Karen called me as I loaded the last of my things into Helga. I learned that one of Taylor's professors had informed her about the expulsion. She asked me what I thought about it.

"That's not exactly on top of my mind right now," I said.

She apologized, noting that Taylor had told her what I'd been dealing with. She offered various condolences, and asked if there was anything she could do.

"Not really."

"What are you going to do now?"

"I bought a stationwagon."

"You're movin' on up, then, it sounds like."

What was that supposed to mean? She asked when we planned on being in St. Louis. I bought an extra day and told her Thursday night.

"You can stay here as long as you need to," she said.

Rhonda grilled bratwursts for supper and then the four of us drank beer and threw dollar-a-game horseshoes until dark. Helga was packed and ready for the big drive. The classic rock radio jock said we were looking at record heat all across the plains states the next couple days. Rhonda was determined to keep the weather at the forefront of conversation, mentioning Helga's lack of air-conditioning and tendency to vapor-lock on hot days, even with the heat vents on full blast. There was some uncertainty as to what vapor-lock was and so Rhonda gave a brief, but satisfactory explanation. Taylor and I made the frown-face and nodded our heads. Shannon blamed global warming.

"Oh, for chrissakes, Shannon," Rhonda said. "Didn't you absorb any automotive knowledge growing up around here?"

Shannon rolled her eyes, and sat forward in her chair as though she were preparing to flee.

I turned to her. "If it'll make you feel any better, I never learned anything about what my parents did for a living."

Shannon looked at me. "Oh yeah?"

"Oh yeah. Absolutely nothing."

Only Shannon seemed willing to believe this.

"Wasn't your dad in the Air Force?" Taylor asked.

I turned to him. "Your grandfather hung out at a bar called the American Legion. Whether he worked there or just drank there was always a big question around the house. What he did before that, I can't really say. Though he did have an affinity for the movie *Dr. Strangelove*."

"I know exactly what my parents did," Rhonda said, as though we were playing a game.

Taylor spoke up. "My mom writes impossible-to-read essays

and books about dead female environmentalists—and grades papers faster than she can read them."

Rhonda turned to Taylor. "And what would you say your father does?" she asked.

Taylor looked at me. "Well, what is it that you do?"

I thought for a moment. "I guess I'm between things. Not very lucrative. I wouldn't recommend it."

Rhonda and I lay on her bed in the dark, naked, watching her ceiling fan. It hadn't been mounted properly, so the central light bulb part of the unit rotated in an orbit all its own, separate from the blades.

"One of these nights that whole thing is going to come crashing down," I said.

"Maybe you should fix it for me."

"I'm not the mechanic. You'd do a much better job of it."

"There's no question about that. I'd just rather you do it."

She'd been making subtle hints like that since Taylor and I finished cleaning out the van—little tasks here and there for me to do, things that would require I stay a few extra days, or weeks. I think she was trying to keep me distracted, and that meant a lot to me.

"I know I keep saying it, but I wish you weren't leaving so soon," she said.

"I need to get Taylor back to St. Louis. He has to start looking for a job."

"Okay, okay. I'll stop."

She rested her head on my chest and closed her eyes. I stared at the ceiling fan, briefly considering the option of sending

Taylor back on a bus or train. He hadn't expressed any desire to hurry back to St. Louis, and I assumed he wasn't looking forward to dealing with his mom and her reactions to the news of his expulsion. Shannon was headed back to Greeley the next day, so he wouldn't have anyone other than Rhonda and me to hang out with. It would've been cruel and unusual to make him feel like a third wheel to that.

It also occurred to me that the drive back might be the last opportunity I'd have to spend time with him for awhile. He seemed like a kid who wasn't likely to stay in one place too long; someone who might be difficult to cross paths with in the future, regardless of where either of us ended up.

Rhonda began humming a melody. I couldn't place it, but it was soft, beautiful, and timeless.

"Ain't that how it seems to go," I said.

"What's that?"

"Just when you're ready to move away from a place, you meet someone that you should've met long ago."

"I guess I wouldn't know," she said.

"You wouldn't?"

"I never moved away."

23

We left Forsyth just after 8 AM, stopping by the library first so I could explain my situation and pay for the sunken cookbooks. It was closed, so I left a note and slipped a couple hundred bucks under the door. A few miles out of town, I pulled an apple from the brown lunch sack Rhonda sent with us. I inspected it for bruising, labels, and other irregularities, and found nothing of the sort. In fact, it was as though I was holding the genuine article—a rare specimen of God's original plan for the apple. I took a bite from it and looked at the sideview mirror. The muted skyline of Forsyth was still visible. Melancholia began to set in. I cycled through my jumbled mental list of valid reasons for leaving, but it did little to suppress the self-doubt I was feeling by leaving Rhonda behind.

It was all I could think about the first couple hours. I knew Taylor wouldn't want to hear me go on and on about it, so we spent most of the first leg of the drive not saying much of anything. Taylor finally spoke.

"You don't really want to leave her, do you?"

"Who, Rhonda?"

"Who else would I be talking about?"

I looked across a pasture to the east. "Ah, she's not the one for me. Or, I'm not the one for her, take your pick."

"That's not the story her floorboards were telling last night."

"Great. We've got a comedian in the car. I should whoop you upside the head." I set the apple in my lap, grabbed the previous morning's issue of the *Forsyth Sentinel* from atop the dashboard, and swatted him with it numerous times. He'd bought the paper so that I'd have something for my "scrapbook." A headline on the front page read: "Nashville star's van dumped in new fun park pond."

"You know, I could take a bus," he said. "You don't have to go so far out of your way. I'll bet I could hook up with one in Burlington."

"I have to settle some things with your mom."

He grabbed an apple from the bag. "Think you'll stick around St. Louis for awhile?"

"That depends on your mother, I guess."

He took a bite. "She's been a good mom, but she can be a real piece of work."

I told him about the lecture she'd given me on the Navy Pier Ferris wheel in Chicago, and he got a good laugh out of it.

"I grew up thinking that's how you're supposed to talk to people," he said. "Man, am I still in for a surprise."

A pack of antelope crossed the highway a few hundred yards ahead. "Yeah, I've never had my life disassembled so eloquently. I must say that I prefer the old ways."

"And what are those?"

"Keeping things bottled up, not saying everything that's on your mind all the time. People used to place a higher value on that sort of thing."

"Repression, you mean?"

"Sure."

"But doesn't that lead to passive-aggressiveness and other negative behaviors?"

"It doesn't have to. Not in the hands of a master."

We eventually got around to talking about his phone conversation with Karen the previous day. The fact that he hadn't told her about his expulsion—not the expulsion itself—was what disturbed her the most.

"Were you ever going to tell her?" I asked.

"Probably not. What would've been the point?"

I thought on this a moment. "I suppose you're right."

He looked surprised to have my support. "You agree? That doesn't sound very fatherly."

"Oh, but it is, son. Get to know this: one of the great freedoms of adulthood is being able to withhold certain knowledge from your parents—for their own good, usually."

"Hmm."

"She probably feels entitled to know everything that's going on in your life."

"That sounds about right."

I took another bite of apple. "You should take pride in the fact that you were trying to protect her from something she didn't need to hear. Maybe she'll realize that someday."

"You should mention that to her. Get it in her head now, before she turns into her own mother."

"I can't wait to see how that goes over."

Helga's vapor locking issue stopped us four times that afternoon, adding almost three hours to the drive. Per Rhonda's advice, we drove with the hood open a crack and the heat vents blowing full blast. This went on for nearly five hours as Taylor and I drank water by the gallon trying to endure the heat, while cursing Detroit engineering, global warming, OPEC, and just about everything else that came to mind.

We parked in Karen's driveway a little after 10:30 PM. Her car was gone, but several lights were on in the house. Taylor let us in with his key. He didn't have a guess as to where she might be. He suggested I call her.

"She doesn't expect us until tomorrow. I think I'll just wait here and surprise her," I said.

I grabbed a High Life from the fridge and sat down on the couch facing the nude painting. Taylor was in the bathroom preparing to go out with friends.

"I didn't know you were a painter," I shouted to him.

"Oh, that? I just wrote my name in the corner. Johnnie painted that."

Karen had left her stereo on a classical station. The house still smelled of garlic and some tangy Asian spice I couldn't identify. Taylor walked out of the bathroom in a change of clothes and wet hair, heading for the front door. "I guess I'll see you tomorrow sometime," he said.

I apologized for the miserable drive.

"Remember to tell my mom I was just protecting her from facts she didn't need to know."

"Will do."

I waited on the couch, drinking my beer, wondering where Karen might've gone; maybe to the store, or out for a couple drinks with one of her colleagues. What if she was entertaining another man that night? I imagined a few different scenarios that the surprise of my being there might complicate.

A mug of coffee sat on her computer desk. I touched the backs of my fingers to the side of it to take its temperature. It was still warm, though not warm enough to produce steam. Her computer was on, so I sat down at it intending to check my e-mail.

The screen saver disappeared revealing a document that she'd been working on. The name of the file was *Essential Carl Mahogany—Preliminary Notes and Outline*. She'd already filled twenty-five pages. I read through the twenty-fifth page, and got a good idea of where she was going with it. I scrolled to the top of the document and began reading.

She was considerate enough to spell out, in plain terms, the purpose of her project within the first couple pages. Some of it read like a witch addressing her coven according to the rules of parliamentary procedure. Phrases like "transgressive memoiring" and "taking pre-emptive control of the present" were set apart from the rest of her gibberish in boldface italics.

Page three revealed that she'd taken a bus to meet me in Kansas City. There'd been no grad student involved.

Page four contained ramblings about the ethics of manipulating the events of my tour to add tension and action to the narrative of her memoir-to-be. Several incomplete sentences hinted at various strategies she could—and did—use to conceal these manipulations.

On page five, she stated that I suffered from "typical, Anglo-Midwestern, ignorant privilege" and that she considered me "illiterate" having "not read a single classic of literary merit."

A few key items marked pages eight through ten: first, she'd been sleeping with someone else during the weeks leading up to the lawn chair attack; second, she'd insisted on him wearing a condom every time; and third, she'd failed to renew her birth control prescription in the heat of it all.

I'd read my fill. I sent the document to my e-mail account, deleted it from her computer, and left.

24

A single night in Nashville was all it took.

I hit a few of my old haunts, looking to catch up with the old rotation of early-evening regulars. Most of them were still there; grayer in the face, and 1,200 drinks closer to death. It seemed as though they resented my having moved away. I doubted this was really the case, but whatever the reason, I'd been gone long enough that we ran out of things to talk about in short time. That was fine with me. I'd successfully disconnected from the old-town Nashville gossip stream, and it felt right.

I suffered through a few house bands for a song or two. The faces of the musicians had changed since I'd last been there, but not the outfits, or the act—dudes with prestigious instrumental performance and musical theater degrees pretending to be hillbillies.

The familiarity began to wear on me, so I landed at a jazz club near my hotel. A tenor sax/piano/double bass combo played to a crowd of six, including myself and the bar staff. Their musicianship and energy was inspiring and impossible to ignore, so I decided to hunker down.

I ordered a tall whiskey sour from the obviously anorexic, but otherwise gorgeous young blonde bartendress, and was taken aback when she asked if I was a musician. She was either being ironic, an insufferable ditz, or was new in town and hadn't gotten the memo that everyone in Nashville is a musician. It's like asking a pancake what's for breakfast.

"No," I said. "How about yourself?"

"Hell no, proud to say. The drink is on me."

I tipped her a couple bucks and held up my drink. "Because I'm not a musician?"

"Exactly. Congratulations!"

It was a nice little gift to welcome me out of my old career.

She began wiping down the beer taps with a rag. "I've known more than my fair share. I'll never get involved with another one, that's for sure."

"I imagine they can be a difficult breed."

"Very self-absorbed and perpetually delusional."

This wasn't anything new—a cliché, in fact—and not insightful enough to convince me that she'd really learned anything the hard way, but I found her attitude refreshing nonetheless.

The jazz trio kicked off an arrangement of Frank Zappa's "Peaches en Regalia," and somehow managed to nail it without the luxury of a dozen expert players. It was triumphant. They had to be delusional to even begin to attempt such a feat. Chalk another one up for the delusional thinkers of the world. It's the only way anything notable ever gets accomplished.

There was one issue left to resolve. I'd managed to save a single copy of the prank edition of the *Essential Carl Mahogany,* and it was now time to get to the bottom of things. So, I finished my complimentary drink, and made the 10-minute drive to Tim's.

I parked across the street from his place—a modest brick and stone house that he bought during the height of our mutual success, in an old neighborhood that has since become fashionable.

A Mercedes was parked in the driveway, which seemed strange to me. I waited and watched. There were lights on in the house, but no movement that I could see, or flashes of television light.

I sat for what seemed like an hour, preparing several different speeches, dependent on who answered the door, and who else was there.

It only took about five minutes of this before I began feeling like a creep. So, I went for the front door, anxious as I could possibly be, knowing the likelihood of me coming out of this looking like a fool no matter what I said or did, was assured.

I stopped just short of the porch and listened for a moment. There was nothing, and still no movement, so I peeked through the big front window. There was a woman moving about the kitchen, emptying a dishwasher. I could tell right away that it wasn't Sheila—blonde, too young, and she was emptying a dishwasher.

It was safe to ring the doorbell, so I did. I noticed Tim had installed a surveillance camera on one of the crossbeams above the doorway. This was new.

"Who is it?" the woman asked. It was definitely not Sheila.

"Sorry to bother you. Is this still Tim Sherrill's place?"

"May I ask who this is?"

I told her, and the door opened right away.

"*The* Carl Mahogany?" she said, looking surprised.

"Fully dressed."

She invited me in, but I hesitated, not knowing who she was, or who else was there. The surveillance camera added some paranoia to the proceedings. She eventually extended her hand and introduced herself.

"Ashley Roosevelt. Tim's fiance. Please come in. I've heard a ton about you."

It was tempting, but I stood my ground.

"Tim's not here, I take it."

She said he was in San Francisco with her father. A business trip. "Tim's completely out of the music business now."

"No kidding?" I wondered if she'd had anything to do with his career change.

"He's in software. On the sales end."

She invited me in again, using sweeping arm gestures this time, and I decided that it was probably safe, as long as I didn't get too far from the doorway.

"You and Tim were pretty much connected at the hip for a lot of years. Your name comes up in at least every other story he tells," she said, before offering me a drink.

I declined, not interested in staying more than a few minutes, or just long enough to mine her for information. I asked how long they'd been engaged. Only a couple weeks, though they'd been dating for 10 months previous to that.

"What brings you back to Nashville?" she asked. "I understand you live in Colorado now."

"I'm between places, you could say."

"So, just stopping by to say hi?"

I pulled the CD out of my pocket and handed it to her. "I wanted Tim to have a look at this."

She took a brief glance, but didn't react in any way that made her look suspicious. "Is this your latest album?" she asked. "Cool!"

"Not exactly."

She set the disc on a coffee table and assured me that Tim would get it.

"I don't intend on leaving it here," I said. "I just wanted him to have a look at it. It's unauthorized."

I asked if she'd seen a copy of the disc lying around, or maybe had heard Tim talking about it, or seen an image on one of Tim's computers. She picked it up and gave it a closer look.

"No. This is all new to me," she said, handing me the disc. "Like I said, Tim's been out of the music biz for almost as long as we've been together. He's pretty set on keeping things that way." While this didn't vindicate Tim entirely, I was satisfied—as satisfied as I was going to get, considering Ms. Roosevelt's limited knowledge. And, so with that, I left.

Sleep did not come easy, so I took a midnight walk from my hotel, past the Symphony Center, and out onto the Shelby Street Pedestrian Bridge. I stopped about midway, and looked out over the Cumberland River. I noticed the CD was still in my jacket pocket. I got it out and had another look at it. The transpositions on the back cover conjured up an old memory.

Sheila and I were at her parents' Belle Meade mansion a few Christmas Eves ago. Her nieces and nephews had been put to bed, and all of her siblings and their spouses were staring at the gas fireplace—three physicians, two lawyers, an orthodontist, one reluctant housewife, Sheila, and me.

There'd been an extended lull in conversation. Sheila's step-mom began vomiting in the least-distant upstairs bathroom. The acoustics were always great in that place, and it wasn't a family night there without a couple of eating disorders asserting themselves.

Sheila's father cleared his throat.

"Don't think of it as a handicap, Carl," he said.

I'd been expecting yet another belittling comment about my profession, as he always had a few ready for me that he saved for mixed company.

"I don't," I said. "Your wife's affliction has never stopped you before."

There was a lot of furniture and clothing noise from the squirming, but otherwise, it was the best silence I'd heard in quite awhile. My tinnitus even seemed to shut down. Sheila's father eventually found the humor in it.

"My daughter just told me that you're a dyslexic."

This was three years into our relationship, and Sheila had known all along. I can only assume that she was afraid the fact of it would offend her father's eugenic sensibilities and squash his hopes for the grandest future imaginable for her.

"Yeah, I was told that several years ago," I said. "I never bothered to get a second opinion. I didn't care for the first one."

He re-lit his cigar, and then took a melodramatic pull from it.

"Well, here's your second opinion," he said. "My daughter doesn't like to admit it, but I know everyone in this city. And, I can tell you that dyslexics often become great people—great businessmen, advisors; a lot of the behind-the-scenes types that really make things happen. They just don't think the same as most people."

I laughed, looking around at Sheila's family. "Don't talk about me while I'm in the room."

The den had already begun to clear. I took another sip of Blue Label and turned to Sheila, wanting to ask her if she'd bothered to tell her father about the CMA award I'd received a few months before. Only one songwriter in the known universe wins this award in any given year. Perhaps I'd been wrong in thinking the award might serve as proof that I'd reached some level of "greatness."

Sheila had passed out.

"I'm not too worried about it," I said. "Expectations of me

were always low, or non-existent. I've never had anywhere to go but up."

He sat forward in his chair and rubbed his brow. "What a great story. You should seriously consider getting your autobiography out on the shelves."

That seemed like a huge leap to make. "Ha. Who would want to read that?"

He took another puff. "Big sales wouldn't necessarily be the point. You should just get it out there."

I wasn't convinced his idea was worthwhile.

"It's unfortunate in almost every case, but people tend to believe the first version of anything they hear, or read," he said. "That's what they're most likely to remember, anyhow. So, it's crucial—especially these days—that a public figure be the first one to tell their story."

"I may not have the genetic predisposition for book writing."

He shook his head. "Ghost writers, Carl. I know some of the best in the business. They've worked the whole Southern circuit: the Clintons, Carter, Duke. Do you know what a ghost writer is?"

As I looked down at the river, it occurred to me that maybe I needed to make like a ghost writer and finish that Clinton opera.

It also occurred to me to frisbee the CD off the bridge. It would've been a symbolic, dramatic thing to do. It would've also been littering, and I'd already littered more in the previous week than I had in my entire life.

I tossed the disc into a trash can on the walk back to the hotel.

25

Karen had left several voice messages by the time I drove back through St. Louis. They were perfect: each one corresponding with a stage in the grieving process. They began with anger that I'd violated her privacy and deleted her outline. Eight messages along, she was apologizing for the whole mess. I didn't take any of it to heart. She'd been given her chances, and had blown each one to bits.

I did call Taylor, and we met at a barbeque joint off the interstate. Karen had apparently been too ashamed to tell him what'd happened, and he was disgusted when I told him.

"Like I said, I had no idea what she was up to," he said. "I'm sorry. That's fucked up."

I didn't expect him to have much else to say about it.

"So, I guess this means you won't be moving back here," he said, looking disappointed.

"Not looking good," I said.

We talked about my brief trip to Nashville as we ate, and I mentioned that I'd been inspired to come out of retirement. He asked if I'd had some sort of vision, or out-of-body experience that'd changed my mind.

"I've been out-of-body for two weeks straight," I said. "I'm kinda ready to get back in there."

"That's good news," he said, through a mouthful of pulled pork. "Now you can finish the Bill Clinton opera."

"You think I should?"

"Hell yeah. You have to. It's got legs. Hundreds."

He tossed some ideas at me, and they were above average for a kid with no experience in the trade. I mentioned this.

"I know a few things about musical theater," he said. "Remember what I told you about the guys mom brings around."

He suggested we collaborate on the project if I decided to move forward with it. I couldn't turn him down. It seemed he already had more invested in it than I did, judging by the ideas he'd shared with me.

"Alright," I said. "Let's see what happens."

Shannon's old bedroom is now my studio. Rhonda ordered some blue-green curtains to match my few things that survived the dip.

The room sits across the hallway from Rhonda's bedroom. I've not taken to calling it "my" or "our" bedroom yet—a residual push to remain on the fence, perhaps. Maybe it's because I still have so few belongings, and just enough new clothes to fill a suitcase, but after a month of living here, I still feel like I'm just staying awhile, though I have no plans to leave.

The window in my office faces south and overlooks the junkyard. There's nothing but miles of pasture beyond the southern wall of the fortress. If I lean back far enough in my chair, this is all I see, but I prefer to look up from what I'm doing and watch Rhonda turning wrenches.

We get up early and eat breakfast together. She goes out to the garage, and I go upstairs to write until lunchtime. I've listened to *My Life* more times than its original audio editor, and have five gems completed, and a good deal of the libretto. Taylor has tossed his two cents in on a couple of things, but I don't hold my breath. He's busy doing the same crap I was doing at his age.

Afternoons consist of helping Rhonda. She's taught me how to run the forklift, and claims that I do it with the precision and grace of a figure skater.

She's appointed me Minister of Pigeon Control. The air rifle she bought me should be delivered tomorrow. It has a scope and all sorts of other cool features.

When it arrives, I'll open the package and hold it out in front of me. I'll feel like I've really earned something. I'm sure of it.

The author wishes to acknowledge the generous support, encouragement, and technical expertise of:

Jan & Major Boddicker, Courtney Boddicker, Maria Winnie, Brad Pauquette & the Columbus Creative Cooperative, Richard Saxton & M12, Gregory Hill, Peter de Kan, Matt Shupe, David Milofsky, Judy Doenges, Leslee Becker, Steven Schwartz, Paul Trembath, David Robinson, Tom Conway, Mia Heavener, Brenna Yovanoff, and all who workshopped the first chapters of this story.

Also from M12 & Last Chance Press

This Road Leads to Nowhere: Pierre Punk
Edited by Josh Garrett-Davis
Contributions from Ocho, Taman Eggers, James P. Leary,
Cynthia Connolly, Richard Saxton, Jenni K. Dillon,
Shiloh Ashley, Elliot Harmon
ISBN 978-94-90322-67-0

An Equine Anthology
Nell Boeschenstein, Josh Garrett-Davis,
Richard Saxton, Kirsten Stoltz (eds.)
ISBN 978-94-90322-54-0

Cool Pastoral Splendor
Richard Saxton, Kurt Wagner, epilogue by Kirsten Stoltz
ISBN 978-94-90322-53-3

A Decade of Country Hits: Art on the Rural Frontier
Edited by Margo Handwerker
Foreword by Richard Saxton
ISBN 978-94-90322-40-3